FROM THE SKY

UNLIKELY HEROES

J. E. PACE

CHAPTER 1

MADIGAN

Who knew how hard it would be to learn to sleep again?

Alone, in a cold bed.

Alfie rests at my feet, snoring softly, so at least a part of me is warm.

I pick up my phone and stare at the time—a habit I know isn't helping. 3:05. As usual. I can't plan much stability in my life, but I can plan on that number. Like...well, like clockwork.

Let the mental games begin.

Sleeping pill? Not enough time before my alarm goes off. Scroll through my phone? Tempting, but obviously a bad idea. Get up and find something to do? Sounds hard. Or maybe I should train my body to stay in bed and at least get some rest? Read a book? Glass of water? Glass of wine?

Not a single good idea among them, or at least not a single good idea that I have the middle-of-the-night energy to execute.

Which is odd when I have so much energy during the day. Or at least enough busyness to feel like energy.

I slump into the pillow, burrowing deeper, tangling my hair as every worry I've ever had cycles through my brain. The perfect distraction. After all, as my therapist says, going through surface level worries is the perfect way to ignore the deep stuff underneath.

Sounds like the right idea to me.

Alfie rolls away from my feet and lets out an indignant snort. He knows I'm awake.

I've got a bottle of Nyquil on the end table. Something that *has* alcohol, but *isn't* alcohol. One gulp should take me down for another hour and a half.

I roll to my side and prop up, pouring a generous dose into the little plastic lid.

It feels like a shot if I think about it. So I don't.

At 4:45, my alarm goes off in earnest. Alarms are always earnest, and that's something I can appreciate about them. Also, they can be counted on. Just like my dog, who is waiting at the foot of my bed, tail wagging. My mouth feels like sticky cotton, the sheets icy, my head achy.

But Alfie's ready.

And that's what I need, every day.

As soon as my feet hit the floor, he's darting to the front door, collecting his leash in his mouth like I've trained him to do. It's definitely his best trick. The trick that kept me from breaking, back when everything else crumbled around me.

Thirty-seven months. That's how long it's been. Such a haggard number, thirty-seven.

One and a half hours later, the dog is walked and fed. Plus I'm showered and dressed, flight suit packed in my duffel bag, boots laced, keys in my pocket. I've got twenty minutes to get to work, which will land me there fifteen minutes early, so I can sign Don out, and start checking the medicines for the helicopter.

Tracey, the nurse who is my partner, arrives about seven minutes after me, and Matt—the pilot—about five minutes after her, always with a coffee in hand. A team of three. The perfect number.

Joshua told me once—okay, more than once, any time I would listen—that in Biblical times three was a number that symbolized completion. *That's why we'll have to have a baby,* he'd said. *Or five.* Because the number of perfection is seven.

I'd always told him that it would be best to start with one, and he hadn't argued.

Turns out that he was gone, so we'd started with none.

And now I'm stuck with the most horrible number of all. One. At least at home.

Which is why it's such a relief to come to work. Which is why I pick up every shift they let me. Even if I'm tired. Even if it's intense. Even if the calls are often stressful and bloody and demanding. I like demanding. It makes all my other thoughts fall away. Some people meditate. I help people in crisis get to the hospital before they die. Well, usually.

When they do die, another little piece of me breaks off. But that's okay, because there's always another way to fill it—another walk with Alfie, another shift, another person I might be able to help save.

CHAPTER 2

ANDY

I wake with a jerk, still wearing yesterday's t-shirt. The beeping that I thought was a flying elevator in my dream is, unfortunately, not. I dig under my covers, then pillow, then roll out of bed onto the floor. There it is, the little gremlin. I pull my phone out from under my bed and notice that it's at ten percent.

Just the way I like it.

Because when you don't charge your phone at night, the minutes feel a little luckier. Plus, I get to see what the day has to offer. Either I'll have a chance to charge it, or—if the opportunity doesn't present itself—well, then I'll go the day without a phone.

Which is its own kind of adventure.

And, say what you want, adventure is lucrative business.

I'm throwing on a pair of muddy-at-the-cuff jeans when my phone beeps again. "You up?"

"Early bird gets the worm," I reply.

"Dude, it's eleven o'clock," he texts. "And we need you down here at The Molehill. We've kind of got a problem."

IT'S MORE THAN A PROBLEM. According to the next text, two kids took off with one of the ATVs at my business, The Molehill, while Tony was getting their parents to sign the release forms.

Which means we have two partially filled-out release forms and two ten-year-old cousins on the loose.

It's time to stop texting and give Tony a call.

He picks up the phone on the first ring. Before he can speak, I say, "Look, just get the parents to finish the forms. Otherwise, Gretchen might kill me. As for the kids, I'm sure they'll be fine. Seems like they've ridden before."

A long silence.

"They haven't?"

"Doesn't sound that way."

A long breath through my teeth. "How'd they even get the guts to steal the four-wheelers?"

"They're ten-year-old kids, dude."

I try not to laugh. After all, this isn't the time for laughing. But, yeah, I would have done the same thing when I was ten—a licking from my Granddaddy or no. "Okay, man, just get the forms. I'm coming over. I'm sure it'll be okay."

It isn't.

By half past eleven, the boys still aren't back. I've sent Tony and Ned out with the Jeep, looking for them, but still haven't heard anything. One of the parents is pacing. The other is on his phone, chuckling to himself.

I plug my phone into the wall, charging and waiting. Because sometimes your big sister is right and you just need to charge the darn thing. Now feels like one of those times.

The skies are gray and summer is brewing. It's hot out there. It might rain. Or the clouds might clear. You never know on a day like this. Whatever it brings, heat or storm, I don't want a couple of kids stranded or lost. Plus, I don't want them wrecking my equipment. Those ATVs cost a fortune, and if anyone doesn't understand that—it's two ten-year-old four-wheeling thieves.

I jerk my phone off the charger. Seventeen percent. Good enough.

I send Gretchen a quick text. My half-sister's not gonna like it, but I know she'll come handle the desk for a few minutes.

Right now, I need to hunt down a couple of punk kids who are probably having the best summer day of their lives.

CHAPTER 3

ANDY

They are not having the best day of their lives.

Neither am I.

I see the smoke drifting up from the trees before anything else, and I kick my own quad into high gear, cursing as I drive.

When I get to the first boy, he's crumpled and unmoving, about thirty feet from the ATV. That's bad.

I hop off my own ATV, turning it off as I move and run to the kid. Touching the vein in his neck, I'm relieved to feel the little tick tock of a pulse.

But the other boy.

I whip out my phone. Fifteen percent. Another curse as I dial 911, panting out the name of my business, the approximate location of where we are on the hill, the status of the first kid. As I desperately run up the hill, toward the wreck, I keep my eyes peeled for the second kid.

Because the thing is—I know he's not okay. If he was okay, even if he'd been a little torn up, he would have been right there by his cousin. And that would have been good.

But he isn't.

He's under the ATV, which is what I'd been dreading. I feel the sick swoop in my stomach, still running, still talking to the dispatcher on the line—trying to answer the questions she keeps asking me with her infuriatingly calm voice.

"There's another one," I say. "Stuck under the ATV."

"Is he breathing?" she asks, like we're talking about the weather, that calm, calm voice.

"Don't know yet," I snap, getting to the kid and squatting down to assess the situation. He's pinned under the ATV, both of his legs and one of his arms squashed underneath it, bleeding from various scratches, with little flecks of blood all over the grass like a horror movie. But I don't even need to check his pulse, because from his four-hundred-pound prison, the skinny little boy is looking at me, face white, blood in his hair.

He opens his mouth, lips pink like a fish gasping for air. "I'm sorry," he whispers.

"Hey, hey," I answer, glancing back at the lump that was the other boy—still not moving. "It's okay. Let's just see if we can get you out from under here."

"Sir," the voice from dispatch interjects.

"The boy," I reply. "He's alive, but, um, trapped under the quad. I'm gonna try to get it off of him."

"I've sent out a unit. I'll contact fire as well." She pauses. "Can you stay on the line?"

"Yeah," I say, jogging around the ATV and trying to find the best way to right it. "Just, they need to hurry."

"They're on their way now."

I glance up to see Ned and Tony zooming toward us in the Jeep. I point to the lump of unconscious kid, shouting instructions, which I'm not sure anyone can hear. But Ned seems to get it. He slows, driving carefully toward the kid. When they're almost there, Tony jumps out of the vehicle, not even waiting for it to come to a complete stop, rushing to the unconscious boy. "Is he breathing?"

Ned rips the keys out of the Jeep and is running toward me, as I position myself at the side of the ATV. "Yeah, I think so," I grunt-shout back. "At least he was."

Tony crouches by the unconscious kid while Ned huffs his way to me and together we roll the quad off the boy.

The kid doesn't look like a flattened cartoon—

not quite. But he doesn't look normal either. His left arm rests at a grotesque angle and one of his legs doesn't look great either. There are scratches and more blood. Ned murmurs a Catholic prayer, which seems like the right idea.

And then we hear sirens, toiling up the dirt utility road.

"Thank heavens," I murmur, as Ned chants another prayer and the ambulance crests the hill.

CHAPTER 4

MADIGAN

We get the call from the ground unit, which is headed to an ATV accident. Two young patients, both with significant injuries. One unresponsive.

"Sounds like somebody's gonna get a ride in the skies today," Tracey says. "You ready, Mads?"

In answer, I grab the cooler of blood from the refrigerator, picking my helmet up on the way out to the hangar.

Matt's already running the preflight check as Tracey and I walk slowly, carefully, around the helicopter, checking each compartment, making sure every latch is tight.

If anything's out of place, we won't fly. If the weather looks bad, we won't fly. If a single one of us feels uneasy, we won't fly. It's how it goes with our job. It doesn't matter how bad a patient might be, if something looks amiss or *feels* amiss, we don't fly. Because three dead flight crew members won't be able to help anybody.

I tap on the firm metal of the helicopter, standing near the nose and waiting with Tracey while Matt makes sure everything on the inside is running smoothly. I hate ATVs. Along with Jeeps and convertibles—all those stupid, showy cars with no nice ceiling to catch you, no walls to protect you from flying debris or tree branches or anything at all.

Though the thing I hate most of all, now and forever, is motorcycles. One wreck, one roll, one collision, and you're gone. Before you can blink, before anybody can get there, before you can even say goodbye.

The engine of the helicopter begins to whir, the blades stirring the air into a roar.

I have to admit that helicopters aren't necessarily the safest means of transport either. In fact, if you think too hard about it, you might realize you're thousands of feet in the air in an oversized metallic bug. But unlike those joyriding vehicles, helicopters have purpose. In this case, they have a whole lot of purpose.

I run through the checklist in my mind, buzz through all the possibilities I can think of with those two kids. What were they doing out there alone anyway?

Hopefully they hadn't gotten hit by another ATV. Hopefully, they hadn't been driving too fast. Hopefully they'd been wearing helmets.

But, yeah, that seems like a lot of hope for a couple of kids on a joyride.

Matt gives the thumbs up.

I haul open the door, climb in. Tracey crams beside me. Seatbelts on. Helmets on.

Tracey gives me a fist bump. But we both know that kids are the worst. There's so much to lose in a kid. You can't say that out loud, at least not to a regular person. You can't go posting on Facebook that a kid is more important than the eighty-year-old with a heart condition. And maybe 'important' isn't the right word anyway. But, yeah, there's more to lose when they're kids. Like, to the tune of another seventy years.

I plug in the cord attached to my helmet so I can hear Matt and Tracey. Matt's humming his usual eighties jams, his eyes on the monitor. The sun is out. At least for now.

Those kids are lucky the weather cleared up. If it hadn't, they'd be out in the middle of nowhere with a two-hour ambulance drive ahead of them. Because flight teams don't come in storms or wind or fog. They come in the sun. That way, everyone lives.

Hopefully.

The helicopter thunders, Matt's voice tapping into my headset. "Y'all ready?"

Of course I'm ready. Being ready is the only thing I'm good for anymore.

CHAPTER 5

ANDY

It's not the first time I've called an ambulance from work. This is an ATV park, after all. We've had a few sprains, broken bones, a concussion here or there. But this is the first time it hasn't felt okay.

Usually when the ambulance gets here, one of the medics hops out, saying, "Andy, boy, whatcha calling us for now?"

This time, they jump out without a word, one rushing to where Tony's standing with the unconscious kid and one dragging the cot as fast as he can over to where I'm kneeling by the boy.

I've been chatting it up with this kid as much as possible. His name is Parker. He likes Minecraft, Lego, and a girl named Jessie, whose mom won't let her go to the movies with him because they're just ten. I laugh at that and Parker kind of smiles too, but he's starting to shiver—a little at first and then bigger and bigger until his whole body is shaking like he's experiencing an enormous earthquake of one.

Ned runs to the Jeep and grabs a blanket. Together we tuck it tight around the boy's waist and chest.

Although as soon as the medic gets over to us, he whips the blanket off, poking and prodding all along Parker's arms and legs, looking into his eyes with a flashlight. Parker's lips are white, fingernails too.

"Glad to see this one talkin'," the medic says. I recognize him. Jimmy. He works weekends for his dad's pawn shop, near my mom's dentistry downtown.

"Care to tell me what happened, kid?" he says to Parker, putting the blanket back on the boy's upper body as he inspects his legs.

Parker does. He and his cousin, Saul, had thought it'd be so hilarious to take the four-wheelers. Their parents were distracted. The keys were in it. "Easier than anything I ever done before," Parker says, as Jimmy tips and taps along his leg.

"You keep the keys in?" Jimmy asks, nodding to me.

"Not usually, but, yeah, I guess sometimes."

"Does it feel easy now, kid?" Jimmy asks.

"No, sir," the boy responds. "I'm freezing and everything hurts."

"Well, in my industry, hurting ain't the worst thing." Jimmy stands up. "I'm gonna get the board off the cot, alright. So don't you move, okay?"

"Guess it wasn't the smartest thing to take that four-wheeler," Parker says.

"Yeah, well, boys your age ain't really known for doing the smartest things," Jimmy replies.

I kind of snort and wink at Parker. "One day it'll make you stronger. I broke my leg once on a four-wheeler."

"You think mine's broken?" Parker asks.

I look at his leg, but don't answer.

Jimmy has no such qualms. "That leg's for sure broken, kid. And your arm too, case you can't tell that. But I think everything else inside is gonna be just fine." He turns to me. "How heavy are those things?"

"Few hundred pounds," I say.

"I seen worse," Jimmy says. "Lots worse." He plunks a stiff board down to the side of Parker, muttering things to the kid, telling him how he's gonna roll him onto the board, then he and I are gonna lift him up real nice.

I hold one end of the board and we lift him up to the cot. Jimmy straps him in. "You help me take him down there over this rocky ground, Andy. And make sure this thing don't tip." He leans toward me, whispering so Parker won't hear. "Listen, we called the flight unit en route. They should be here real soon."

"What's the point of doing him up on the cot then?" I whisper back.

"Oh, the copter ain't for…" Jimmy starts, but then stops and just looks at the other kid—the one down the hill. The kid's got some kind of contraption in his mouth. The other paramedic has him hooked up with an IV, though I'm not sure why.

"What's wrong with Saul?" Parker asks, which just goes to show how pointless whispering around kids is.

"Oh, he done bumped his head real good," Jimmy replies. "We can't get him to wake up yet."

"But he ain't dead?" Parker asks.

"Nah, he ain't dead," Jimmy says.

Parker sighs, like a huge load has lifted off his shoulders, but something about the way Jimmy phrased it, about the way the sentence hung at the end like it wasn't finished. He ain't dead… *yet*.

I open my mouth to ask more, but Jimmy needs my help loading the kid into the ambulance and just as soon as we're done with that, I hear the whir. Distant at first, but it grows quickly to a solid buzz, then a rumble, then a roar.

"Cavalry's here," Jimmy's partner says.

"Good. We need to get this one to the hospital

'fore that adrenaline wears off and we've got a wailer on our hands."

I watch the helicopter, utterly mesmerized. I've never been this close to one, never had it blow my hair, my clothes. Tony and Ned stand back. The skids bump onto the ground, the blades slowing as the helicopter settles.

And then the most remarkable thing happens. A woman hops out. Probably no more than five feet tall, dark hair, positively black eyes. It feels just like the movies, like she's moving in slow motion, though she must be moving really fast. She tears off her helmet as another woman in a flight suit comes around to help her.

A flurry of questions for the medics that blur in my brain, then, "You better get another unit out here just in case," the other woman says, glancing nervously at some clouds in the distance.

"We already got one coming," Jimmy says. "Though I'm sure hoping we don't need it."

"Aren't we all," the other woman says, casting a glance to the pilot who's still in the cockpit, checking a tablet or computer or something. And then the other medic is talking to the nurse, showing her the tube in the kid's mouth, their voices low as the team works to load the kid into the helicopter.

The black-eyed woman turns to me, Ned, and

Tony, who are all standing around like the most useless dudes on earth.

"Who's in charge here?"

I lift a finger, a little tentatively since it doesn't seem like being in charge is the desirable position to be in right now. "It's my park," I say.

"You're the owner?" she asks.

I clear my throat, because I feel like I'm in trouble, although I wasn't the one who stole a four-wheeler. "Yes, ma'am."

She sizes me up from top to bottom, which under normal circumstances I might find flattering, but then she mutters, "Of course you are."

"Excuse me," I say.

She shakes her head like she can't be bothered with an answer while she and her partner secure the kid into the helicopter—it's not a lot of space.

"Where's his parent or guardian?" the dark-eyed woman asks, getting the boy positioned.

I clear my throat again. I'd forgotten about parents, hadn't even called. I look at Ned and Tony.

"I gave them a call," Tony says. "Gretchen said she'd get them out here asap."

Thank you, Tony. And Gretchen. I smirk back at black-eyes, like I had it covered the whole time.

"I was hoping they'd be here to see him off," the woman murmurs, glancing down the hill. And then, as though she hadn't said anything, as though that soft blip of emotion was all in my mind, she turns back to the helicopter. "But we've got to go before the weather turns."

"It's just a few clouds," I mutter, squinting to see if there's any sign of a vehicle making its way up the hill.

"Well, we don't have time for 'just a few clouds' to become a storm."

I hold up my hands in surrender. I wasn't trying to suggest that they wait around.

The other woman hops into the helicopter, right behind the pilot. "Ready, Mads?"

Without an answer, the black-eyed woman called "Mads" swings up through the door of the helicopter, sitting behind the unconscious boy. In the small aircraft, it looks almost like he's resting on her lap.

I cast another glance down the hill, hoping to see a parent. I mean, what if the kid… Like, what if he never….

I don't even dare to finish the thought. The blades are speeding up and we all take an unconscious step back. The helicopter lifts, and I see that the black-eyed woman is looking down the hill, just like I was. Almost like she's still hoping they'll come, if for nothing else than to wave goodbye.

It's a thought that unsettles me. I hadn't thought too much about parents, partly because, well, there was an ambulance and a helicopter here, so things were going to be just fine, right?

Right?

I shove the thought away, turn back to my friends. "Alright, who gets to file the incident report?" I say with the lightest voice I can muster. Just as a small SUV trudges its way up the hill.

"Oh, crap," I mutter, as their faces come into view, a teary woman in the passenger seat.

"I'm on it," Tony says, skedaddling away to the Jeep. Ned follows, leaving me with a mother who just missed her child being air-lifted to a hospital.

CHAPTER 6

MADIGAN

The kid doesn't code on the way to the hospital, so that's good. The ground paramedic had tubed him up real nice before we got there. Also good. So now he's dreaming with a little Ketamine.

Too bad that idiot of an owner didn't think to call the parents sooner. Not that they could have flown with us. There's not room for so much as an extra elbow in the smaller helicopters, but it's still nice when the family can show up. Gives people closure. For better or for worse.

Whether this kid will wind up as better or worse isn't really my rodeo.

As we hit the helipad, a tech hurries out with a bed.

We transfer the litter, monitor, and ventilator to

the bed. Then we all wheel him to the trauma room. Nurses, doctors. A whole team. Tracey gives the hospital nurse the report. I stare at the kid, watching his breathing, looking for little twitches, signs of life.

There's nothing more foreboding than a quiet kid.

Kids are supposed to cry and yell and burp and vomit. Just lying there—it isn't right. I want him to blink and flutter just like they do in books.

But it's not a book. If there's one thing I've learned in my life, it's that nothing's like it is in fiction. And we've got him drugged up pretty good. The doctors will likely keep him that way—under a drug-assisted coma while they run a bunch of tests.

We're gone way before that point. We're like the knight on the horse. Swoop up, save the dude or damsel, drop them off at the castle, and on to the next patient.

Honestly, it's what I usually like about my job. Not knowing. Not having to cope with anything beyond the stemming of the initial disaster.

I can do disasters. It's why I'm here. To pause the initial emergency, to buy the patient time he wouldn't have had without us, to keep the body alive, and then get the patient to the experts so they can do their thing. I don't usually *want* to know if they succeed. That's their demon to conquer or carry home on their shoulder.

And heaven knows I don't need to be adopting other people's demons.

But this time I kind of do.

Tracey claps me on the back as we leave the room, turning our backs on this unconscious kid. "His mama'll get there," she says.

I nod. What else is there to do. "Thanks, Trace."

We fly back.

No calls.

Trade out Matt for another pilot.

No calls.

Everyone loves these nights—a full eight hours of sleep. But for me, tonight, it just means more time to think, in another lonely bed—this one at the station.

I wish something would come in so I can get my mind off that kid—or at least get my mind onto something else.

Just after six, when I've finally fallen into a tossing sleep, we get a call. And even as tired as I am, I'm glad for that call, for that old woman with her two hurt knees. Glad she's light enough to fly. Glad for the lump of paperwork we get every time. Glad, glad, glad for having things to do.

"Get some sleep," Tracey says when we're all done. As if she knows.

"I've got another shift in the afternoon. Picked one up with the ground crew."

"Then it goes double," she says, looking into my

eyes. "Get. Some. Sleep. And stop picking up so many shifts. You know it makes me nervous."

"You know I love it," I counter.

"I know you think you need it," she says.

And I let that one sit, not willing to touch it with a twelve-foot pole.

"You buy that eye mask I told you about?" she asks, trying to lighten it up.

I don't answer.

"You know what," she says. "Never mind. I'm just going to get it for you. Smells like lavender. It'll help."

I nod, smile, like lavender is the only thing that I need, the magic potion that will make me sleep.

And then I drive back to the house that I shared with my husband of two months, walk myself over that empty threshold, past the shelves that used to hold his textbooks and my old journals, and into the bedroom so I can stare at the bed that is much too big for just one person.

"Alfie," I call. But he's already there, already running to me with his leash in his mouth.

Thank goodness for that. We'll walk. We'll walk till my breath finds a pace, till my nerves settle into a rhythm, till my rushing, worrying brain finally slows down and my legs don't feel like they can walk anymore. And then, and only then, will I be able to get some sleep.

CHAPTER 7

ANDY

"The paperwork is gonna be a nightmare," Gretchen is saying, though I'm not listening. I keep hearing Jimmy's voice telling Parker that his cousin isn't dead. That sentence that should have been comforting, except for that pause at the end, that unspoken question mark.

I keep seeing the female medic's black eyes through the helicopter window, gazing down the hill, looking, hoping for someone to drive up it and say goodbye.

Goodbye. It's a nice thing to say and all, but it's only truly *important* when there's a lot to lose.

"Andy!" Gretchen whacks me with the stack of papers she's holding. "You're going to have to handle this. I've got to get back to the house."

"You think they're gonna be okay, Gretch, those kids?"

She softens, lowering the stack of papers onto the desk. But she still doesn't answer me, not directly anyway. "Don't worry, Andy. I'm glad you got to them quickly, found them as soon as you could."

I shrug. "Doesn't really feel like I got to them fast enough."

Gretchen blows a hair out of her face. "What's fast enough? You got to them as soon as you could. They were both still alive. You called the ambulance. You and Ned lifted an ATV off of a kid. That's a lot of heroics for one day."

"One of the helicopter medics…" I begin.

"Yeah?"

I want to describe that look she gave, the sound of her voice, *I was hoping someone would be here to see him off.* The longing behind it, like she wasn't sure the kid was going to make it. Instead, I just say, "She was kinda rude."

"Aw, Andy, don't let that get to you. Things get tense in these situations. That's not a you problem."

I stare out the window of my shop. We closed it for the afternoon. We've got to get the four-wheeler cleared off that side path anyway.

She glances down at the papers. "Listen, Andy,

maybe I'll just take these over to the house, see what I can fill in."

She goes to pick them up to take them with her, but I place my hand on the stack with a thunk. "I got it," I say.

"You sure?" she asks.

"Yeah, yeah, now go get ready for the next wedding or book club or whatever it is you have going on tonight."

"No events. Just a consultation for a bridal shower," she hums with a hint of gossip in her voice. "Miss Hedges."

"Nellie?" I ask. "The librarian?"

"The one and only. Finally getting hitched. I think every woman over fifty in this town is excited. Come to think of it, I am too."

"Well, have fun." I stare out the window, toward the hill where the helicopter landed.

Gretchen wrinkles her forehead. "You know, I really can take some of these. Maybe I should do half."

"I've *got* it," I say, a little more forcefully than I mean to. "Now go have fun." I give her my best get-out-of-here gesture, and she surrenders, leaving me to myself in the office.

Once she's gone, I sit for a moment more, then take a set of keys off of the hook, and head outside. My favorite ATV—I call him Rico—is sitting in its stall, all shiny and just cleaned, waiting for me like I imagine a horse might do. I pull Rico out and turn toward my favorite trail—one that rides into the woods and over a little creek that's only there in seasons when it's been raining.

This summer it's been raining. Which is good. Because I need a little mud to clear my head.

CHAPTER 8

MADIGAN

I work too much.

It's what everyone in my life says.

Lucky for me, there aren't that many people in my life, so it doesn't get too overwhelming.

I've worked eighteen hours of the last twenty-four. With another shift coming.

It's for the best—to keep moving, to keep working, to keep doing.

When Dad brought Alfie over for the first time, that's what I learned. You can't stay in bed forever. You've got to get up. You've got to move your legs. You've got to do something. That's how you survive.

And I was surviving.

I was more than surviving. I was strong. I was healthy. I was earning plenty of money, even in a profession where it's tough to earn plenty of money.

I even had a few friends at work. At least in the helicopter.

On the ground, it was a little harder since I just picked up shifts for whatever crews needed it. The shift I had today was at the south station of Midvale EMS—a station I try to avoid, mostly due to the fact that it connects to the local fire station, which means that quite often it connects to Terry Steiner.

And Terry Steiner very much wants to connect with me.

It's not a brag. There aren't a lot of single ladies in EMS, so I guess I'm just the thing that's available on the menu.

And I kind of hate that.

Especially since Terry is a class A, muscle-brained, pinheaded jerk who believes it is my ultimate privilege to work next door to him.

But my engagement anniversary is this weekend, and I desperately need a shift to distract me—which came in the form of the overworked, run-to-death staff at the south station. Maybe I'm not the only one who doesn't want to pick up a shift next door to Terry.

TERRY'S up in my business before I've even got the ambulance fully cleaned for the start of my shift.

Santos, my partner for the night, hears the door open and he takes the antibacterial spray out of my hand.

"Hey, Sandman," Terry says to Santos, who is clearly trying to be ignored. "You missed a spot." He smears an invisible line along the ambulance and then leans his three hundred pounds of hulk against it. I see the ambulance move. Fire gets about a quarter of the calls that the ground crew does. Which gives Terry all the time in the world to get in our way. Well, my way. Santos has somehow managed to scamper out of sight. Which I don't super appreciate, even if he did finish the cleaning.

"Heard you were working tonight, Mads," Terry says, sizing me up like I'm a burger on the menu.

He does *not* have permission to use Tracey's nickname on me.

"Madigan," I correct.

"That's not what Tracey calls you."

You're not Tracey. That's what I want to say, but I clamp my teeth shut.

"You doing anything after your shift, *Madigan?*" Terry says, with emphasis that I do not appreciate.

"Gonna catch up on a bit of sleep," I answer.

"Mmmm, wish I could get a picture of that," he croons, and I *really* do not appreciate that.

"Then another shift early in the morning," I continue, ignoring him.

"You don't have to be there *that* early," he says.

"I've got to take care of my dog," I reply. "And my house and everything else."

"Next weekend, then?" he asks.

I make a mental note to absolutely pick up an extra shift, two maybe. "Let me check my schedule."

Terry lifts an eyebrow. There's accusation in the gesture. "Give me your number and I'll text you," he says.

How about a fake number, I want to reply. But instead, I just smile, ignoring the request for a minute as I bustle around, pretending Santos really did miss a spot and I've got to make the ambulance sparkle.

Terry stands there, watching for another minute, but then—in an act that can only be called mercy— the tones go off at the fire station.

"Duty calls," he says, strutting away like he's about to save the world. "I'll get your number and call you."

I won't answer, I hum in my mind.

You want to know the truth? I haven't been on a single date since Joshua died. I don't really want to go on one again. But IF I do—and it's the biggest 'if' in the whole world—I sure don't want it to be with this lump of muscle and crude jokes and absolute lack of ability to correctly read body language, or at least to correctly respond to it.

CHAPTER 9

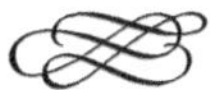

ANDY

I'm folding napkins.

Yeah, yeah, it's not in my usual line of work, but one of Gretchen's waitstaff called in sick. And I need something to get my mind off of the week. Or, at least, to get my thoughts out into the open. And Gretchen's good for that sort of thing.

"You think I'll get sued," I ask. "About those boys?"

"Not really," she says. "It wasn't negligence on your part any more than it was their own parents."

"I left the keys in," I say. "I always leave the keys in."

Gretchen lifts an eyebrow without comment. She's tying bows. I've never seen anyone as devoted to the tying of a bow as my sister.

"I stopped, in case you're wondering," I say, as I

stack the folded napkins on the counter. "Leaving the keys in, I mean. Two days ago, I bought thick envelopes for the keys and have been keeping them tucked neatly in a file drawer. It's an absolute pain in the butt, if you want to know."

"Mmmm, sounds hard," she mutters.

"'K, it's not that hard, but it was a lot easier to just leave them in the vehicles."

Gretchen makes a face that says she doesn't think I've lived a hard enough life. She's not wrong. "Look," she says. "I know you're worried. I can tell by the way you're folding those napkins."

I look down at the napkin in my hands. It should be in neat thirds, but looks more like an accordion—an accordion that someone threw down an elevator shaft and then stepped on.

Gretchen refolds it, creasing it softly.

"Yeah, I guess I'm a little worried," I say, trying to copy her with a new napkin.

"The parents were there," Gretchen says. "Right there, when those kids took off. I don't think that can really be counted as your fault."

I nod and tuck napkins in thirds, letting my fingers fall into a rhythm. When I've got a neat stack of them, I add, "And that kid's mom—the unconscious kid—his mom didn't get there on time. She was pretty upset about that."

"Again, not your fault," Gretchen says. "She can't

sue you for being the one to find her kid and get him on the helicopter as quickly as possible."

"I wasn't worried about the suing part, not with that," I say, moving on to the silverware and sorting it neatly into shiny piles. "More with the happening part. It just kind of played out real sucky, you know."

"It did," she said. "But you're not really one to worry about the happening parts. Usually you can let that stuff go."

"Yeah," I say. "But one of those medics, she seemed upset about it. Kept watching for the parents, even as they were lifting off the ground. It made me paranoid, like the kid was going to die."

"Did he?" she asks.

"I don't know," I answer, dropping a fork.

Gretchen stops her bow tying and turns to me. "You didn't ask."

"Well, he's not at the hospital here. I honestly don't know where he is."

"I'll ask Jackson to find out. You've got a name, right? 'Cause you've got a release form."

"Yeah, I've got a name," I say.

"You gonna give it to me?"

"I will when I look it up, Bossy pants."

Another lift of her dark eyebrow. "You don't need to be looking it up. If I was a gambling woman—which I'm not—I'd say you already know it, but you don't want to tell me."

Well, she should be a gambling woman, because she's right. Not that I tell her that. Instead, we set tables in silence, lighting candles in the center of each. With the burgundy napkins and the tiny lights, it looks almost like Christmas.

"You're good at what you do, sis."

"Yeah," she says. "You know, I kind of am."

She puts an arm around me, gives a little side squeeze. "It's gonna be okay, Andy. That kid, The Molehill. All of it. Doesn't seem like *that* long ago that you were laid out right there on an unfinished wood floor in front of the fireplace with a broken femur. That didn't end too badly."

"You mean, you and Jackson hooked up."

"We didn't *hook up*," she says defensively. "We lovingly cared for your moaning butt all night long."

"You're welcome," I say. "And look at you now."

Gretchen nods. "Speaking of, how is it with the new girlfriend?"

"It's not," I say. "We broke up a few weeks ago."

"I'm behind," she says.

"To be fair," I add. "It's difficult to keep up."

"You can say that again," she grumbles. "But I'm not going to break my femur and spend a night trapped in a house during a snow storm to help you find the right girl."

"Who said I needed help?" I ask. "Settling down

would only make it harder to run The Molehill. Keep me tied down."

"Eh," Gretchen says. "You could use a *little* tying down. And you might be surprised how much *more* you can accomplish with the right person, not less."

"You know old man MacArthur is selling his lot."

Gretchen looks up quickly. "Really?"

"Kind of a steal," I say.

"You're going to expand," she says.

"Thinking about it," I say, putting scented sprigs of some kind of herb on each plate. "Just thinking."

"When have you thought a day in your life before doing?" she says, laughing.

"Hey," I reply. "I've thought. I just do it faster than most people."

"So how much was the earnest money?" she asks.

"A couple thousand," I answer.

"All paid?" she says.

"Not exactly," I answer. "Though I took it out of my account. So I guess I might be doing a *little* more than thinking."

"You act. It's kind of your super power," she says. "Now hustle your butt into a little more action and go get dressed. These guests aren't going to serve themselves."

"You know I hate those suits your waitstaff wears."

"But the ladies love them," she says. "And we're going to have a bunch of ladies."

"Well," I mutter. "I guess there are *some* things worse than helping your sister out."

She smiles, real wickedly.

"They're old," I say, catching on.

"Nellie Hedges' bridal shower."

"Ah, Miss Nellie," I say.

"The one and only."

"Well, then. I'll get my suit. Ain't nothing Miss Nellie deserves more than a good send off."

"You're a good kid, Andy," Gretchen says, her smile going all soft and gloppy.

"Not a kid," I say, hustling out of the dining room to get changed.

CHAPTER 10

MADIGAN

I haven't worn a dress for months. Years actually. It's not that I don't appreciate a good dress. It's just that I rarely have any reason to wear one anymore. Not since Joshua died. After that, where was I going to go in a dress? Not to a nice dinner. Not to a conference with him. Not even to the different churches we'd loved to explore. Definitely not back to a church.

And my job certainly doesn't call for a dress, or anything besides our flight suits. As for the moments in between work, sweat pants or pajamas do just fine.

Which leaves me with precious few places to go that require an actual outfit, much less a pretty one. I certainly haven't spent any time in the last few years wrestling with panty hose. Or supportive undergarments for that matter.

I pull my ratty bra out of my drawer and wonder when the last time was that I'd bought a new one. Then I stop thinking about that, because I know when it was. Of course I know when it was.

I put the bra on without looking at myself, wonder if the dress will even still fit me.

It's been nearly four years. I slip it over my head. It's dark coral with lace along the hem and sleeves. High neckline, though my collarbone still peeks a little above it. I put in the pearl earrings Mamie gifted me from her own grandmother, dig around my closet for some appropriate shoes. I guess that's the type of thing I should have bought. But didn't.

I've got some black pumps and that will have to do.

Makeup is a whole other beast. I haven't worn lipstick for as long as I haven't worn a dress. But I know that somewhere I've got a tube. I pull it out, wondering if lipstick goes bad, then tuck it back in my makeup bag and start with my eyes instead. I'll sometimes throw on a little eyeliner and mascara if Tracey and I get lunch, which means that at least I can put those things on my face without too much effort.

Digging through the little makeup bag, I'm surprised at how much other stuff I have—several palettes of eye shadows, mostly browns and grays, a little sampler of blush, even a bit of concealer. I go for the gray palette for my eyes, add a touch of color to my cheeks, and then confront the old lipstick.

I could skip it, I guess, but I'm wagering all those older ladies who are my aunt's friends will be wearing it. It's a bridal shower. In the South. For my dad's only sister. When in Rome…

I untwist the lid, trying not to remember when I got it, which only makes me remember harder.

Joshua and I were in France for a conference—the city of love. Yeah, yeah, we were already well in love. He was busy during the days, which meant I got to wander every café and bistro and book shop I could dream of. Except on that particular afternoon he would be reading his own paper. Numerology, of course. Something that sounds like the most boring thing in the world, until you realize that it's history and mystery and ancient coding all wound up together in a strangely academic suit. Joshua always did look good in a suit, especially that suit. Studying and reading. Deciphering manuscripts, learning dead languages.

I'd wanted to look good for him that afternoon when he read his paper, so I'd let a Mamie and a French sales girl talk me into a stupid expensive lipstick that was—to put it mildly—a very brave shade.

Brave shades weren't exactly my thing.

But I did it then. Wore that lipstick all through his presentation and then dinner after.

And if I did it then, I can do it now too. I bring up the lipstick, paint it carefully onto my lips, trying to push away the memories that keep flooding back to me.

Joshua had loved seeing me at his presentation. And I had loved his paper. I wasn't the only one either. Everyone else liked it too. It was the last thing he published, that paper.

I squeeze my lips together, smoothing the color.

Knowing what I know, looking at that lipstick.

Joshua had proposed to me that night. He'd given me the ring as we'd stood in an ancient church under a glowing stained-glass window depicting a dove with a cascade of colors raining down. They'd sparkled and it had seemed in that moment that nothing could ever go wrong for us, that our lives would always be a rush of sunny yellows and warm greens and electric blues.

"You see the frames," he'd said. "The black that holds in the glass. That's me. Symmetrical, reliable. And all the shards of color in all the different shapes. That's you. Together we make the art work as one piece. Will you…will you make the art work with me for the rest of our lives?"

I had cried, blubbering out words as he'd slipped the ring onto my finger. *Yes, of course, yes.*

And now he was gone. And the art didn't work. It had just been me with all my shards, messy and broken without that framing.

So I'd become the frame.

Only now there was nothing beautiful to fill it.

I look at the lipstick, perfect on my lips even now, all these years later. And then I don't want to look anymore.

I wipe it off in a rush, smearing it in ugly lines, until it's all gone. In fact, I wash my skin, scrubbing until it's fresh and pink, leaving only the eye makeup.

Those ladies will have to make do with me showing up in drugstore lip balm today.

I step back quickly, looking at the rest of me. The dress fits well enough.

I'm a little skinnier, especially around my hips, which isn't perfect. All those walks with Alfie must have eliminated them, though the walking has toned my butt, so I fill the dress out decently from behind.

I grit my teeth, gathering my courage. Then pick up my wallet—I haven't bothered to buy myself a new purse—and head to my car.

I've only been to one wedding since Joshua died. It was every bit as terrible as I'd thought it'd be, though I'd managed to smile until I finally escaped to my car. But I'd vowed not to go to another wedding for at least a decade.

This event with Aunt Nellie wasn't quite a wedding, though it was a little close for comfort.

Still, I can console myself in knowing that it won't be as much lingerie and dirty jokes as it will be wine and gossip and finger foods. And I can do that.

Can't I?

CHAPTER 11

ANDY

A guy doesn't admit that he's excited to wait tables at a bridal shower for a bunch of older ladies. But—off record—I may know someone who is excited to wait tables for a bridal shower for a bunch of older ladies.

If you want to know what's going down in a town, you plant yourself in the center of a group of older women, preferably older women on their second glass of wine. This was the perfect group for that. Bonus points if the belle of the ball—Miss Nellie—was the type of librarian to sneak a kid survival books on a regular basis when he was younger.

Maybe it goes without saying, but I wasn't exactly a library type of kid. I was definitely more of a play-with-friends, build-ramps-on-the-sidewalk-for-our-skateboards,   hang-upside-down-in-a-tree kind of kid.

But when I moved here, I didn't have friends or a skateboard or even a climbable tree in our new yard. It was the perfect opening for my mama to take me to the library every Saturday. And I just hated it.

It didn't help that Mama always wanted me to read great works of literature or something. I remember her finding this kid version of *Moby Dick* and being so excited and, well, as a grumpy and lonely junior high kid, all I could do was snigger at the Dick part of the title. That didn't go down great with Mama. She was always worried I'd wind up a little like she had as a teen—running off to sow wild oats and stuff.

And apparently sniggering about the Dick of Moby only fed this fear. She made me check that book out and told me I'd be grounded if I didn't read it.

"Grounded from what?" I asked, as we neared the checkout desk.

Which is when Miss Nellie piped in, interrupting us and raving about a new book she'd just gotten into the library. It was also about water life, she told my mom. Super factual, interesting.

Mom huffed, but she did agree that I could get both.

The book Miss Nellie had offered was a survival

guide. About shark attacks. And *that* was right up my twelve-year-old alley, even if I was a born and bred Kentucky boy who hadn't seen an ocean in his whole life.

I devoured that book and then every other survival book Miss Nellie saved for me. After that, it got harder, but she still found books that could engage me. Things with gross details about cutting off your own arm to escape a fallen boulder or big adventures that boys did alone. That kind of stuff. I never graduated to *Moby Dick*, or even *Robison Crusoe*, but I did learn to like to read. And I still like those types of books when I get the chance.

Mama was supposed to come to the bridal shower and then we were going to go out for dinner afterwards. But she'd just texted me that a patient had come in with a broken tooth, so she would have to miss the shower. Maybe the dinner too.

I'd get us a table later anyway. If she didn't show, I'd get our food to go and we could eat it later.

As Gretchen bustles around, chatting it up and checking on hors d'oeuvres and worrying over napkins, I fill glasses and mugs, make jokes, give compliments.

If I do say so myself, I can really *kill* it with the older ladies.

And, you know, those old ladies aren't so bad themselves. "You clean up alright, Andy," Miss Nellie tells me, sipping her drink.

"I do my best, Miss Nellie."

"Look at you, all grown up in that bowtie," another woman says, reaching up to give it a tug. "Never thought I'd see the day."

"Me either," Gretchen quips from a table over. And those ladies, I'll be darned if they don't guffaw.

"Your mama's done a right decent job on you," Nellie continues. "Now when you gonna be the one sitting in this house, getting ready for your nuptials?"

"I don't know, Miss Nellie. I ain't managed to get myself too close yet."

"You *haven't* managed..." Miss Nellie corrects. "And I'm not sure I'm the one to give advice to a young thing like yourself on getting married..."

More guffawing. This time at Nellie's expense.

"But in your case, there certainly doesn't seem to be any reason to wait as long as I have," Nellie laughs along with her friends. And then the front door opens, and then Nellie's eyes light up.

I turn to see who has come in, just as one of the more tipsy women topples a wine glass.

I shoot forward, catching it just before the glass

hits the floor, although I do manage to splash the red stains up my sleeve.

Gretchen hurries over, dabbing at me with approximately twelve thousand napkins. "Thanks, Andy. Go clean up. I think I have a spare jacket in the coat closet. I'll take care of things in here." She sets the glass back on the table, and I go through the door to the kitchen as Miss Nellie coos to the new arrival. "Oh, Madigan, sweetheart. I'm so glad you made it this party with all of us old fogeys."

"Who you calling old?" one of the other women chimes in.

"We can't hide from the truth," Nellie replies as the kitchen door shuts behind me, drowning out their voices.

I make my way to the coat closet to try to find a spare jacket. I have a few stains on the cuff of my white sleeve as well, which I try to wash out with a little dish soap, though I only manage to make a bigger mess. At least it gets rid of some of the smell.

The truth is that after Mama had me, she never touched a drop of alcohol, at least not in front of me. Apparently, my daddy had had a bit of a problem with drink. And by 'bit of a problem' I mean that it most likely killed him. That was Gretchen's story to tell, since she'd been the one to find him. But it wasn't a great story. And it wasn't one Mama had wanted me to repeat. We'd been a teetotaling family ever since I'd arrived on the scene, and I'd never quite gotten used to the casual smell of booze.

The jacket Gretchen mentioned is way in the back of the closet, a little dusty and a little tight. I slip into it anyway, doing my best to get it over my shoulders and across my chest.

Gretchen finds me in the kitchen, fussing over the dirty sleeve of my other jacket. "I'll take care of that," she says.

"You sure?" I reply. "I'm not sure this one fits me right."

Gretchen steps back, surveying me, then laughs.

"I told you," I say, starting to unbutton it, so I can put my dirty jacket back on.

"No, no," she says, waving her hand to stop me. "I'm not laughing because it doesn't fit. I'm laughing because it looks great. You're just so used to baggy t-shirts and, I don't know, cargo pants or whatever it is you wear, that you don't understand a well-fitted suit when one falls onto your shoulders."

"You don't think I look stupid?" I say.

"You look fantastic," she replies, straightening my bowtie and handing me a fancy porcelain coffee carafe. "Now go out there and woo those ladies some more."

"Yes, ma'am," I say, walking out into the dining room, carrying the carafe, like I've come to save the day.

And then something weird happens. As I walk in, every eye in the room turns to look at me, like they've made some collective pact.

Miss Nellie smiles. "Andy, dear, come here. Let me introduce you to my niece, Madigan."

I see Madigan, seated to the right of Miss Nellie. She's young—the only young woman in the room—and there's something familiar about her. I can tell from her eyes that she's thinking the same thing about me.

Her eyes, those dark, dark eyes. The shine of her hair, the tilt of her head. And then it clicks. She's the medic from the helicopter.

I won't say that my mouth doesn't fall open.

I also won't say that I hadn't spent at least a little time thinking about that face since she'd gotten back on the helicopter. After all, it was a very nice face. So why had it taken me so long to recognize her? She was wearing makeup now, so there was that. Though I think that the biggest difference was that before I'd come over, she'd been smiling.

I square my own shoulders, paste on a smile.

The woman, Madigan, she hasn't placed me yet, though from the intense look on her face, I can tell she's still trying.

"Well, I'll be darned," I say, giving it my best Kentucky drawl. "I do believe we've already met."

She squints at me, and then I see a bit of the

dawning. A small shake of her head, as though she's trying to unsee what she knows she saw.

"Miss Madigan stopped by my establishment the other day," I say, keeping my voice a little too light as I poor one of the ladies a cup of coffee.

Madigan's lips droop.

"Your ATV park?" Nellie says, her voice a bit confused, as though she knows that under normal circumstances her niece wouldn't be caught dead at something so lowbrow as that.

"A kid almost died," Madigan adds, her voice pinched.

Nellie looks between the two of us, Madigan's dark eyes boring into my face, my smile boring back. "Oh, no," Nellie says. "How awful for the two of you. Did the child, did he, um, survive?"

"So far," Madigan says, taking a large swig of the wine that sits in front of her.

"Yes," I answer.

Again, Nellie looks between the two of us. And—for the record—no one ever accused Nellie of being dumb. She knows when it's time to abort a match-making plan. And this is that time. "Well, now, Andy, I do believe I could do with a little coffee."

I tip a steaming stream into her white and blue mug. "Cream or sugar?" I ask.

"Both of course, dear," she says as Madigan continues to drink her wine. She's getting through it pretty quickly. I resist the urge to stare at her, instead focusing on making Miss Nellie's coffee as sweet and creamy as possible.

Nellie leans closer. "You better make the rounds," she whispers. "I have a feeling a lot of these ladies could do with a cup of coffee after all that wine."

I give her a wink and then do as she says, making my rounds to the different tables, offering coffee and as much charm as I can muster, casting the occasional glance back at the woman next to Nellie.

Her dress fits her perfectly, her arms tight and strong against the tanned shoulders, which hold up her long, pretty neck.

I look away every time I catch myself staring. She is definitely not watching me. In fact, it seems that— if anything—the thing she's most interested in watching is the bottom of her glass. Which doesn't really speak volumes about her excitement level about me, or maybe even being here in general.

I try to give her the benefit of the doubt.

But who wouldn't want to attend a party with the coolest, sweetest old lady in the world, especially when it's to celebrate that she's finally found her soulmate and is getting married?

Even I had been having fun. Why couldn't Madigan?

I taste her name on my tongue, try to remember what her partner on the helicopter had called her.

Mads. Yeah, I like that better, though I have to admit that it fits worse.

"Andy, dear," Miss Nellie's voice calls out cheerfully.

"Yes, ma'am," I say, sliding over to her table.

"Could you show my niece where the lady's room is, please?"

I nod, noticing that Madigan looks pale and, well, not so great.

"Of course," I say. For any of the other ladies I would have pulled out her chair and offered my arm. But Madigan is already scooting out.

"It's right through that door, and to the left."

"Thank you," Madigan says formally, wobbling just a bit as she makes her way through the double doors.

I glance at Miss Nellie, trying to ask with my eyes if I should follow her to make sure she gets there okay, but Nellie isn't looking at me. She's watching her niece. When Madigan is out of sight, she lets out a sigh.

"That girl," the woman next to Nellie says. "She's still struggling. How long's it been?"

"Over three years," Nellie says, and I admit that I suddenly become very interested in slowly filling everyone's coffee cups. "I thought she'd be alright here, since I'm so old and it's basically just a luncheon. It's not like we'll be opening gifts with lace panties."

"Hmmph," the woman beside her sniffs. "We'll see about that."

Nellie smiles, but she's still glancing toward the doors that Madigan went through. "I just thought she'd be okay."

I delicately hold up the cream for the ladies at the table, but most of them aren't paying attention to me.

"It takes time to get over a thing like that," one of them says.

"I just don't want her to miss out on her youth," Nellie murmurs. "But who am I to tell her what to do or how she should live? Losing a boy like that would take its toll on any girl."

General murmurs of understanding around the table.

And then a click of heels as Madigan comes back through the door.

"Coffee, dear?" Nellie says cheerfully.

"I don't think so, auntie. I actually should probably be going." She leans over to give Nellie a kiss.

It's a sweet thing, but everyone—even me—is aware that the party has barely begun and she's already leaving.

"Why don't you have Andy show you out the

door, dear," Nellie says. "You've got an Uber coming?"

Madigan glances at her phone. "Yup. It'll be here in four minutes."

She doesn't look at me. Which means I'm not quite sure what to do. I definitely don't want to show someone to the door who doesn't want to be shown. But then Nellie gives me a quick nod. I set down the cream and trot to catch up with Madigan so I can get the door for her.

She steps through and I follow. "Do you want me to make sure the Uber gets here?" I ask, glancing at the stormy clouds hanging low in the sky.

"You don't have to," she says, glancing down at her phone.

I nod and turn to go inside.

"Hey," she says.

I turn back.

"Thanks for being so sweet to Nellie," she says, setting her phone down on the concrete banister. "She deserves it. She deserves this." She waves an arm at Gretchen's Cottage.

"Of course," I say. "Nellie's the best. She used to sneak me books."

Madigan almost smiles. Almost. "They had to be snuck, huh? That sounds nefarious."

"Well, they were mostly about sharks," I add quickly.

"Of course they were. Anyway, thank you for making it a good day for her."

"Do you have to…be somewhere?" I ask, because there's no way to politely ask why she's leaving so early.

She raises an eyebrow at me. "After three glasses of wine? No," she says. "These things are just tricky for me."

And I know her openness is surely the wine speaking, but I still want to ask her more. Unfortunately, at that moment, her Uber pulls up.

"Make sure Nellie has a good time," she says as she slips into the back seat.

"Not sure I could stop someone like Nellie from having a good time," I say, shutting the door, like I'm the chauffer.

She nods at that, through the window, and something about her face looks almost pinched—that tight look people get when they want to cry but don't.

Or maybe I'm just imagining it.

I watch the car drive off—not too long or anything, not creepy-style. Just a few seconds as it heads down the drive. And then I straighten my tight jacket and turn to go back inside.

But right there, still sitting on the banister of the porch, is Madigan's phone.

I hold it up, trying to catch the attention of her or

her driver, but they're heading onto the road now and can't see me waving.

When I go back in, I set it at Nellie's table. "She left this," I say, looking guilty.

"Now, Andy, that was your one job, to make sure she got into her car…"

"I did that part," I interrupt cheerfully.

"…with everything she needed," she concludes.

Nellie taps on the phone. "I suppose I'll drop it by after the party," she says. But the collective group of women has turned to me again, that secret-pact look returned their eyes.

"Unless, of course, you'd be a dear and do it for me," Nellie says. "I'm so busy today with the wedding preparations."

All the ladies are smirking.

"To be honest, Miss Nellie, I'm not sure she'd like me dropping it off," I say.

"Well, then, she should have been more careful and taken it with her," Nellie says, "now shouldn't she?"

I pinch my lips together. I'm *really* not sure if Madigan is going to be thrilled to see me show up at her doorstep, especially after the three glasses of wine have burned off a bit more.

Nellie seems to sense that. "Tell her I sent you," she says. "That I had too much to do to do it myself. Tell her, honey, that I *begged* you to take it."

I take the phone, a little tentatively. It's a plain phone, black, nondescript—exactly the type of thing I'd expect from a woman like Madigan. "Yes, ma'am."

"I'll give you the address at the end of the party," Nellie says. "And, sweetie, when you head over, do me a favor and wear something nice."

There's no collective guffawing. It's been replaced by a collective clucking. Heaven hath no energy like a bunch of older women on a matchmaking mission.

I'm not sure I'm the right man for the job. But what can I say, I've been given worse jobs in my life than to show up at a pretty woman's house to return her phone.

CHAPTER 12

MADIGAN

I've kicked off my shoes and fallen asleep on the couch when Alfie starts barking. His 'someone's here' call. Something that sounds aggressive, but is really just overly excited.

Alfie *loves* visitors. As opposed to me.

I try to uncrumple from the couch. My tongue feels starchy and gross. "No one's even at the door," I mumble.

Just as the doorbell rings.

"Okay, someone's at the door." I dig around on my couch for my phone to try to see what time it is. With my job, I get all kinds of messed up. It could be midnight for all I know. But I can't find my phone.

I look down at the dress, wrinkled and off-kilter, and consider not opening the door at all. After all, it's probably just someone trying to sell me new broadband. But Alfie is going nuts. And I know if I don't get it, he'll give me that really sad look, like he knows I could have, but chose not to just to deprive him of the company.

"Alright, alright," I grumble, smoothing myself out as best as possible and running a few fingers through my hair. "Crate."

He obeys very reluctantly, but I can't have this wild dog out here, jumping around with strangers.

When I open the door, I really wish I'd ignored it because, standing there, is the guy from the luncheon. He's still got the suit on, but has taken off the tie and unbuttoned the top button, which gives him this unintentional GQ look. And I have to admit that he looks…really nice.

Which kind of stinks because I know I don't.

I square my shoulders and set my jaw. After all, why do I care what I look like? I don't even like this guy with his stupid ATV business that must not even be doing very well since he has to wait tables at Gretchen's Cottage in his free time and…

He holds out my phone.

I stare at it. Kind of like I've never seen it in my life, though I know exactly what it looks like with the scratched corner and the magnet on the back. It used to be Joshua's.

"Oh," I say.

"You left this," he replies, like he doesn't want to

be there, just as much as I don't want him to be here. "And Nellie asked me to drop it by. She said she had a lot to do with the wedding preparations and stuff."

That's a lie. I almost speak the words out loud and catch myself just in time. After all, it's not his lie. It's Nellie's. That woman would do anything to have me coupled off again.

"Thank you," I manage to stammer out, then run my tongue over my fuzzy teeth. I should never have agreed to go to that luncheon. I knew it would be hard. And I also knew I'd picked up a shift tonight with the ground crew. Which I've got to get ready for. Starting with a solid cup of coffee.

Alfie is turning circles in his crate, like he's about to lose his mind.

The guy—Andy or something—tips his head in Alfie's direction. "Does he know he's not locked in?"

"Oh, yeah," I say, giving a quick sign with my hand that brings Alfie to my side. I motion for him to sit and he does.

"Whoa," Andy says, like he's never seen a dog obey a basic command before. "He knows sign language?"

"I mean," I say. "He's a dog. He can learn all kinds of things. They're some of the smartest animals on earth."

"I think dolphins are considered the smartest,"

Andy says without skipping a beat. "No offense, dude."

Alfie does not appear offended. He's wagging his tail like it's his personal mission to shake it off his bottom.

"Can I pet him?" Andy asks, just like little kids do at the park when I take Alfie for his walks. And I have to admit that there's something sweet in that.

"Yeah, sure, of course," I say.

Andy squats down to Alfie's level and holds out his hands, like he's reaching out for a hug. Alfie is ALL about that, and practically throws himself into Andy's arms, making it look like all I do every day is crate him and give him sign language commands.

"He's very friendly," I add, because I feel the need to explain that Alfie isn't really a prisoner in my house starved for love and attention.

"I can see that," Andy says, rubbing him all up his neck and ears. And there's no denying that it really is incredibly sweet.

"Thank you for the phone," I say when Andy has thoroughly massaged the entirety of Alfie's neck and back and Alfie has trotted off contentedly like that was all he'd ever wanted in life. "Sorry you had to bring it all the way here."

"No problem at all," Andy says, brushing his legs. He's got dog hair on his pants, which makes me feel a little embarrassed, but Andy doesn't seem to care.

"Well," I say. "I'd better get some coffee going. I've got a shift later tonight."

"'Course," Andy says, just as Alfie runs into the room, carrying his leash in his mouth. His best trick indeed.

Andy laughs—this big sound. "He can do everything, I guess."

"Yup, he's pretty smart," I say, staring daggers at Alfie, the little con artist. It's *not* time for a walk. We always go right before I leave for work. "A little too smart, honestly. He's trying to take advantage of having a visitor to get his walk in early."

"Can't blame a dog for that," Andy says. "What's his name?"

"Alfie," I reply.

Alfie nudges him in the knee with his nose and tips his face up imploringly—leash still in his mouth.

Andy's eyes light up like he's just had the best idea in the whole world. "You know, I could take him. What would you think of that, Alfie boy?"

Alfie clearly thinks it's the best idea that's ever been thought in the history of human thinking. He wags his tail like his backside is going to fall off.

"Oh no, really," I say in a rush. "You don't have to do that."

I bend down, trying to wrestle the leash from Alfie's mouth. "Now you're just trying to make me look bad," I murmur.

"I really don't mind," Andy says.

"I mean, don't you have to…" I stop myself before finishing my sentence *be somewhere*. Like at work. And then I realize it's Friday night and that normal people don't have to be at work on Friday night. Though it still seems that a guy like Andy would be out with friends on the weekend.

"I was supposed to have dinner with my mom," he says. "But she had a little emergency come up, which means I got cancelled on. So I've got a few minutes to walk this desperate dog."

"He's really alright," I grumble. "We really do walk every day. Twice. Once when I get home from work and then when I go back. When my shifts are long, my dad comes over and takes him."

"I mean, he's just a dog," Andy says. "And a dog's gonna take advantage of a walk whenever he can."

"Apparently," I grumble. The truth is that I can't remember any other time Alfie has shown up with his leash for a stranger.

"Why don't you enjoy your coffee," Andy says. "And I'll take this guy out for you. We won't go too far."

"No, it's really okay," I say, but then I look down at Alfie, into those dark brown eyes, into that ridiculous face that saved my life and is still holding a leash between his teeth. "You know what," I say suddenly. "There's a coffee shop about a half a mile away. I'll come with you and just grab an espresso or something there."

Alfie dances in a circle, the leash beginning to wrap around his legs. "You ding dong," I murmur, bending down to unwrap him as the realization dawns on me that I've just agreed to—no, that I gave the invitation to—go for coffee with some man I don't even know, that I'm pretty sure I don't even like. *Oh Alfie, what have you done this time?*

CHAPTER 13

ANDY

We walk there in silence. Not quite utter silence, but real close. At one point I literally comment on a tree.

Alfie trots and wags and occasionally yips at a squirrel or bush, but he seems to be the only one who understands how the three of us got into this predicament. I had just meant to bring Madigan her phone. Truth be told, I hadn't even really wanted to do that. And she had definitely not wanted me to show up at her doorstep, much less be forced to share a warm drink with me.

If it wasn't so painfully awkward, I might laugh. Because the whole thing is freaking hilarious. But it doesn't seem like a big, unexpected giggle would be the right thing to make Madigan feel more comfortable.

Occasionally, she tugs Alfie back to her side with a word. Though she doesn't need to. He's the most well-behaved dog I've ever seen in my life. Lassie could take lessons from this guy. I think Madigan just wants someone to be able to say something to, so occasionally she'll do this clucking noise with her mouth, followed by a 'heel, boy.' And Alfie, trained soldier that he is, steps right next to her heel, even though he'd only strayed maybe an inch.

Madigan is still in her dress from the party. She's thrown on a practical pair of slip-on shoes. As we walk, the hot summer air blows the cotton dress against her legs. They're nice legs—strong and tan. I imagine with her work she has to stay somewhat fit.

I open my mouth to say so, but as it replays for that instant through my brain, I realize it could come out sounding creepy. *Hey, honey, looks like you work out.* So again, I say nothing. Neither does she.

Alfie stops to enthusiastically mark a piece of territory just outside of the coffee shop and Madigan waits for a moment before I hold out a hand for the leash. "Go ahead and order yourself something," I say.

She reluctantly relinquishes the leash. "What would you like?" she asks. I think it's her first full sentence since we left her house.

"Oh, I'm good," I say. "I'll get something when you come back. Do you want to sit outside or in?"

"Alfie usually prefers out, though it's really hot today, but yeah, outside I guess," she says. "And I'm going to get you something, so tell me what you want. I appreciate you bringing my phone to me and all this." She gestures at Alfie.

I glance at the shop. This will probably not come as a surprise, but I'm not exactly a coffee shop kind of guy. I'm not particularly interested in froth and foam and whipped cream. In fact, I don't often drink coffee at all—I get my kicks in different sorts of ways.

"Just…anything decaf," I say.

"Decaf," she replies with no small amount of disdain.

"We don't all want to stay up for work all night," I reply with a smile that I hope feels good-natured.

"'Cause you're just going to go home and tuck into bed on this Friday night?" she asks in a slightly saucy voice. I can't tell if that means more disdain or if it's her own attempt at being good-natured.

"I never know what I'll do," I reply. "But that's definitely one of the options. Truthfully, I might hop over to Mama's house to make sure her procedure went well. And then I'll head over to the park to check on things there. First Fridays we always stay open late."

She nods, but it's in this of-course-you-do way. "Decaf it is," she says.

And, maybe it's just to annoy her, but I stop her just before she goes in. "I don't suppose that fancy shop has milkshakes, do they?"

"A milkshake?"

"Sure. If I'm honest, that's what sounds the best of all."

Another of-course-it-does look. "I'll ask. Flavor?"

"Vanilla," I say. "With a shot of caramel."

Alfie has long-since finished his business and is sniffing at the flowers along the path, but Madigan goes in alone anyway.

"Your girl can't get away from me fast enough," I say to Alfie. "I suppose we ought to find us a table."

Which isn't too hard, since there's only one left, directly in the sun, and next to a group of young girls out for a night on the town—junior high style.

Alfie doesn't mind. He wags and wiggles and the girls coo over him like he's the best thing since iced coffee with cream.

"I just *love* your dog," one of them coos at me through an excess of lip gloss.

"He's not actually mine," I say.

"Oh, your girlfriend's," another asks.

And then I get stuck. *Well, no, but also not really my friend. Truthfully, a random stranger whose name I only actually know from overhearing it, but I somehow let her dog talk us into a coffee date together.* "A friend," I say, stretching the meaning of the word to the utmost.

Several of the girls give we-know-better looks. Alfie and I let them slide.

"Aren't you the ATV guy?" one of the girls asks.

"Yeah," I say, a little flattered that anyone knows. But, well, that's rural Kentucky for you.

"My brother likes to ride at your place. Mama's throwing a fit, though, since them kids got hurt."

"Yeah," I say. "That was real rough, but so long as your brother doesn't steal any keys, he should be just fine."

"Is that what happened?" one of the other girls squeals.

I'm rescued by Madigan, who shows up with our drinks and another judgmental look about my table choice and a suggestion to go inside where it's cooler.

But Alfie has settled his rump under the table, and doesn't seem invested in moving.

"We like your dog," the girls coo.

"Thank you," Madigan replies, her look softening slightly at the compliment. She settles into the seat across from me and hands me my shake. She's got ice in her coffee though it looks black. I guess when you work nights, that's how it's done.

"So," she replies, casting an awkward glance at the girls, though they've stopped paying attention to us and have moved on to some bit of juicy gossip.

"Your, um, park stays open late on the first Friday of each month?"

"Yeah," I respond. "We get a few food trucks out there, have a good time."

"But you weren't going to go?" she asks.

"Not tonight. At least not till later. Mama and I had us a nice date."

"Oh," she says. "That reminds me. I figured you might be hungry and want some protein to go with your sugar bomb." She opens a little bag that came with the drinks and pulls out a wrapped turkey sandwich. "For you."

I'm legitimately touched. "Oh, thanks. You didn't have to…how much do I owe you?"

"It's on me," she says with a wave of her hand. "I appreciate you bringing me my phone."

"Thank you," I say, since there's nothing else to say.

"So, um, your mother. Is she, uh, okay?" Madigan asks tentatively.

"Yeah, of course," I say, digging into my sandwich. "Why?"

"Oh," she says, like she's not going to pursue it.

I stop eating, look at her, wait.

She picks up her coffee. "I just thought you said she had a procedure, an emergency or something."

A smile tickles my mouth, though I don't let it out just yet. "Oh, yes, the procedure. So you thought that my mother—who I was supposed to have dinner with tonight—had some emergency procedure, and that instead of me being by her side, I came to your house to, uh, bring you a phone and woo your dog."

"Um, maybe," she says, swirling a finger nervously around her glass. "But not when you say it that way."

"She's a dentist," I say. "One of her patients broke a tooth, so she went in to help with that."

"A dentist?" Madigan asks, as though that detail is more unbelievable than the idea that I would abandon my mother to an emergency procedure.

"Yup," I say. "Dr. Putman."

"Oh," Madigan says, recognizing the name. "My hus—" she stops herself. "I know people who've gone there."

"Well," I say, my smile creeping out. "Best one in town."

"I'm really sorry," she says, taking a gulp of her drink. "I didn't mean to assume that…"

"I'd leave my mother alone in the hospital." I finally stop trying to hold back my smile and laugh.

"I'm so sorry," she says. "Really. Obviously, that was ridiculous, even with—"

"With?" I ask, still teasing, but genuinely curious about what she's going to say.

"I guess, um, your job and everything. It seems risky and impulsive and—"

"—irresponsible," I finish for her.

She doesn't reply. Just gulps her coffee. And messing with her like this is, well, it's kind of fun.

"So back to your, uh, park—it's open tonight. First Fridays."

"Yeah," I say.

"And I don't suppose that after dinner, you were going to take your mother there, show her a good time?"

I tip my head to the side. Did this woman, who barely ever cracks a smile, just make a joke? "She's been a time or two," I reply. "Not her favorite thing though. Teeth and all. She's not a fan of things that can knock them out. I tell her she should be grateful for all the business I send her."

Madigan pales.

"I'm kidding," I say. "No one's ever knocked a tooth out since I opened the place. Though they *could.*"

She's staring at my teeth.

"You know, if you weren't going to work," I say. "I might invite you over to The Molehill for a ride."

She laughs then. Okay, it's more of a twitter, but it's definitely more than a smile. "You know what *I* do for work, right?" she says.

And it's meant to be a joke; it *is* a joke, but at that

moment our eyes meet and we both remember that kid and feel the weight of it.

I clear my throat. She reaches under the table to check on Alfie.

"I better get going," I say, wadding up my napkin. "Thank you for dinner." I peek under the table and Alfie is lolling on the warm sidewalk, half asleep. "Tell Alfie I said thank you as well." He hears his name and his ears twitch. "But I really better be going."

I pause. She pauses.

"And, hey," I say. "I *think* we know each other's names, but just so we're clear, I'm Andy."

"Madigan," she says softly. "Thanks for bringing my phone by."

"No problem, Maddie," I say, the name rolling off my lips before I can think about it.

She opens her mouth like she's going to correct me, but doesn't.

"I'll see you around," I say.

And then, a smile touching her lips, she adds, "But hopefully not when I'm at work."

"Why, Miss Maddie," I say. "I do believe that's your second joke of the night."

She smiles then, full-toothed. She has truly beautiful teeth—white and square. My mother would adore them. "Who said I was joking?"

"Well," I say, holding my empty milkshake glass up as if to say cheers. "Here's hoping."

And Madigan, she lifts her own empty cup and clinks it against mine.

CHAPTER 14

MADIGAN

"**W**hat just happened, Alfie?" I say, looking down at my dog, who is fully committed to sleeping under the table.

It wasn't a date. I didn't go on a date. I'm sure of that. And somewhat relieved.

But it was still, somehow, *something*.

"Come on, boy," I say, clucking my tongue in a way that signals it's time to get home. "Mama's got to get dressed for work."

Alfie rolls over, as though he's hit his teenage years and isn't invested in moving or listening. I suppose he has hit his teenage years, or at least his young adulthood. "Come on, boy. I'll get you a treat."

I never buy the pup cups the coffee shop offers. The cream is terrible for Alfie's digestion, but I've got some tooth-cleaning treats at home.

And something about the tooth-cleaning makes me think about Andy's mother, the dentist. Joshua used to go to her office; he raved about her. I think he even got her a Christmas present once.

What a strange degree of separation, like the Kevin Bacon thing. That's how I choose to think about it as I head back to my house. Just a weird little circle of people who know of each other in sideways ways and smalltown connections.

I pass the church Joshua and I used to attend when we weren't travelling. Methodist, though neither of us had been baptized into that faith. But Joshua liked the architecture and he'd had some good chats with the pastor about history and numerology.

It *is* a beautiful building. Or was. Now the steps to the door are crumbling and the front door has a huge 'closed for renovations' sign on it, though I don't see any renovations happening. A few of the windows are boarded up and the door is locked with a chain and padlock.

Through that door used to be a small prayer room open to the public. Homeless people would make their way there during the winter months, though it would have been empty on a night like this in the summer. For just a moment, I touch the door, practically smelling the polish of the wooden pews.

But then I remember how Joshua and I used to

stop there sometimes, usually after getting dinner, sometimes even on a lazy Saturday afternoon together. And Joshua would make jokes and I would act reverent, even though back then he was definitely the most reverent one.

I step back from the church with a jerk, looking down, ignoring the steeples, the art deco—if that's even the right name—the things that Joshua would have pointed out.

Alfie hurries with me, staying right at my side—as always—even if I am forcing the poor guy to trot just to keep up. Sometimes, some things—well, I just can't get away fast enough.

CHAPTER 15

ANDY

Mama shows up at The Molehill around 9:00, looking exhausted.

"How'd it go?" I ask.

She wiggles her head back and forth in a so-so kind of way. "His tooth broke because of some decay that was already a problem, so it wasn't a simple fix."

"No glue job, huh?" I say.

"Definitely not," she replies. "More of a consultation. Parents don't love that. But what can I do, create teeth where there are none?" She glances around my sparse office—a couple pictures of quasi-famous people who visited on the walls—no one truly big-time, but still some fun folks. In addition to pictures of slightly-famous people, I've decorated with an old desk that literally came from a second-hand store, a file cabinet, laptop, and my mini fridge.

That's where Mama's eyes settle. "So what'd you get?" she asks.

"Get?" I say, confused by the question.

"For dinner," she replies.

Ah, yes, dinner. The one we didn't go to, but I promised my mom I would get food from anyway, and then I spent the afternoon with a beautiful woman *and* a turkey sandwich, and completely forgot.

"You forgot," Mama says, before I can.

"Sort of, yes," I say.

She glances out the window. "Any food trucks still out there? I'm starving."

I almost—almost—say, "You're not starving." Which is exactly what she used to say to me when I was younger, but looking into her nearly-hangry eyes, I decide against it. "Where can I take you?" I say, getting my keys for the Jeep.

"Oh, it's okay, honey. I'll just get something at home."

"Nope," I say, opening the door for her. "Anywhere you choose. As long as it's open past nine. Which limits us to—I think—McDonald's and Smithy's."

"Smithy's then," she says.

"Good choice," I reply.

"What did you eat?" she asks as we walk to my car.

I pinch my lips for a second, trying to decide what to tell her. I go with the perfect truth. "Turkey sandwich."

"At Biggie's?"

"Nah, just some coffee shop."

Now, this may come as a surprise, but I'm not the best liar in the world. I had a little practice in my teen years, but never enough to really master the skill. Mama gives me a classic side eye.

"What coffee shop?" she asks, as I open the door for her.

"Honestly, I couldn't even tell you the name. It was close to—" I stop myself, but it's too late. I've said too much.

"Close to what, honey?"

"To the house of this person who left her phone at the luncheon."

A truth that oddly seems to satisfy my mother. Apparently, she's assuming all the ladies at the luncheon were in the over-sixty crowd.

"How's Nellie?" she asks.

"Glowing," I say, staring straight ahead and starting the ignition.

"And Gretchen?"

"Good. Business is booming. Glad I could help her out today."

"You're a sweetheart, Andy. You've about given

me an ulcer a thousand times in my life, but you're a good kid."

And now—even though I didn't lie at all—I kind of *feel* like a liar since my mom thinks I spent the whole day helping my sister and serving a group of old ladies. Which is only mostly true. "I think it was by that big church," I say. "The coffee shop."

"Ah, near Panning Street. It's gotten a little gentrified, that area. It's nice."

"Yeah," I say.

And then my mama hears it. It might even be possible that I'd put that pause in my voice there on purpose, so she'd ask me more questions. She bites. "So who'd you take the phone to?" she asks. "Edith? She's always leaving hers at my office, poor thing."

"No," I say. "Not Edith." Okay, so I'm not going to let my not-lie drop, but I am—for some reason— going to make my mom drag the truth out of me.

"Who then?"

"Her name was Madigan."

"Madigan?" Mama says, like she's testing the name. "I don't know that I know her."

"I don't think you do," I say, scooting into Smithy's nearly empty parking lot.

"Was she one of Nellie's friends?"

Ah, there it is, my entrance. "Her niece, I think."

And then Mama's face goes blank, like she does in fact know this woman, and she's now the one with the not-lie to hide. "You went for coffee with her?"

"Technically I got a milkshake," I say, making my mama work harder.

"Well, that's going to be all the talk if it gets out," Mama murmurs.

The host pops out of nowhere like he was just waiting for a juicy piece of gossip to drop into his ears. "How many?" he asks.

I hold up two fingers.

"Why would it be all the talk?" I ask Mama, realizing that this is why I baited her, why I made her drag the full truth out of me. Because of that pact-gaze all the older ladies gave me, because of the chit-chat when Madigan went into the restroom. The talk of the 'lost boy' and the 'poor girl.'

"Let's just get our food," she says.

"SPILL THE TEA," I say once we're seated.

She picks up her menu, all innocent. "What tea and why would I want to spill it?"

"You know what I mean, Mama," I say. "What's the deal with that girl?"

"Woman," Mama corrects me. "You can't go around calling every young female a 'girl.'"

"Okay, woman," I respond. "Now will you tell me?"

"How did you wind up taking Madigan her phone?" Mama asks.

"She left it," I say, leaving out the part about three glasses of wine.

"She just left her phone at Gretchen's?"

"No, Mama, I stole it so I would have the chance to take it to her."

"Truly, that might be the most believable thing about this whole tale." Her eyes settle on the shrimp scampi, like I knew they would.

"And what is so unbelievable about me taking someone her phone and us going out for coffee?"

"Nothing," Mama says, making eye contact with the waiter, who hurries over. "The scampi," she says to him.

"And for your date?" he asks and Mama giggles, though I'm not entirely sure the waiter meant it as a joke. Mama was young when she had me and she looks younger than she is; people occasionally mistake us for a couple.

"What do you want, Andy?" she asks.

"I'm still full," I say.

"Nothing at all?" she asks.

I wave the waiter off, trying to remember where we were in our conversation. Mama is really good at derailing these things.

"Why is it weird?" I repeat. "People get coffee together all the time. Especially friends."

"Mmmm," Mama says. "So you're friends?"

I don't answer.

She raises an eyebrow. "You're not friends."

"Well, we're not more than friends," I say, now on the defensive. "I took her phone to her and we took her dog for a walk and wound up getting coffee. It's not that weird."

"No," she says. "Of course not."

I'm about ready to bang my head on the table. "Okay, Mama, explain this—at the luncheon, Madigan went to the restroom and all the ladies clucked and cooed over some boy. She lose a baby or something?" I ask.

Mama looks off into the middle distance, like she's contemplating the fate of the world.

"Nah," she says. "She lost a husband."

I sit back in my chair, tipping onto the back legs just a little so Mama won't notice. "Ouch," I say. "He run off?" That's usually how the husband-losing scandals go in this neck of the woods.

"He died," she answers.

I plunk my chair back suddenly onto all four legs. "You're kidding," I say.

"Don't I wish it," she replies. "He was my patient and everyone was so torn up about it. It happened the spring after you broke your leg. You were still recovering and starting your business with Gretchen and just about giving me a heart attack every ten seconds, so I don't think it was really on your radar."

"That sucks."

"Don't say 'sucks,' honey."

I try really, really hard not to roll my eyes at my own Mama, who—at my age—was a single mom raising a little boy and trying to pull her life back together. She'd been way wilder than the word 'sucks.'

"But it does suck," she continues. "They'd only been married for a few months. He was some kind of up-and-coming scholar. He moved to town with his new bride—her daddy's from here. They'd bought a little house here while he was on a sabbatical doing research. The whole town expected him to be working at Harvard in a few years. 'Course that's just smalltown talk."

"So Madigan hasn't dated anyone since then?"

"Don't know how I would know who she has or hasn't dated," Mama says coyly, digging into the scampi, which has just arrived as though to thwart my mission of learning more.

"But you know what people say..." I begin.

"I know people around here say a lot of things," she ends.

"Come on, Mama, throw me a bone."

"Baby boy, I threw you a whole lot of bones,"

Mama replies. "Probably told you more than I should have. If you want to find out more, you're going to have to get it from the horse's mouth."

"I'll tell her you called her a horse."

"If that means you're talking to her instead of the gossip vine, go ahead," Mama says.

And she means it. She doesn't give me a single other detail the whole night as she gobbles up her scampi.

We talk about the business and Nellie's bridal shower. I order each of us a piece of pie and then Mama starts yawning, since she is *not* a night owl.

"Come on, Granny, I better get you home," I say.

"I'd like to become a Granny," she grumbles as I get her chair.

"Ah, now, Mama, you always told me not to rush it like you did."

"I suppose I did tell you that," she says with a sigh. "And it was good advice. But not rushing it doesn't mean skipping it altogether."

"I've got no plans to skip it. Just need to find me the right girl. Maybe I'll ask Maddie out on another date. An actual one."

Mama doesn't comment, which makes me wonder if it is a good idea.

"Got to get things straight from the horse's mouth and all," I say.

"You can ask," Mama replies, leaving the sentence

hanging like she doesn't know what Madigan will answer.

I pat Mama's cheek. "You know I like a good challenge."

"I know you like a good risk," she says.

"Sometimes that's the same thing," I reply.

"I suppose it is," she says.

"Speaking of," I begin, handing her a mint as we walk out into the beautiful starry night. "There's a bit of property come up for sale right behind mine."

"And?" she asks, unwrapping the candy.

"I'm thinking about making an offer."

Mama doesn't reply right away. It's one of her best mom talents and the type of thing that has kept us from butting heads too much in the last few years.

"Don't get in over your head," she finally says as we both pause to take in the twinkling sky.

"It's just a bit of land," I reply. "But it's nice. There's a pond on a big chunk of it."

"Is it ridable land?" she asks.

"Honestly, I wasn't thinking to use it for riding. I was thinking that it might be the perfect little shooting range. Far enough away from The Molehill to not be dangerous, with the pond separating everything."

"ATVs and now rifles," she says. "What are you going to do next? Anacondas?"

I rub my chin as if pondering her suggestion. "I'll

put it into the idea sack. Next time I draw one out, then maybe."

Mama rolls her eyes.

"Or…hear me out," I say. "Next up. Ski lift."

"I'm listening to that one," she says as we walk toward my Jeep.

"Only problem is, I have to buy more than a *little* molehill to make that happen. More like a whole mountain."

"Well, if anyone could buy a mountain and make it work, it'd be you, hon," Mama says, reaching up to tousle my hair.

"Aww," I reply. "Now let's get you home before you turn into a pumpkin."

"Too late," she murmurs sleepily, as I hold the door open for her to climb into the Jeep.

CHAPTER 16

MADIGAN

 stare down at my phone as the coffee drips into my mug.

Thirteen little words. An unlucky number in almost every culture. Unlucky enough that many elevators—even in the 21st century—skip it in skyscrapers and hop from twelve to fourteen.

Thirteen little words from a man who shouldn't have my number in the first place. After all, having my *phone* and having my phone *number* are two very different things.

I wonder if Nellie gave it to him. It seems like the type of thing she'd do. Though somehow it hadn't really seemed like the type of thing he would do—ask for it, or take it if offered. He'd seemed so uncomfortable when he'd first shown up on my doorstep, like he hadn't even wanted to be there. At least until he and Alfie hit it off.

Alfie is sitting at my feet, leash in mouth.

"I know, boy," I say, setting my phone down for now. "I just need to get a little bit of caffeine into my system."

He looks at me with raw judgment. But he's not the one who came home at eight this morning after a twelve-hour shift where we ran ourselves to death. I prefer working in the skies. Midvale EMS is always understaffed. And could use another truck.

I yawn.

Alfie stares.

"We can't go yet anyway," I say. "We have to wait for Grandpa. He'll be here in just a few minutes."

Alfie wags his tail at the word *Grandpa.* My dad. Aka, dog grandpa extraordinaire. He would have been a great regular grandpa too, but right now, that's not looking like it's ever going to be in the cards.

The thirteen little words from the text tap into my mind involuntarily. Pesky things, words—and the way they never quite leave me alone.

I dump half of my coffee down my throat like a proper addict. "Okay, boy," I say, leaving my phone where I can't see it. "I'll get dressed."

Alfie follows me into my room. Privacy is not his strongest suit.

He settles himself by the door of my spartan room. A bed for me, a bed for Alfie, a dresser, one end table, a lamp, and a desk. I boxed up most of the books and moved them out after Joshua died, along with his end table, papers, glasses, everything.

And when I say I boxed them up, I mean I didn't object when my dad did. As for me, in those first weeks, I just lay on my bed, unmoving for days. I honestly don't know how many. The only calls I took were from my dad and he would always tell me to get up and I would always tell him I would, and then I would always *not* get up. I barely moved. I barely ate. I lost over twenty pounds.

And then one morning, or maybe it was afternoon, my dad called. "I'm getting up," I said, not moving a single muscle.

"You're not," he said.

"I can't," I responded.

"That's scientifically untrue," he replied.

"I'm not a scientist."

"Listen," he said. "Just get up to walk the dog."

"I don't have a dog," I'd said.

Which is when the doorbell had rung.

The doorbell had rung a lot in the days after Joshua died, then less and less the more I ignored it. If there wasn't a Grubhub notification on my phone, I was *not* opening that door.

"Get the door, Maddie," Dad had texted, like he was some kind of creeper in a thriller movie.

"Dad, why are you here? I'm not even dressed," I'd texted back.

"Well, then get dressed, and answer the door."

I had not gotten dressed, but I had rolled out of bed and found my filthy, stinky robe. My legs were wobbly, my hair almost impossibly oily, my nails chewed to scabbed nubs. But I wasn't going to leave my dad standing on my doorstep.

"Dad, I—" I said, my voice rising as I opened the door.

And then there he was, with this box in his hands. And in that box, a scruffy little ball of floof.

"I said you need to walk the dog," he said again, grinning like an absolute lunatic.

"Oh, Dad," I said, trying to look away from the little creature who was literally trying to chase his tail within that tiny box. "You know I can't possibly—"

Dad cut me off. "Dogs need to be walked. Morning and evening. He'll need potty-training as well. I've brought some supplies."

I noticed the little bag hanging off his arm.

"Some food and some pads for him, a few toys. Leash and collar, of course. There's a dog park not far from here."

"Dad, I know you mean well, but I don't know

the first thing about dogs," I'd said. "Neither do you." But I'd made a tactical error. I'd reached into the box with that little ball of floof and I had touched his velvet soft snout and now he was licking my hand.

"Which is why I also bought this how-to book for you," my dad was saying as the little tongue slurped at my fingertips. "I know you love a good book."

I did, in fact, love a good book, and now my hand had travelled to the dog's neck. He was leaning forward, little paws on the edge of the box, threatening to topple it out of my dad's arms. "Oh, here, let me get that," I'd said, reaching to take the box. But instead the dog had leaped into my arms.

And that was the beginning of the end.

He was licking my neck, snuggling into my stinky robe, which he seemed to find quite adequate. And then Dad was hooking a collar around his neck.

"Maddie," he said. "Go. Get. Dressed. Otherwise, he's going to wee on the floor."

And what can I say? I got dressed.

I lean down now to give Alfie a nice neck rub, just like he's always loved. And just like he did that first afternoon, he practically leaps into my arms, only now he's so big, he almost knocks me down. It reminds me, for just a moment, of the other day— when he had leapt for Andy. I push that thought away, burrowing my head into that soft floof of Alfie's neck. "I know," I say. "I love you too."

The doorbell rings.

"Come on in, Dad."

If it's ever a killer, I'm probably in trouble, but so far, it's always only been my dad. "Go get him," I say to Alfie, who is wagging in the knock-off-his-tail kind of way.

Alfie bounds out of my room and I throw on a clean t-shirt.

Ever since that first day when Alfie had arrived, I'd walked him morning and night. My strength came back; my appetite came back. My life, piece by broken piece, came back. And then, one day, a little bit later, when my dad had asked what I'd needed help with, I'd asked him to clear Joshua's things out of my room.

"You sure, honey?" he'd asked.

I'd been too choked up to answer, so I'd just nodded.

"You don't seem sure," he'd said.

But I was. I needed them—not gone, not all the way—but not in my sight every single day.

The week after that, I replaced my books with a training manual for my new course. EMT Basic. To make room for that, I cleared out all of my college classics, my cheap paperbacks, even a few special editions of my favorite novels—replacing all my old books with encyclopedic tomes about anatomy and physiology. I'm not really one to go partway in.

The only old book I left on my shelf was a collection of poetry by Alfred Lord Tennyson—Alfie's namesake.

"You decent?" Dad calls down the hall.

"Coming!" I say, grabbing a hat and my wallet.

At that moment, my phone dings with another text message.

"Your phone, honey," Dad says, picking it up and handing it to me. "Looks like work," he says, his voice a touch disappointed.

I swipe my phone away from him. They need a shift covered—Sheila had to go home sick.

"You can go into work if you want to," Dad says, his voice even, which is actually his tell. His voice is never even except when he's trying to be cool with something he's not cool with. "I can dog sit."

"Nah," I say. "We already planned to spend the day together." I click away from the message, and there, sitting near the top of my texts is the one from Andy. Those thirteen unlucky little words. I read them again, almost against my own will.

What would it take to get you to go to dinner with me?

"Something wrong, sweetie?" Dad asks, hooking Alfie up to his leash.

"Oh, no," I say, distracted. "Just…did you know that in a lot of skyscrapers they don't label a floor as the thirteenth?"

"You thinking of a new book idea?" Dad asks.

I shake my head. I haven't thought of a book idea in years. "Just thinking of…numbers."

Dad puts his arm around me and gives me a tight squeeze. "And what's the happiest one?" he asks.

"Oh, that's easy," I say. "Three."

"Three?" he says.

"Of course," I answer. "You, me, Alfie."

"That *is* the perfect number," Dad says. "So how is three so different than thirteen? Isn't thirteen just three combined with ten, which—if I recall from holiday dinners—has a meaning of completeness and divine order?"

"I never should have let you and Joshua chat it up over a turkey," I say. "And you'll have to tell your theory to the elevator-making people, because historically they were afraid it was so unlucky that fires would break out on the thirteenth floor."

What I don't say because the words won't quite leave my mouth is that in many Asian cultures they distrust thirteen because one and three combine to make the number four, which is a homonym for death. They avoid it.

Just like I do.

I shove my phone into my pocket, ignoring the text.

CHAPTER 17

ANDY

I get to The Molehill, about thirty minutes before it opens. Ned has just unlocked the door and is opening things up for business.

When he sees me, he holds his hand over his heart as though he's having a heart attack.

"Yeah, yeah," I say. "Save it for acting school."

"You're just here a little earlier than usual, that's all," Ned says, laughing.

"You know when I first opened this place, I was here from dawn till dusk—doing everything myself."

"Right," he answers. "Which is why you hired me, so you could sleep in every day."

"Not entirely true," I respond. "I just sometimes need a little creative time in the mornings to think."

"If by thinking you mean dream," Ned says.

"Sometimes," I respond. "But this morning

instead of thinking, I have other matters to attend to."

"You calling that girl?" he asks.

And now it's my turn to feel like I'm having a heart attack, because how would he even know about her.

"I'm headed over to the lake to check out a new property."

"Tell me more," Ned says, as I dig my keys out of my desk, and unlock Rico, my favorite vehicle.

"Can't," I say. "Top secret. Just a little bee I've got in my bonnet."

"I think you'd look real nice in a bonnet," he says. "What do you hope to do with the property?"

Okay, so apparently I'm bad at keeping secrets because I say, "Thinking of a rifle range."

Ned looks out the window, rubbing his chin and kind of nodding. "I can see it," he says.

"Me too," I answer, grabbing my helmet.

"You're driving over?" he says.

"Best way to clear my head."

"Speaking of heads," he says, looking down and fiddling with some paperwork. "You ever hear anything about that kid?"

I clear my throat. I had, in fact, heard a bit about that kid—the one who hit his head. And it wasn't the greatest. "He's alive," I say.

"You know when that's the report someone gives, things aren't usually super great."

"Things aren't super great," I reply, another bee tickling into my bonnet. "But hopefully they'll get better soon."

I put my sunglasses on, and head out into the morning sun.

Maybe I should do the early shift more often because there's nothing quite as beautiful. I hop onto the ATV, and head out over the hills. It feels almost like a workout, the way you shift your body left and right with the four-wheeler, bouncing around, keeping it under control. I've actually wanted to add some mountain bike paths to the property, but I'm worried the ATVers will drive them, making it unsafe. Ah, adulthood, to worry about those things.

I crest a hill, catching a bit of air, bracing my core, letting the wind catch me. When I was a kid, I used to dream about flying. Now I get to do it instead. In that moment, right before you come down, when you're just suspended, when you're almost an angel—that's what I love about riding.

I guess that's what I love about risk. The chance to fly. If only for a moment.

I think about my unanswered text from Madigan. She left me on 'read.' All day, all night.

Mama said it would be a risk. And I'd told her I liked risks. Not a lie.

I take a sharp curve, leaning, my arms and chest tense and strong. The day is going to be a hot one, and I'm glad to be out here in the beginnings of it.

Ned can pretend I never get up before noon. But it's not usually true. What most people don't know is that I sleep with my curtains open. That way, when the sun rises, I have the option to rise with it. Rise being figurative of course. Because most of those mornings, I stay in bed, taking it all in. It's my time for ideas, for inspiration, for *joy*.

I see the lake as I come through the trees. It sparkles in the sun. A sapphire of a thing.

I think it's then that I know, really *know*, I'm not backing out. I'm buying the property. I could put the range on the north side, so that the sun won't hit too hard in morning or evening. It's already got a building there, and then the shooters can look out over this gorgeous lake the entire time.

Who wouldn't pay good money for that?

Though, who am I kidding, that's only half my motivation. It's love as much as money. I want people to wake up each day as excited as I am about the day ahead.

I brake suddenly, skidding up a wave of dirt. Because right there in front of me is a tall barbed wire fence. Well, that'll have to come down.

I slow down, ride around it, figuring there must

be an opening somewhere. After all, it's not really a fence, unless there's an opening, right?

About a mile around, I find the gate. It's still locked, but I figure Bill will be here soon to open it. I glance at my phone. Five minutes early.

I use the time to ride the periphery of the property.

Thick cattails on the southern side, a worn pier on the east. Ducks float through the morning waters, bathing and preening, bottoms tipping up when they find something good to eat.

In the distance, I see a plume of dust as a truck pummels down the dirt road toward me. Right on time.

Now I suppose I have to play hard to get to try to get a good price. Playing hard to get has never been my strongest suit.

I think again about my text to Madigan.

I figure that one good risk deserves another. By the time William MacArthur has swung out of his truck, all six foot seven of him, I've sent Madigan a second text. I'll give it four tries. My lucky number.

CHAPTER 18

MADIGAN

The thing about flying, it sets you apart, makes the world small, helps you understand your tiny place within it. The lights of the Riley Children's Hospital in Indy sparkle ahead of us.

Matt tips the helicopter to the south and my little patient stirs. She's got a long gash deep on her head. Apparently, she climbed up her brother's basketball hoop so she could "dunk" the ball, only her weight caused it to tip, landing on top of her.

Pavement, little girl, heavy basketball pole.

Not great, but it could have been worse. We're taking her up north because the doctors in Midvale felt like she should get pediatric care. And she should.

"You doing okay, sweetie?" I say into my headset.

She doesn't answer. She hasn't spoken since we got on the helicopter. In fact, we had to disentangle her from her mother's arms to get her on, and it wasn't my favorite moment ever in my career. She was crying and her mom was crying and we all looked like the wrong end of a Hallmark movie. Or maybe we looked like an action movie where I was the bad guy.

We'd even tried to get a bigger helicopter on scene so her mom could come with, but nobody was close enough. Unfortunately for this little girl, time mattered more than space. Which meant her mom got left behind.

Tracey and I have been making bad jokes and pointing out sights and trying to coax her out of her funk the entire time. She hasn't even cracked a smile.

I'm in the seat behind her, which in a tiny helicopter like the Bell 206 means she's pretty much in my lap, though she's facing forward so it's difficult to see her face.

"We're coming up on the hospital. Can you see the lights?"

Her head flicks to the left, the smallest movement, but I notice it.

"Your mama and daddy are driving up right now. They should be there really soon too."

The girl doesn't answer, except to sniffle, so maybe it was the wrong thing to say.

"We'll be landing, just like in the movies, and you can tell all your friends. Bet none of them have been in a helicopter."

The sniffle stops, and she watches the lights grow in the distance as we approach the landing pad on the top of the hospital.

I've almost forgotten what I said when she murmurs, "Not Chase neither." She has the cutest, thickest little accent.

Tracey gives me a side-eyed wink.

Chase, I'm assuming, is the big brother she was trying to impress with her basketball stunt. "No way, not him either. And guess what else?" I whisper, leaning forward, like I'm telling her a secret through the headset. "We'll be landing on the roof. How cool is that?"

"Kind of cool," she mutters as Matt circles the helipad before we prepare to settle onto the roof nice and soft, like a bee on a flower.

"Ma'am," the little girl says, with all that thick southern politeness. "Do you think you could take a picture, send it to Mama so she knows we got here real safe."

"I'd love to," I say as the blades slow and I open the door. "We'll get an epic one to send to your brother too."

She smiles then, the first of the night. "You know,

it kinda looks like Christmas up here with all them lights."

And, you know, with a talking, smiling patient, it kinda does.

I hold up my phone to snap a picture of her and notice the little text bubble at the top. Dude is not taking my not-so-subtle hint of completely ghosting him. This must be his fourth text. I'm gonna have to reply at some point and ask him to stop.

Unfortunately, as I try to click away so I can share the picture to the little girl's mother, the text box to him pops up automatically and I accidentally hit one of those auto reply bubbles, the one that says, "Great! What time?"

"Oh no," I mutter, checking my language in front of our young patient.

"Did it not go through?" she asks.

"Oh, sorry, yeah, I'm sending it right now," I mumble, looking at my phone, the little checkmark filling in so I know Andy's seen my response. I quickly send the picture to the girl's mother, then click my phone off, shaking away the sense of dread, and coming back into the moment. "Now let's get you inside."

"Do you think there's angels up here, this high in the world?" she says as we wheel her toward the elevator.

"Angels?" I ask, dodging the question.

"You've got us," Tracey says, rescuing me from the question and punching the elevator button. "Don't you think we look like angels?"

The girl giggles, which means 'no, you look like two ladies in weird jumpsuits.'

"I think there's angels," the girl says. "Angels and Christmas. You can't have one without the other."

I look out at the lines of lights that brought us here, the helicopter still lit in red and green, the dark black sky above us with the dim stars that twinkle stubbornly through the cityscape—nebulas thousands of years away that have already burst and died. "Let's get you inside, sweetie, so you'll be all patched up when your mama gets here."

CHAPTER 19

ANDY

old you it was my lucky number.

I quickly text her back, thinking about some of the nicer restaurants in Midvale. After all, there's no reason to blow this chance on a cheap burger.

"Do you like pasta?" I type, then delete it. For some reason, I get the sense that I shouldn't give her the chance to back out by saying she's gluten-free or something. *Meet you at 7:00* feels like a better bet, though I really do need to check date and time since she works so much. "Is Friday or Saturday better?"

She doesn't respond, not for hours. That feels like a bad sign, though I guess she could be at work, or sleeping, or something. She was just so quick with the first response. But I'm not in middle school and I can wait.

Besides, I've got plenty to do. Bill and I are drawing up the papers this week and I'm hoping Gretchen can recommend a lawyer to me.

So I shake off the hopefully-not-ghosted text thread and give Gretchen a call.

"Hey, sis."

"That's your need-something opening," Gretchen says.

"Am I that obvious?" I ask.

"And then some," she responds. "So…what's up?"

"It's a secret," I reply.

"No, it's not," she answers. "You already told me you've got that earnest money stashed away. And I've been talking to your mama."

"Okay, it *was* a secret," I quip away.

"You're buying that property," Gretchen says, "and now you're calling me with your need-something opening. So…?"

"I'm drawing up papers this week and wanted to talk to a lawyer."

"This week?" she says. "Kid, you move fast."

"Is there any other way to move?"

"Not for you," she replies, and I can hear the clink of china as she sets something up. "Though the rest of us have several other settings. Anyway, are you sure about the whole rifle range thing?"

"What's not to be sure about?"

"You'll need specific release forms," she says. "Special insurance."

"I've been there and done it before," I reply.

"You mean I have," she responds.

"I helped."

"You watched." She quickly adds, "And I'm really glad you did. It's great for learning. But doing is different and I'd love to help, but things are crazy here at this time of year and I'm not sure how much help I'll be."

And she and Jackson have been talking about getting married. That's something *I* know because *I've* been talking to my mama. But I'm not in the mood to tease her for that right now. At least not until I get the name of her lawyer.

"I don't need your help," I respond, trying not to sound touchy. "Well, except for the name of your lawyer."

"Done," she responds, sending me the contact card.

I'm not exactly offended that she's nervous about me striking out on my own. After all, I'm her little brother and all. I'm just ever-so-slightly offended that she thinks I wasn't paying attention the first time around when we got the ATV park all set up and squared away. I mean, of course, I was paying attention.

⸻

Madigan

HE WANTS to meet at Gandolf's at 7:00. Friday or Saturday—that's the only choice I've been given here. I mean, I guess I technically had the choice to say no, but I already kind of messed that one up, didn't I? I wish we could just blow this off with a cheap burger and be done with it.

"I work all day Friday," I text back. All day and all night. Plus a twelve-hour shift with the ground crew on Saturday, though I'll be done by six. Which I guess leaves Saturday night.

"Should I tell him that?" I ask Alfie. "Or should I try to back out?"

Alfie gives me a look like he would never back out of an outing in his life. Which is true.

"I guess I should just go," I mutter, because backing out seems harder.

He thumps his tail on the floor.

"I wish I could bring you with me," I add.

He thumps harder.

"And I hope that with a name like Gandolf's we're not expected to dress up. Like, it's not *Lord of the Rings* or something, right?"

Alfie thumps again like he knows the answer and would tell me if he could, but he can't, being a dog and all.

"I'll look it up."

Alfie comes over beside me and snuggles into my armpit.

"What would I do without you?" I ask him.

He thumps very zealously.

It's a strange thing to have your life saved by a dog, or maybe it's more common than we think. Alfie trots away to do some important dog stuff. I open up my phone and pull up Gandolf's. It looks like the restaurant is just a basic Italian place, not fantasy themed—just kind of Olive Garden goes hometown—so that's a win.

When I look down, Alfie is holding his leash in his mouth, and I laugh. "You'll always be enough for me, you know that, right?" I say.

And Alfie looks happy, but he also gazes at the door in this small way like he sort of hopes someone else would walk through it to keep us company. Yeah, I get it buddy. I wish he was still here too. I wish you could have known him. We would have been perfect together, the three of us. The perfect number.

But then I remember that Joshua had a horrible allergy to dogs, and animals in general. He couldn't even ride a horse after an allergy attack when he was a kid. Guess that's why he'd chosen a motorcycle instead.

<hr>

Andy

I WAS *NOT* PAYING sufficient attention when Gretchen got The Molehill set up. I mean, I'd thought I was. I'd been trying. But sitting here, in a leather plush chair, with the lawyer talking circles around me, I'm completely lost. I'm struggling to keep up and definitely wishing someone smarter than me was sitting right here, beside me.

I look over the papers he's supposedly explaining, as though I know what we're talking about. He nods and murmurs and says comforting things. I nod and murmur back.

"It's pretty standard," he concludes.

Which sounds like a good thing.

"Okay, we'll probably be closing in about a week."

He nods and doesn't warn me off of the deal. That also feels like a good thing.

After that, there's not much to do but pay his bill, a hefty chunk of change. And wonder why I even bothered with a lawyer, if none of it even makes sense.

But whatever. I'm off to buy a hillside. And that's pretty cool.

CHAPTER 20

MADIGAN

You know how in movies they always wear a dress to dinner. Yeah, I do *not* do that. Jeans and a decent shirt. That's how I'm doing this. I'm just relieved it's not *Lord of the Rings* themed.

I'm also relieved when Andy shows up wearing jeans and a decent shirt. It's what I *expected* from him, but I have to admit that he's surprised me a couple of times. I also have to admit that I haven't quite shaken the image of him showing up at my house in his black suit jacket and white shirt. He had looked...*nice.* Really nice.

If I'm honest, he doesn't disappoint tonight either. He's wearing dark blue jeans, almost black, not too tight, but not skater boy loose either, which is what I would have pictured. Green button-down shirt, which makes me realize his eyes are also green, which is a nice complement to the sandy blond hair.

"You look nice," he says when he sees me, and I look down at my clothes, wondering if maybe I could have tried a little bit harder.

To cover my awkwardness, I say, "Funny name, this restaurant."

"Gandolf's," he says. "How so?"

"Well, you know," I say. "It's like *Lord of the Rings*. Gandalf…the wizard."

He clears his throat.

"You haven't read it," I say.

"I haven't," he admits.

"But you've heard of it?" I press.

"Yeahhhh," he says, in a way that makes me wonder if he has.

"It's a great series," I say, not managing to crest out of the awkward zone. "You should give it a try sometime."

"Maybe I will," he responds. "I don't know if it can compete with the shark survival books your aunt Nellie used to slip me."

"Yeah," I say, imagining Nellie doing exactly that type of thing. "It might be a tough act to follow, but in *Lord of the Rings*, there are Orcs and wars and things, so…"

"Is there a movie?" he asks. "Could I cheat?"

"Yes, there's a movie. And, yes, it's good," I say.

"But, no, you can't cheat. You've got to read the book first."

He laughs, this big, happy sound. If Alfie laughed, it's exactly the sound I'd imagine him making.

I look down at my fingers, at my ringless hands. And feel suddenly, hopelessly lost.

Fortunately, at that moment, the host calls Andy's name.

Andy

I HOLD out an arm in a 'ladies first' gesture and watch as Madigan follows the host to our table.

She looks so fantastically, amazingly beautiful. Snug shirt, barely any makeup to hide those deep dark eyes, perfect posture, hair that tumbles over her shoulders.

Which is why it's unfortunate that I'm totally striking out here.

She's fidgeting and uncomfortable. A little out of my league if I'm honest.

I definitely did better with the older ladies at the luncheon. Maybe next time Nellie can play matchmaker with one of her granny-aged friends. They seemed to like me.

"You know," I say, as soon as we're seated. "I really have heard of it—that book."

"Series," she corrects.

"And I knew it was a movie before I asked."

"Have you watched it?" She lifts an eyebrow. "Be honest."

"Nope," I say, holding my hands up. "Remember how I didn't know the, uh, head wizard's name. Totally ignorant here."

"Well," she says. "Totally ignorant is better than watching the movie first. Just remember, you've got to read the book first. Everybody knows that."

"Except for the people who don't read the book first."

"Is that you?" she asks.

"Not on purpose," I say. "But I'm sure there are some movies I've watched that were books, and I was just too dumb to know it."

"You're not dumb," Madigan says.

I'm smart enough not to respond to that. "I see where you and Nellie are related now. You both obviously care about books a lot."

She doesn't answer. In fact, she looks even more uncomfortable. Another strike.

I clear my throat, wondering if there's beef between the two of them.

"So Nellie gave you my number?" she asks.

Ah, there it is. She thinks her aunt was giving out personal info to set us up. "Actually, no, why do you ask?"

"Well, you had it, my number."

"Yeah, I say. I brought you your phone."

"My phone," she replies. "But not my number."

"You know your number pops up on your phone with the screensaver."

"It does?" she asks, pulling it out to look at it.

"Yeah," I say. "It's a setting. Usually people will use it to put something like, 'If lost, call X number.' Though obviously that wouldn't work if it was your own number."

"I didn't set it up," she says, staring at it a little dumbfounded.

"Yeah," I reply. "Maybe it's a weird default or something."

And then, this understanding dawns in her eyes and she looks really sad. "Oh," she says in this small voice.

I lean forward. "Is that okay?"

"This phone," she says. "It used to belong to someone else. But then he, well, he's gone, and my phone broke, so I just took his, but changed it to my number. But I'm not very good with tech, and I guess he just had this as the setting, on the front. My number."

I clear my throat. I know who she's talking about, but she doesn't know I know who she's talking about. And that makes it real awkward. "Oh," I say. "Got it."

She looks at me as if to say *You don't got it.* And there's nothing truer than that.

The waiter rescues me by plunking a basket of bread on the table and taking our orders. I order the special, like I always do, and Madigan reads the menu and asks a bunch of questions and finally settles on lasagna.

"Lasagna's always safe," I say, smiling.

"I like safe," she responds. "That special had mussels in it."

"Hopefully I like them," I reply.

"You don't know?" she says.

"Never had them before."

"Oh." She dips a piece of bread into the olive oil, swirling it around like she's creating art, not eating food. Then looks up with a squint. "So my number was on my phone as the screensaver, but you, did you memorize it?"

"I didn't memorize it on purpose." I take my own chunk of bread. "It was just there, and I noticed it. And I'm pretty good with numbers, so it stuck. And then after we went for coffee, well, I thought I owed you a meal."

"Owed me, huh?" she says, before taking a solid bite of her crust.

"Yup," I reply, deadpanning. "That's the only reason I'm here."

"Well, I'm glad I paid for your sandwich then."

And I don't know if you've ever gotten a compliment from the type of person who doesn't give compliments, but the feeling I get is kind of like that—warm all the way up from my toes to my fingertips, like someone just inflated me with dopamine. "Maybe we should do it again sometime."

But that, apparently, is too far. I see her jaw clench—a tight bite of her teeth.

She opens her mouth to answer, and I know it's not going to be the answer I want to hear and all that dopamine just drains right back out, but at just that moment this guy pops up at the table. I think it's the waiter and glance up, but it's this big dude, muscles pretty much bursting out of his t-shirt. Kind of like an angry superhero. And much like an angry superhero, this guy has this furious throbbing vein at the top of his neck.

"Hey, Mads," he says. His voice is pitched to a tone one could only call *mean.* "Thought you had an extra shift this weekend."

And Madigan, I've got to respect her, because she doesn't even answer right away. Just takes her napkin real slow and wipes her lips. "Hey, Terry, nice to see you too. And I did have an extra shift this weekend. Two actually. One last night. One this morning."

"None tonight apparently," he says.

"No," she replies. "Tonight I'm out with my friend Andrew. Andrew, Terry. Terry, Andrew."

I nod like I'm being polite, though I'm also trying to figure out how to handle it if things go south, which kind of seems like Terry's personal plan. If you've ever been out on a first official date with someone whose evil ex, or whoever this guy is, shows up, well, it's not exactly ideal first date material. Especially when he's clearly up for a fight and he's got a good hundred pounds on me, and he looks like it's his personal goal to drag someone by the hair out of the restaurant and I'm not sure if it's my date or me, but either way I'm unwilling to let it happen. Yeah, that's where my head is when he says to Madigan, "I asked you out."

I open my mouth to say something that has not been premeditated, so it's probably good when Madigan speaks first, "And I said I had things to do this weekend. Which is clearly true."

The host is glancing our way and I see him and the waiter share a look. They are also formulating a plan. It's nice to have backup.

"And the truth is that you didn't actually ask me out on a date," Madigan says, her voice picking up a little prickle. "You asked me if I was busy. Which I both was and am. So, if you don't mind, I'd love to continue my dinner with Andrew."

Terry shoots me a look that I believe is intended to kill me.

And I, because I'm an idiot who clearly welcomes death, offer him my best smile and give him two thumbs up. And, you know, if Mama's worried about my teeth, she should worry less about ATVs and more about the asinine looks that I can give a man almost twice my size.

Terry stalks away, which—by the way—is to a table with a date who is perfectly gorgeous and looking a little miffed.

"Andrew, huh?" I finally say when Terry is gone. "You know I haven't been called Andrew, well, ever. I didn't even know it was my actual name till I showed up in kindergarten and my teacher kept calling an Andrew Putman for attendance. I got in trouble on that very first day for ignoring her—missed half of recess."

Madigan kind of sniggers at that. "So I guess you *have* been called Andrew. And, hey, if you can call me Maddie, then I can call you Andrew."

I smile at her. "Seems fair." The waiter brings us two steaming dishes of food. They smell amazing.

"So who was that anyway? Ex-boyfriend?"

"Are you kidding?" she says. "Surely you think better of me than that."

"Hey," I say, tearing the last piece of bread and handing her half. "No judgment zone here."

"Well, do me a favor, *Andrew.* If I ever decide to go on a date with that jerk, please judge me. And hard."

"Yes, ma'am," I say.

"You know what," Madigan says, waving the waiter back over. "I'm ordering dessert."

"After you eat all that food," I say, nodding to her lasagna.

"If we have to, we'll share."

TURNS out we're both lightweights, because we can barely get through a quarter of the double chocolate cake, even sharing. We talk about Kentucky and hiking and how unholy hot it's been this summer. She even laughs at a few of my jokes.

And then she leans forward, resting her fork on the plate. "I think that's it for me."

I settle my fork down beside hers and when I do, my thumb brushes against her pinky and she doesn't move it. And I don't know what's come over me, but I just hold my hand there, unmoving, like the time when I was five or six and a bunny came into our yard almost at my feet. I'd stood like a statue for at least five minutes, until it had sniffed its way away from me, to a fresh patch of grass.

That's what I do now, feeling the touch of heat from her finger, until she leans back, patting her belly as though she never even noticed the touch.

But I'm staring at her and feeling kind of gooey and soft when she says, "Better get the checks. I'm covering dessert."

"It's okay," I reply. "I've got it. All of it."

But she's waving the waiter over and asking for the check and I still don't have my feet quite under me. And then there's cash on the table, and we're walking out.

"You know you never told me who that guy was," I start, looking for something to say. "All I know is he's *not* your evil ex."

"He's a firefighter at one of the stations where I work sometimes."

"On the helicopter?" I ask, confused.

"No," she says, shaking her head. "I work full-time for the helicopter, but I pick up shifts here and there at other places."

"Busy lady, huh?"

"I try," she says.

And then, because she doesn't say anything else, I add, "I'm gonna be getting a little busier myself."

She doesn't ask a follow-up question, but I keep

going, like I lost all my social skills over dessert. "A rifle range, next to my property. I'm planning to buy it."

"A rifle range," she says, turning to me with this little squint to her eyes.

"Sure," I say.

"Sounds dangerous," she replies, like she'd forgotten for a moment who I was and what I did, and everything else about me. Like she'd thought for a second that I really was *Andrew*, her friend. But now she remembers, and she's disappointed.

"No," I say, walking her to her car. "It's…there are a lot of safety precautions, even ear plugs. Trust me, dinner with that jerk Terry would be more dangerous than my rifle range."

I'm trying to make it a joke, but it's not landing.

We arrive at her car. The days are long and hot and the sun is just beginning to set, the humidity of the day settling like a blanket over everything. She pulls her keys and phone out of her purse.

"You know," I say. "This was a lot of fun…"

She interrupts me. "My phone," she says, staring for a moment at the screen. "With my number on the front. It just says 'Call' and then gives my number. But if it was my phone, why would you assume it's my number?"

"I took a weird gamble," I say. It's true.

"You texted to ask what it would take to get me

to go to dinner," she says, lifting an eyebrow in a way I'm not sure is amused or accusatory, or maybe just confused. "What if it had been some other woman?"

"Well, then, maybe that would have worked out too. Would have been fun no matter what happened."

"But what if it was a man? Or she was married? Or old? Or homeless?"

"I feel like you don't understand how gambles work," I say. "You win some; you lose some. But if you're lucky, you can win big."

"And are you lucky?" she asks.

"You know," I say, laughing and leaning forward (another gamble), "I kind of am."

She nods, this little furrow on her brow. I want to reach up to touch it, as though I could wipe it away.

"I'm not," she says.

I tip my head to the side, confused.

"I'm not lucky," she replies. "Look, I really appreciate you not pressing earlier. About whose phone this used to be. But the truth is that it was my husband's. And he died."

"I'm so sorry," I say, thrown off of my usual game by her honesty. Her face looks a little like a fissure that is about to crack open.

"Sorry for what?" she replies. "It's not your fault."

"Well, no, of course not, but I'm just… that's hard."

"It is," she replies. "And now it's my turn to say I'm sorry. Because even though you called that number and even though you got a hold of me, it really wasn't very lucky. Because I'm really not in the market for a—" She waves her hand toward the restaurant. "—a relationship or another date, or really anything."

I nod, feeling—I've got to admit—a little less lucky. "No worries," I say. "And I'm still lucky. We had a fun night. I got to pay you back for the sandwich and the walk. And you can give Alfie my regards."

"I will," she says.

"And if you ever need a pet sitter, give me a call. After all, Alfie and I kind of hit it off."

She smiles. "I'll do that."

She clicks the lock on her car and I open the door for her to get in. She nods a thank you and then her eyes narrow and I think I've done something wrong again, until I realize she's looking past me.

I turn around to see that guy, Terry, hustling toward us, his date missing.

"Crap," she mutters. And under different circumstances, I would think this would be the perfect moment to fake a kiss—you know, for her benefit and all—but there are limits to what I'm willing to gamble.

She slips into the driver's seat, fiddling with her keys.

"Madigan!" he calls, holding an arm up in a way that makes me feel slightly sorry for the guy. At least until he strongarms his way past me, holding the door open so she can't shut it.

"Oh, hey, Terry," she says, forcing a smile.

"Next week," he says.

"I'm working Friday," she says.

"What about Saturday?" he presses.

I'm not sure if I should be offended that she was willing to give me the not-in-the-market-for-a-relationship talk, but not this dude.

"I don't remember," she stalls. "I'd have to check."

"You've got your phone," he says. "So check."

She clicks it reluctantly, turning it on.

"Look, dude," I say. "I hate to tell you this, and I know Maddie is trying not to hurt your feelings, but…"

The daggers that get stared—they are impressive.

"But next Saturday is my birthday party."

He tips his head to the side. "And Madigan is coming," he says, like he can't imagine anything less likely. "As friends, I suppose."

"Of course," I answer, wishing that the fake kiss had worked out because that would have been so much more fun. And then, because I can't seem to stop myself, I say, "You should come too. I'm having a bunch of friends over. Seven o'clock."

"Well, unfortunately, I'm not your friend."

"Very unfortunate," I say. I give him my best smile. "But we could change that."

"Are you seriously going to this guy's birthday party?" he asks, turning to Madigan.

"It's his freaking birthday," Madigan says. "Let it drop."

"And how old is he?" Terry asks.

"Twenty-nine," she says, without a beat. "Last year of his twenties. Got to make the most of it."

"He doesn't look a day over nineteen."

Another winning smile from me. And then I see his date. She's out in the parking lot, looking around for him.

"Dude," I say, tipping my chin toward her.

"We'll figure out a day next time you're at the station," he says.

And I realize something. He doesn't have Madigan's number. But he doesn't want to ask for it in front of me, because then I'd know he doesn't have her number.

He stalks away and Madigan leans against her seat with a sigh.

"Thank you," she says, rolling her shoulders like she's trying to get loose after a boxing match. "I was about to crack. And—wow—you really are a gambler."

I tip my head to the side. "It's an addiction."

She shakes her head, almost laughing. "And an alarmingly quick liar. I can't believe you invited him to your 'birthday.'"

"Actually, I'm kind of a terrible liar."

"Well, you thought that one up fast," she says, putting the key in the ignition.

"I didn't," I say. "Saturday really *is* my birthday."

"You're kidding." She turns back to me, tipping her head up so that she's all eyes and lips and I can't help but notice that I've leaned down as well so that we're a good bit closer than we were.

"I'm not," I answer, smelling the sweet scent of her skin. "Though I'm only turning twenty-seven. But that was your lie, not mine."

"Yeah," she murmurs, tipping her head back down and looking forward. "I guess it was."

"I'm meeting some friends at Louis's at seven." I hold up my phone calendar, as though to prove it.

"Not at your ATV park?" she asks with this funny, crooked smile.

"I don't actually spend *all* my time there," I say.

She adjusts her mirror. "Well, then, maybe I should come to your party. We don't turn twenty-seven, excuse me—*twenty-nine*—every day."

I shut the door, feeling that lit-up feeling again, even as she drives away.

CHAPTER 21

MADIGAN

I get home and slip into my house, ready to drop my clothes in my room and take a hot bath. Or a cold shower.

I mean, what just happened back there? And did I actually agree to go to Andy's birthday? And why? And also, I'm turning thirty this year, which means he's nearly three years younger than me. Rob the cradle much? But also, no one's robbing the cradle, because it's just his birthday party, not a date. Which brings me back to the basic question: What on earth? What on earth am I doing?

It's then that I notice something is wrong in my house. The kitchen light is on. And I never leave it on. But maybe I did tonight.

I pause in the front hall of my tiny starter home, the one I was supposed to share with my husband,

and think. I came out with my purse, got my keys off of the counter. And, yes, yes I definitely turned the light off. I can feel the switch under my fingertip.

"Hello," I call tentatively, but no one answers. Not even Alfie.

That part makes my skin crawl.

"Alfie," I say, a bit more frantically.

Nothing.

Sweat prickles into my shirt. I slip my keys between my fingers, so that I can jab an eye if necessary, searching for another weapon of some sort. Just coats and shoes. Not even a nice, sharp umbrella.

"Alfie," I call again. Only the whir of my refrigerator answers back.

"Is someone here?" I ask, wishing for a moment that I'd chosen to be a cop instead of a paramedic. I take a step forward and listen. Still nothing.

Has someone broken in, robbed me, let Alfie out when they did?

Although the door was locked, wasn't it? I'd assumed so, so I'd put my key in, but what if it hadn't been locked?

For a second, Terry's face flashes through my mind. He'd been a creep all night, but he doesn't have my number, much less my address, and just because he's a little too assertive doesn't make him a stalker. Does it?

I take another step forward and then realize I've gone insane. A woman armed with her key and a half-full water bottle is not the right person to confront whoever turned my kitchen light on. Even if they're probably gone.

I turn quickly to the front hall, fumbling with the doorknob, my palm sweaty. And then I realize why everyone in horror movies always gets killed. Because we're a bunch of morons, that's why. I can barely get my sweaty palm to turn the knob, and when I do, I burst out of my house. And barrel straight into someone.

I scream.

A dog yowls.

And my dad curses.

"Dad?" I say, trying to gather my wits and adjust to the darkness outside.

"Madigan, honey. What are you doing? Running like a wild boar out of your house. Are you okay?"

I'm shaking my head, trembling, trying to put it all together. This is my dad. Next to him is my dog. On a leash. "Someone's in my house," I say. "Or was. I don't know."

"Really, baby," my dad says, taking my arm and pulling me closer. "I locked it. Was the door broken in?"

"No," I say. "And what do you mean you locked it? Were you in my house?"

I feel like my brain is under water, moving slowly, everything out of focus.

"Of course I was," my dad says. "I came to get Alfie. Truthfully, I came to get Alfie *and* you. It's Saturday. I thought we were going to the dog park together. But you weren't there. I texted. Didn't you see?"

I shake my head and it's the stupidest thing, but I start to cry.

Dad wraps me up in his arms. "Honey, what's going on? Is something wrong?"

"I'm so sorry I forgot," I blubber through my tears. "I'm such an idiot."

"You're definitely not," he says, shuffling me and Alfie into the house before the neighbors start peeking through their curtains. "Are you okay?"

"Yeah," I say. "So *you* turned the kitchen light on?"

"Probably," Dad says. "Yeah, I guess. Do you want me to check the house?"

"I can," I reply, but Dad is already walking into the kitchen, looking around. And Alfie has plopped his bum down beside me, tail wagging, which feels like a good sign. Aren't dogs supposed to sense danger?

"Hey, buddy," I say, nuzzling my face into his neck.

"Nothing," Dad says, coming back into the hallway. "Coast's clear. Not so much as a hairbrush out of place."

"I'm so sorry," I say again. "Looks like I'm losing my mind."

Dad looks at my outfit that is not sweatpants, at my slightly made-up face. "Looks like you did something fun. That's good."

I wipe my face, forgetting all about the mascara, which I smear, and try to regain my composure. "Yeah."

I feel all fuzzy headed, though I didn't drink a single drop of wine. Maybe I should now. I get a bottle down, along with two glasses. "I, uh, went out with a friend."

"Tracey?" he asks.

"Someone else," I say.

Alfie is sniffing me, his tail thumping.

"Someone Alfie knows?"

"Yeah, I guess."

"You guess," Dad says, as I fill my glass. "Not that guy that's been harassing you at work?"

"No," I mumble, taking a sip of wine and opting to skip the part about how we saw Terry there. Twice. In fact, opting to skip all the parts about everything.

Dad covers his own glass before I can fill it. Instead, he runs water from the tap.

"You can't drink tap water in a wine glass," I say, trying to change the subject.

"Watch me," Dad replies, taking a few swigs. "And don't think I didn't notice the subject change. You seem a little frazzled, hun."

"Well, I came home and thought someone might have broken into my house and that threw me off a bit," I said. But is it really true? Or was I already thrown off and that's why I freaked out and didn't remember I was supposed to meet my dad, whom I know has a key to my house.

"Just me," Dad says. And then he waits. It's one of his superpowers.

I take a few more sips of wine. Sipping wine is *not* a superpower. My fuzzy head is just getting more fuzzy.

"I agreed to go to some guy's birthday party next week," I say.

"Great," Dad says, nonchalantly. "Sounds nice."

"It's not nice," I say. "How can I go to someone's birthday party?"

Dad gives me a funny look. "You've been going to birthday parties since you were four. I think you'll be okay."

Another sip of wine.

"And where, where exactly did you meet this guy?" Dad says, swirling the water in his glass like it really is wine.

"Just this call. At work."

"That's unusual."

"And then again at Nellie's luncheon," I add.

"Also unusual. I thought it'd be all ladies. After all, I wasn't invited." Dad stops suddenly, his face going slack, like all his thoughts just drained. Until he starts smiling, and then grinning and then sort of snorting little pieces of laughter out of his nose. "Tell me it wasn't," he says, trying to get the words out through snort-laughs. "Surely not."

I shake my head. "Are you okay?"

He's guffawing now, like hiccups, only worse.

"Dad?" I say.

"Did someone hire a stripper for Nellie's shower?"

"Ew, gross, Dad, no. Gross, it was Nellie."

"Oh, honey, you just never know with older ladies. Things go wild after a certain age."

"Yuck, Dad. Ugh, no. It wasn't—he wasn't—a stripper."

"So why was there a single, solitary man at Nellie's shower?" Dad asks.

"Well, that just shows what a weird potty brain you have," I say. "He wasn't a stripper. He was just a server. Like, for food. Ew, Dad, seriously. This has been the weirdest night." I finish off my glass of wine before Dad has even gotten through his water.

"You're telling me," Dad says. "My daughter goes

on a secret date with someone who may or may not have been a stripper at my sister's bridal shower. And in the process, she absolutely forgets about dog park night with her dad. Nice."

"It wasn't a date," I bark as Alfie's tail wags at the hilarity of it all. Dad is still sniggering. Good thing Dad didn't have any wine, or he would have collapsed from the absolute glee of it all. "I mean, it was just dinner. Nothing fancy."

"Oh," he says. "And that's the part that's important for you to emphasize. That it wasn't a date, not that he wasn't a stripper."

"Yes," I say. "And no, neither. He wasn't a date or a stripper."

"But you're going to his birthday party next week. A second date. Will he be popping out of his own cake?"

"Not even a first date," I sing-song. "Well, sort of a first, but not a second. And no cake popping. It's just a few of his friends, very low key."

"So he wants you to meet his friends?" Dad is teasing now, full-tilt Dad mode, like I'm in high school again.

"No, he just. Well, I had to escape from Terry, so now I'm going to a birthday party. And he's too young for me anyway."

"Wait, Terry—who's Terry?" Dad asks, and then without waiting for a response, he continues, "And how young is this man?" He's a little more serious now, as though slightly worried I really might be going to a birthday party with a nineteen-year-old stripper.

"Twenty-seven," I reply.

And Dad snorts again, setting his water down so he doesn't spill it in the glee of his laughter. "You know your mom was a full five years older than me, right?"

"It's not a date," I say, and something about the mention of my mom drains all the everything from it, because I kind of stomp from the room, leaving both Dad and Alfie to their fun.

MY MOM WAS five years older than my dad. An exchange student at their college. She was there for one semester. A whirlwind semester apparently. Because it was long enough for her to get pregnant with me. She left that Christmas without ever telling my dad she was pregnant, maybe not even knowing herself, and with lots of promises to write to my dad.

She didn't write. Except for once, eight months later. In that letter, she said she'd found someone new—a fact my dad had already surmised from the context clue of being pen-pal-ghosted. But she also said she had something important that she needed to discuss with my father. And she was travelling to the States to do so.

Which is how Dad and I first met—me as a tiny newborn. She said her new boyfriend didn't want someone else's baby and she was planning to put me up for adoption, but thought she should approach Dad first.

She had all the papers filled out and everything. She was sure Dad didn't want to be saddled with some baby when he was the ripe old age of twenty.

She was wrong.

The way Dad tells it, it was love at first sight.

So he went to the airport expecting to meet an old ex, and came home from the airport with a brand new love of his life.

Dad's words, not mine.

Grams and Grandpapa wigged out (which, to be fair, is understandable, considering they went from having a son with no girlfriend to having a grand-daughter in the space of twenty-four hours, give or take some paperwork). The whole town wigged out.

But then they did what good people do, and they figured it out.

After the gossip died down anyway.

Dad dropped out of college (he'd just been partying anyway) and became a machinist. And the rest, as they say, is history.

It's a sweet story. At least my Dad's side of it.

When I was eleven, I begged my dad for my birth mother's address, so I could write. Nothing came back. I sent letter after letter. Waited each day for a response. Which is probably why Dad decided to dig up her parents' information and write a letter of his own. Turns out my birth mother wasn't neglecting me after all (well, besides the giving-me-up-without-a-backward-glance part). A few years earlier, she'd died in a car accident. I grieved that woman I'd never met.

Though I did start to receive letters. From my mother's mother—a woman just as shocked as Grams to be a grandmother (apparently my birth mother was good at keeping secrets). And also just as pleased. She even came one summer for a visit, speaking fragmented English and beautiful French. No wonder my dad had fallen in love with a Frenchwoman. I did too.

After that, Mamie, as she insisted I call her, sent me gifts every birthday and Christmas.

When Joshua and I were married, Mamie sent chocolates, her own grandmother's pearl earrings, and a plane ticket to visit her in Paris. We did, exploring the cathedrals, the ancient buildings, the quaint streets. Just like we'd done on the night he'd proposed.

The last letter I sent her was to tell her Joshua was gone.

She'd wired money and penned a short condolence on beautiful paper. But I hadn't written back. She hadn't written either, perhaps reminded too much of her own daughter's death. So similar, the tragedies that seemed to follow me.

DAD TAPS ON MY DOOR. "MADIGAN," he says. "Madsie." My childhood nickname.

"Don't call me that," I mutter.

"What?" he asks. "Can I come in?"

"Sure," I say.

"I'm sorry, baby. I didn't mean to upset you. Just trying to tease."

"I know," I mutter. "It's your dad duty and stuff. Just hit wrong, I guess. It was a weird night."

"That you don't want to talk about?" he said.

"Not really," I reply.

"Sometimes I wish you'd had a mother in your life," he says, as though he knew I'd been thinking about her. "Someone to tell all your secrets."

"I don't need a mother," I say, opening the door so I could see him. "And I definitely wouldn't tell her my secrets. All I need is you."

"Is that really all you need?" he asks, reaching up to pat down a stray hair.

"You and Alfie," I say. "I tell *him* my secrets."

"Well, he's good at keeping them," Dad says.

But I can also feel what my dad doesn't say, that he thinks I need more than my dad and my dog, that he wants me to go out, to be young. Blah blah, the same thing every person over fifty in this town seems to think I need. But I don't. How could I need, could I want, another person who might end up leaving me in the end?

Dad sits next to me on my bed, until I lean my head onto his shoulder. "I really *am* sorry I forgot," I say.

He laughs, a sweet small sound this time. "Oh honey, don't go living your life sorry about what you forgot."

"Can I live my life sorry for what I remember?" I ask.

"Nope," he says. "That part is a gift, even when it don't feel like it."

CHAPTER 22

ANDY

For my birthday, I close on the MacArthur property. Gretchen is right. I don't have a mode outside of fast.

It hasn't been used as a rifle range, or anything else, for a while—so it's looking a little rough. Still, it's got a nice building that could be used for almost anything, a wide-open space to the north, and loads of wooded areas everywhere else. And then of course, there's the lake. I'll drag Gretchen and Jackson over next week. This is their area of expertise, fixing stuff up real pretty.

For now, I've got to get ready for my big night. Admittedly, I hadn't exactly had a *firm* plan to meet at Louis's. Truth be told, all I really had *planned* was to get together with my friends. And let's face it, 'planned' was a pretty generous word for the level of thought I'd put toward it.

But as soon as I invited Madigan, I knew that had to change. Even a gambling man knows his limits.

So I'd chosen the venue, told all the guys. Also had them bring their girlfriends and wives.

Which meant that now I had twelve guests, plus me and Maddie, going to a little bar-restaurant at the south of town.

And I'm just now realizing that I probably should have called ahead.

APPARENTLY, it doesn't really count as calling ahead if it's only an hour and a half before dinner and you're bringing fourteen people to a little place. "You'll have to take it outside," the tired woman on the other end of the line had said.

Yeah, sure, cool.

Except that storm clouds were gathering, low and heavy.

"You got a date, huh?" Ned asks, as his wife slides a slender finger along the drink menu.

I nod, glancing toward the door, hoping I have a date. Madigan is late.

"Leave him alone," Ned's wife scolds with her

touch of a Mexican accent. "It's his birthday. A guy don't have to get harassed."

In other words, Nina is also not confident that my date will be arriving.

"So who'd you ask?" Tony says, popping some complimentary peanuts into his mouth. "Originally, this was going to be a guys' night."

His girlfriend gives him a playful shove in the ribs.

"Yeah," Ned pipes in. "I coulda gotten a night off while Nina took care of the kids for free. Those babysitters cost a fortune."

"What Ned means," Nina says, landing on a drink and waving to a waiter, "is thank you. It's so nice for me to finally get a night out."

"Don't thank him yet," Ned says. "From the looks of it, we're all going to be sopping wet in about ten minutes."

Gretchen and Jackson pop in the door, Gretchen with an elaborately wrapped gift, Jackson holding a white box.

"Hey, you two!" I say, dodging the conversation with my friends to greet my sister and her boyfriend.

"So where is she?" Gretchen asks, glancing around.

Apparently, me having a new date is way more interesting than me having a birthday.

"Not here yet," I answer in my lightest voice.

Jackson raises his eyebrows in a bro look of solidarity. I think it means, 'It happens to the best of us.'

And then just as Nina is getting her drink, a ripple of lightning rips open the sky, followed by a crash of thunder. Several of the women squeal and cover their hair.

"We've got maybe thirty seconds, bro," Ned says.

The women hurry inside as fat drops of rain strike the patio pavement. All except Gretchen, who loops an arm through mine as we stand under the doorframe. "It's pretty packed inside."

"Yeah," I mumble.

The night isn't quite shaping up how I'd wanted. Stood up by my date. Now packed like sardines into a tiny bar and grill. The waitress is looking at us like she wishes she had a stomach bug so she could go home early.

But I've never been a guy to let stuff get me down.

"You know," I say to our little cluster. "Plan B. Let's head to my new place. Closed on it today. It ain't fancy, but it's got tables and a kitchen area. Y'all head on over, and I'll order us some food."

"And I'll bring some tablecloths," Gretchen says. "Maybe napkins and silverware, so we don't have to eat like savages."

"Nothing wrong with a savage," I say.

Gretchen throws a quick glance at the box that Jackson is holding. "Don't forget that," she says with a sweet smile up into his face.

I roll my eyes, though neither of them is looking at me, too caught up in their own gazing.

And then the door swings open, and Madigan shakes off a sopping wet jacket.

"Maddie!" I say, without thinking, hurrying over to her.

She glances around the dark restaurant, trying to get her bearings.

Somewhere in the din, I hear Gretchen murmur, "Is that his date?"

Madigan is wearing black pants that hug her hips with a short blue shirt that gathers at the waist. Her hair tumbles in loose waves behind silver earrings so long they nearly brush her shoulders. I feel like the whole restaurant is turning to her, but maybe that's just because I can't stop looking.

Several members of my birthday party are moving past her like they're part of some Biblical exodus.

She looks confused, glancing at the couples leaving the building. "Sorry I'm late. It was a little tricky to find parking."

Another couple wiggles past her through the door.

"Did I get the time right?" she asks, as the group inside thins.

If she is secretly hoping she got the time wrong, I can't tell from the look on her face.

"No. You're right. You're perfect," I say, stumbling a little on the words. "It's just that our reservation was for the patio, and, well…" I look outside at the rain pouring down on the sidewalk in sheets.

"Oh, shoot," she says, glancing at the sopping jacket in her hands. "I'm so sorry."

"No worries," I say. "I was just about to order food. We're actually going to head over to my place. My new place. The, uh, rifle range. You know, just to eat."

Madigan nods, but for reasons that could only be called insanity, I keep talking. "We're not going to shoot anything. Not tonight."

Madigan continues nodding.

"Don't have my paperwork done for that sort of thing yet. Though I guess as long as no one's paying, there isn't really any liability."

Gretchen gives me a weird look, then a little shake of her head. *Stop talking.*

I stop. Look down at the menu. "What would you like to eat?"

Madigan glances down at a menu that is on the take-out counter. "I don't really know," she says. "Just, I guess, whatever's good."

"Not the calamari," I say. "Mama learned that once."

"Not the calamari, then," she says.

"So you're Andy's date?" Nina says, from the stool where she's finishing off her drink.

Madigan opens her mouth and I know—deep down in my bones—that she wants to say it's not a date and she just came for my party. But instead she just smiles. "Looks like I'm late though."

"Girl, there's no late with Andy." And then she leans in. "Though I admit that I haven't seen Andy that frazzled for a while. You get it, girl."

Madigan turns pretty much as red as a human being could turn. And, honestly, I'm not sure I'm much better.

"I think maybe a bunch of sandwiches and appetizers," I ramble on in an effort to distract from Nina's comment. "That seems easiest since we're taking it elsewhere."

"The spinach dip sounds good," Madigan says, focusing her energy on the menu as well.

I give Ned a look. There are a *lot* of looks being given tonight.

He just smiles and hands Nina her coat.

"You gonna hold that over my head, baby?" she asks.

"I guess I probably am," he answers.

"Good," she says, "'cause I don't want this shirt to get wet."

"I do," Ned says and she gives him a playful bump with her ample hip as they head for the door.

Madigan is looking like she's really, really invested in the menu, like it's her new life's mission to memorize the appetizer list. "Maybe also the fried cheeses," she says. "Can't go wrong with fried cheeses."

"Indeed you cannot," I say.

And then to save us from ourselves, Gretchen comes up and holds out a hand. "Nice to meet you. I'm Gretchen. Andy's sister."

"You own The Cottage," Madigan says, taking her hand.

"Yeah," Gretchen says.

Madigan looks at me then, like she's remembering something. "And Andy works for you?"

"Not most days," Gretchen says with a laugh. "But we co-own the property—our Memaw's old land— and we try to help each other out."

Madigan tips her chin up, a bit of understanding dawning.

"See you there," I say to Gretchen as she and Jackson glance at the rain, which doesn't look like it plans to let up any time soon.

I turn to Madigan, the last member of my

birthday party still here. "Should we, uh, drive together?" I ask. "Might be easier."

Madigan looks like she is about to say no, but then the appetizers start stacking up. Several boxes of food, multiple drinks in the little drink holders. She swallows—like, it's a deliberate enough pause that I can see it—and glances out the door at the rain.

"Sure," she says finally. "I can help you carry these."

CHAPTER 23

*O*kay, so now I'm on a date headed to a rifle range. Two things I definitely wasn't shooting for. Pun *intended.*

But I draw the line when I see his car, which is not the correct term. Because it's a Jeep. Not a fancy soccer mom Jeep, which is just an SUV with standard steel walls and normal car stuff. Nope, this is a bona fide lowercase 'j' like the-kind-they-use-in-wars-jeep with an open frame that is covered only with a flimsy plastic thing. Which at least Andy had the foresight to put on before it rained.

But, yes, rain. Pouring, pounding rain. Obscuring the road, making the pavement slick, especially since it's been several weeks since it rained. Fun fact: Roads are slipperier when it hasn't rained for a while because the oil residue from the cars has built up and then when the rain hits, it's like skating along on an oil rink.

Nope.

I stop outside the door, which Andy is unlocking. He's not wearing a jacket and he's just getting pummeled with water. I know my car is at least four blocks away and I know he's not going to like what I'm about to say, but I also know that I'm going to say it anyway.

Have you ever had the cops show up at your house, hats off, held in front of them when you open the door?

Well, I have. And I'm not getting in that car.

"I'm sorry," I begin, the rain dripping off my hood onto my cheeks. "But I'm actually not comfortable riding in a Jeep, especially in these conditions." I feel like I'm explaining an early curfew to some kind of kid too cool to even know what a curfew is.

Andy turns to me with this look that feels like slow motion. "I have a cover," he says, as though he can see no other problem with a Jeep in the rain. I'm sure he can't.

"I know," I say, the bags with the food dripping like we just threw them into a pool. "But Jeeps are really unsafe. Especially with the roads like this. And I'd just rather not."

Another slow-motion turn, this time toward his vehicle, as though considering it for the first time.

"You can take it, of course," I say quickly, holding up the food so he can have it. "I'll just walk back to my car."

"You don't have to walk to your car," he says. "At least I could drive you there."

And I mean, it probably wouldn't hurt, those few blocks, but I feel a hard clench in my stomach and I just can't. Yeah, me, the girl who gets into a helicopter every time she has a shift. But this is different. At least it feels different to me. Those slick, slick roads.

In the air, we have a rule, a policy actually. It's called the 51% rule. It means that each of us has a 51% vote. So if one person doesn't feel good about flying, doesn't think it's safe—it doesn't matter if it's me, the nurse, or the pilot—if one of us says, 'No, I don't have a good feeling about this,' then we don't fly. Period. I feel that way now, that pit in my gut.

"I'll go slow," he adds.

"No," I say. "It's okay. Here." I hold up the food again.

And Andy, I'm gonna have to give him credit, because he just starts to laugh. "You know what," he says. "It's okay. I'll come with you. Just hang on a sec." He opens the door and digs into the backseat, coming up with a beach towel and a spare t-shirt, which he stuffs into a spare plastic bag. "Okay, ready," he says. "Lead the way."

"Are you sure?" I ask.

"Now, Maddie, you can't get rid of me that easily," he says. "If that Jeep isn't safe enough for you, I probably shouldn't get in it either, don't you think?"

His tone is light, teasing. I still feel a little embarrassed.

He nudges me in the shoulder. "A guy can't get in a wreck on his birthday."

"Yeah," I reply, feeling the tightness in my gut loosen, relax. "It's not really great on any day. But on your birthday it would definitely put a damper on the festivities."

"So how far is your car?" he asks.

I pinch my lips together, a little piece of a smile teasing against my face. "Oh, you know," I say. "Only about four blocks."

"Man," he says, his shirt sticking fully to his core and chest. I can't help but notice that it's not an incredibly *unpleasant* core and chest for a shirt to be sticking to. "You really *did* have a hard time finding parking."

And then, there, in the pouring rain, I start to laugh. He does too. And it's a sweet feeling—one that I haven't had for so long that I'd almost forgotten it.

"I don't suppose you're any good at running," he says.

"I have a dog," I say indignantly. "I am queen at running."

"Well," he says, taking half of the bags from me and grabbing my free hand. "Then what are we waiting for?"

DESPITE MY SANDALS, which are literally squishing with every step, we get to my car in record time. And still laughing.

I have to fumble in my rain jacket for my keys, Andy just standing in the downpour watching.

"You know, sometimes it feels like you're doing it on purpose," he says. "You probably just want to see this wet t-shirt contest in action." He flexes for effect.

And I laugh again. But—truth—he looks *very* nice flexing in his wet t-shirt.

I find my keys and beep my car open.

Andy very considerately puts the towel over the passenger seat and then crawls in.

"Wow," I say, watching the rain hitting the windshield and stuffing my soaking wet jacket in the seat behind us. "Aren't downpours like this supposed to let up after a few minutes?"

We can barely see a thing and I'm really relieved to be in my car, not his.

"I kinda like it," Andy says, admiring Mother Nature's commitment. "There's nothing like the rain around here. Did you know that an area can be considered a rainforest just dependent on rainfall alone. So, even though the Amazon is the biggest rainforest—and it's tropical—it's not the only one. There are actually several temperate deciduous rainforest regions. And Kentucky is part of that."

"You're teasing," I say.

"Nope," he answers. "Look it up."

And I cannot resist this kind of challenge. I take out my phone. He's right.

"How do you even *know* this?" I ask.

"I'm pretty sure I got it wrong in some trivia game. So then I had to look it up to see if it was true, just like you're doing right now. And it was. And I remembered it."

"My dad says one of the best ways to remember something is to do it wrong the first time," I reply.

"Well, then I should know lots of stuff," Andy replies.

And I'm not sure where my usual rod-up-the-butt self has gone, but I laugh yet again. In fact, it seems almost as though I can't *stop* laughing.

"You better turn this thing on," Andy says, nodding to the windows, which are fogging up. "Otherwise, rumors might fly about what we're doing in here."

And then I remember where my rod-up-the-butt went. I turn my car on real quick, hit defrost, and set it to hot, despite the temperature outside. These windows need to un-fog.

And now it's Andy's turn to laugh. "I knew I could get you to warm this car up," he says, and then—with no warning whatsoever—he takes off his shirt.

His shoulders ripple with the movement, along with his arms and back. Each part of him covered in sharp lines and edges that flex and move as he does. Joshua was strong too, but fuller—broad back, thick arms, not the wiry muscles that run up and down Andy's body.

He pulls up an edge of the towel he's sitting on and dabs the moisture from his torso and chest, running it along his arms.

And then I realize. I'm staring.

Staring at this half-naked man in my passenger seat.

Just as the windows of my car are un-fogging enough that any passerby could look in.

Fortunately, it is still pouring so there are no passersby getting an eyeful. Just me.

I shift my gaze, fiddling with the settings so that the heat is now largely blowing onto Andy. "Is that better?" I say, without looking at him.

"Yeah, thanks," he answers, pulling the fresh t-shirt out of its bag and over his head, letting the dry fabric settle onto his taut frame. "It's not quite a blow dryer," he says, shaking his wet hair in front of the heater. "But it'll do."

To keep the heat from creeping up my neck and into my face, I say, "That's how Alfie likes to do when he's wet too."

It's meant to be funny, though I'm not sure it is. At any rate, Andy isn't offended. Instead, he gives his hair another good shake.

"Here," I say, fishing around in the backseat of my car for a hand towel I keep there. "I think this is clean."

"Thanks," he says.

I place the towel over his head, just like I might have with Alfie, dabbing at the water. Which is absolutely the wrong thing to do. We're super close now, with me leaned over the center console, basically massaging his head.

I jerk back, leaving the towel abandoned on Andy's head.

He pats at his hair, wrapping it up in the towel like a turban.

"Nice," I say.

"Bet Alfie doesn't do this," he says, pointing to the turban.

I cast a little side eye look his direction. "He probably should."

"That's not why you have this towel, right?" Andy

says. "Like, you don't use it to towel Alfie off when he, you know, barfs in the car or something."

"If I did, I wouldn't tell you," I reply with a prim look.

"Then tell me this," he says, leaning way over the armrest now, his warm breath close to my face.

My own breath catches, the heat creeping over my chest and neck.

"Do I smell like a wet dog?" he asks, his voice serious in an exaggerated way, as he unwraps the turban.

His hair is still wet, though no longer dripping, his left hand gripping my seat, forearm rippling up into that bicep, which is now partially hidden by his dry t-shirt. And he just keeps leaning.

I sniff delicately, trying to keep my face light, playful. "I think you're good."

"So does that mean I smell like a dog or not?" he says, giving his hair a little shake in my direction.

"Hey!" I say. "I'll tell you this much. You have about the same level of respect for personal space as my dog does." And then, before I know quite what I'm doing, I've taken one of those wiry shoulders and pushed it back. Playfully. Like I'm…like I'm flirting or something. "Also you don't smell like a dog. Just like the rain." It's true. And it's a nice smell. One of the nicest in the world. "You smell like the deciduous temperate rainforest region."

He leans back against his seat. "You know that might be the nicest thing a woman has ever said to me."

I don't quite trust myself with an answer. Instead, I begin to back the car out—checking all my mirrors first even though I've got a backup cam too.

We drive through the next few minutes in silence. Well, not silence really—the rain is pounding in waves along the car, hitting us from all sides—a rhythm it seems we both appreciate.

"Probably *is* best we didn't take the Jeep," Andy finally says. "It's been known, on occasion, to leak. And this is probably that type of occasion."

"It does *seem* like it might be that type of occasion," I say, turning onto a gravel road as we head toward his new rifle range. It winds and dips through a canopy of trees, which are hopelessly pretty. I'll give him that. Although it might also become hopelessly muddy if rain like this kept on for days, which it sometimes does.

"You might have to pave the road to your new place," I say, clicking the windshield wipers up a notch.

"I might," he says, looking through the window at the blur of trees. "After all, not everyone's got an off-road vehicle like myself."

I smile, though it's a little tight since I'm having

to concentrate on the road, which is pocked and flooded in parts.

We hit a hole, sending a wave of water along Andy's side of the car.

"Do you really think we would have gotten in a wreck in the Jeep?" he asks, turning from the window to me.

And then I remember—why I don't flirt, why I don't giggle, why I don't shamelessly stare at a man while he changes his shirt. Because it's dangerous. No matter how fun it seems in the moment. "Probably not," I say. "But it's a chance, and I'm not a fan of chances."

"Isn't life kind of a chance?" he asks as I dodge a deep pothole puddle.

"Yes," I answer, and don't say anymore. He doesn't understand the chance that life is. And what it means to take a chance on it and lose.

CHAPTER 24

ANDY

No one ever accused me of being Sherlock Holmes, but the way she closes up, the way she watches the road like a hawk, the way her shoulders have tensed, her neck in tight lines. It could be her job, sure. But it feels like more than that.

There's no way in heck I'm asking Madigan what happened to her husband, how he died. Not when I've finally gotten her laughing and smiling.

But something happened. And I'm gonna guess it wasn't some slow illness where she got a peaceful goodbye.

When I have a chance, I'll ask Gretchen to do some gossip sleuthing. For now, we park right in front of the building for the new rifle range. And race inside. I want to grab Madigan's hand like I did when we were running to her car, but something has changed in her face, in her posture.

I get the door for her, hold it open despite the rain.

She rushes in and I follow. Gretchen has outdone herself. In the thirty extra minutes it took to wait for the food and then to get here, she's hung white Christmas lights all along the ceiling, and each table has a white cloth draped over it with blue linens. My favorite color. She's even got candles at each spot like we've all got a wish.

"Happy birthday!" everyone shouts. I'll be darned if it doesn't feel like a surprise party even though I was the one who planned it.

"Aww, y'all," I say, looking around for the food.

It's then that Madigan catches my eye.

"I'll get the food," I say. "It appears I got so excited about my birthday that I left it in the car."

Ned's giving me an I-know-what-you-got-excited-about look that I will him not to express in words. The last thing I need is for one of my friends to shout, *What were you doing in the car anyway?* That would pretty much cost me another date with Madigan ever. And maybe I'm not the only one who knows it, because no one says anything.

Except for Madigan, who says, "I'll get it, Andy. You don't have to get wet again."

"Are you kidding?" I say. "Remember how I love the rain?"

A bit of that lilting smile is creeping back into her face. "But it's still your birthday." She beeps the lock on her car and is jogging back out before I can stop her.

When she comes back, she is not sopping wet (though the bags are still dripping a bit from earlier) and her eyes are big and glowy.

"There is the hugest rainbow out there," she says. "It drapes across the full horizon."

We all crowd out the door to see it. And she's right. It forms a full arc across the sky—the kind of arc so committed that you'd definitely find gold at the end.

But just above the big arc is another, fainter rainbow. "See that?" I say, pointing. "It's a double."

"Now, that's downright Biblical," Tony says. "A rainbow that size."

"Genesis chapter nine," Madigan murmurs. "Whenever the rainbow appears in the clouds, I will remember the promise..."

I give her a sideways glance, not sure anyone else heard. To be honest, I hadn't pegged her for the religious type, though she's definitely staring at that rainbow with a look of devotion.

"Guess God loves you," Ned says, giving me a

punch in the arm. "He'd have to with all the risks you take and survive."

We all laugh, the whole group. Except Madigan, who is still looking at that rainbow, the sides of her mouth soft and thoughtful.

"So is that the horizon we're all gonna be shooting into?" someone says and laughs.

The lines of Madigan's mouth tighten.

"Now, now," I reply. "Not till we get everything in good order. I've got to get this place done up real nice, with all the safeties in place. Plus, paperwork."

"Good thing you've got your sister to help with that," Tony says with a grin.

"Hey, I can do it myself," I reply.

Madigan is watching, real careful.

"I already started," I add. "Met with the lawyer and everything."

"I *can* help if you have questions," Gretchen adds, squeezing in next to me.

In front of us, the rainbow is fading, the double one almost completely gone. "I got it," I say.

"Tell us what you've got in mind for it," my friend Tim pipes up.

"Well, I *am* planning to have the range in this direction," I say, pointing in the direction of the fading rainbow. "That's how it was years ago, so it seems easiest to leave it that way and I don't think there'll be too much to do except to inspect equipment and stuff."

"Didn't you have it inspected before you bought the place?" Gretchen asks.

"Not the machinery. Just the building. That's pretty standard," I say, a little defensively.

She doesn't argue, which I appreciate.

"But the real fun," I add, leading the group back inside, "is that I'm going to have an ax and knife throwing room over here. It's plenty big. I've been researching it, and we can set up nets and sandbag walls and things. It should be fun and relatively cheap to keep running."

"That's a good plan," Gretchen says, walking along the room, gazing from ceiling to floor. "And those are super popular right now. Just make sure you get all the details you need in your paperwork."

"I plan to," I say. "But even more than that," I add, looking at Madigan, who trails after the group with a stoic look in her eyes. "I plan to not have any injuries. I want this place to be as safe as possible."

"Now that's a good plan," Ned says.

"Though injury is often part of risk-taking play that this is," Gretchen adds.

"Doesn't have to be," I say. "We'll have thick nets up between the stations, and the knives and axes will be somewhat dull. You don't need a big, deadly knife to hit a straw target."

"But you'll have people pulling their arms back over their heads with a heavy ax," Gretchen presses.

I give her a look that I hope says, *Are you trying to wreck my love life?* "We'll be sure to do classes beforehand, maybe a safety video."

Maybe she gets it because she backs off just a bit. I cast a glance at Madigan. She's wandering the room, a little like Gretchen did. And then she surprises me by asking, "Have you heard of those 'Wreck It' rooms—the ones where people destroy old junk and stuff? You could probably use this smaller side room for that, as long as everyone was in a safety suit with glasses and a helmet."

"I've heard of those," Gretchen says thoughtfully, coming up behind her and peeking into the smaller room.

I'd planned to use that room for storage, but it really is a good size. "We'd have to limit the number of people," I add.

"Definitely," Gretchen says. "But those rooms are really popular too. You could have divorce parties or..." She stops midsentence. "Never mind, the whole idea of that makes me sad."

"Some people use them to grieve," Madigan murmurs.

Gretchen and I share a glance.

"Have you ever gone to one?" Gretchen asks, her voice as light and casual as possible. "Are they fun?"

Madigan turns like she just snapped out of a trance. "No, actually. I haven't gone. But I've been invited."

"Nothing wrong with banging up some junk," Tony says. "You could think of it as upcycling."

"You could," I say. "The stuff would be easy to get. I bet I could make a cheap deal with the dump, maybe even a free deal." But something about the idea rubs me wrong. "Anyway, we'll have to see," I say, shutting the door to the side room. "For starters, I'll just be using this room for storage."

As we walk back to the main room, the rest of the group ahead of us, Madigan leans toward me. "You didn't really like the idea, did you?"

"Oh," I say, caught off guard. "It's a really good idea."

"But you didn't *like* it," she presses.

"I…" I begin. "It would be profitable."

"But…" she says.

"I guess there's something about it that feels off to me. I guess I'm not crazy about the idea of destroying your way through your grief, or just destroying stuff because it's…fun."

"And how is it different than throwing axes against a wall?" she asks.

"It's kind of hard to articulate," I say, walking a little slower. "But in one, you're having fun, laughing, trying to hit a target, even using some hand-eye coordination—that sort of thing. It takes some skill. With the other, you're just...demolishing. All fury, no grace."

We're trailing behind the others who are already in the other room. I hear chairs scraping as they sit, voices rising and falling in chatter. Above it all, I can hear Gretchen opening up the bags with sandwiches and dips, and I'm glad I mostly picked things that won't need to be rewarmed.

"You don't think there are times for all fury?" Madigan asks, interrupting my thoughts.

Normally, this is when I would make a joke, try to lighten things up. Instead, I stop walking and turn to look at her. Her face is hard lines and dark circles. I want to lean toward her, move a lock of hair off of her face, give her a smile.

Instead, I say, "I'm sure there are times for it. Times when fury takes over, when it demands to be noticed and felt. I guess the question is, should you feed it?"

"Has it ever taken you over?" she asks. The hall is dark, her voice quiet, especially against the din in the other room.

I want to tell her that of course it has, that of course I understand, of course this is something I can speak about with authority. Instead, I take a deep breath. "No," I say. "Not really. I've had some hard times. Raised by a single mom. Never knew my dad. Crap ton of broken bones, including my femur. But I had the best granddaddy in the world. Grandmama too. They helped Mama get back on her feet. Which she did, and then some. So that she could take care of all those broken bones of mine. Honestly, even when I broke my femur in the middle of a snowstorm, there were people there to help me. And one of those people turned out to be my half-sister. So I guess I've had more grace than fury. If I'm being honest."

"You are," she says, her face tipping up to mine. "I appreciate it. It's a fair answer. Your question was fair too—about what we feed," she adds. "Even though I didn't like it."

"It's okay," I say. "Liking it wasn't one of the requirements. Maybe it was a dumb thing to say anyway."

"It wasn't," she says and for this weird moment, I think she might start to cry. I lean forward, not sure what to do to help when she says, "And maybe it's not even that you've had more grace than fury. Maybe the grace is just the thing you've fed." Her eyes are almost black in the dim hall, her cheeks and neck flushed, body just a few inches from mine.

I do brush a lock of hair off her face then, tuck it carefully behind her ear, my thumb brushing the soft skin along her ear.

"Andy," she says.

Just as we hear Gretchen's voice. "Where is that brother of mine?"

Madigan takes the opportunity to jump about three feet away from me.

"Coming!" I say, as I walk through the door to the main hall. "Just thinking about that room."

"Well, get in here," Gretchen says, her voice a light scold, though her eyes are full of about a trillion questions. "It's time for cake."

And is it ever. Gretchen is holding the most beautiful homemade cake. Three layers. Blues in ombre down the sides. Flecks of edible gold across the top. Like the sun kissing a Kentucky sky.

She's made me a cake ever since we figured out we were half-siblings. "Aw, Gretch. You've outdone yourself," I say, settling into a chair.

She smiles. "I'm just glad I have a brother to outdo myself for. The layers are caramel."

"Well, what are we waiting for? Let's dig in."

"Nope," she says. "Not yet."

"You're not gonna make everyone sing, right?" I whisper.

"Of course I'm gonna make everyone sing," Gretchen says, tapping her glass.

"Hey y'all," she starts, walking along the table and lighting the candles that are at each spot. "It's time for cake. But first, I gave everyone a candle, because I knew Andy would want y'all to be able to make a wish. There are twenty-seven, one for every year. So, when we're done singing, let's get 'em blown out."

"You ready to make a wish?" I ask Madigan as she settles into the seat to my right.

"I'm not really a wishing kind of person," she replies.

"Well, get ready to be," I say, as Gretchen lights our candles. "Because that candle isn't going to blow itself out."

My friends begin singing the most off-key version of "Happy Birthday" I've ever heard. I'm not gonna lie—it makes me tear up just a little.

As for me, I know what I'm going to wish: a second day like this with Madigan.

If only I can figure out how.

Because the thing she doesn't realize is that I'm really not a wishing person either, more of a doing one.

CHAPTER 25

MADIGAN

It's our third trip to Riley in Indy in the last three weeks. And this time it's worse than a brave little girl with a gash on her head.

Tracey looks down to the baby in the seat in front of me. Still unconscious. Still unmoving. Tracey records the vitals, looks out the window, sighs into the headset. It's been that kind of trip.

Babies are never good. Never fun to transport. Not when they're critical enough to need an air lift. This one looks okay on the outside—no huge bruises or welts, which makes her unconscious state all the more concerning.

But she's breathing, so there's that. There's always that, I tell myself as we descend to the helipad at the children's hospital. If no one's breathing, then we never even make it on scene. And there are plenty of those calls too, I remind myself. Plenty of deaths where it's the coroner who makes his way to a house instead of us.

We begin our descent and radio in. Within minutes, I see the security guys on the roof.

The helicopter lands with a soft bump and Tracey and I crack our doors open, moving as quickly as possible, removing the litter with the vinyl car seat from the patient's seat up front.

Security opens the doors and we hurry down to the pediatric ICU. There we're met by a small team —a couple nurses and a tech.

"Geez, another one," the head nurse says, glancing down at her paperwork.

I want to say that she says it sweetly, but she doesn't. In fact, the way she says it makes it sound like we are intentionally knocking children out so we can bring them to the children's hospital in Indy. "This hospital was closest for peds," I reply.

The nurse makes a clicking sound with her teeth, checking the baby. "Let me guess. Mom says some terrible accident happened—a dresser fell on her or something."

"Probably a shaken baby," Tracey says flatly.

We settle into the silence—the truth—of her comment.

And then the head nurse nods tightly as the other nurse sweeps the baby down the hall and out of view.

These calls suck, and even though Nurse Groucho is not my favorite, I can't blame her for the absolute awful that some of this stuff is.

"The cops are looking into it," Tracey says.

I think about what Andy said, and wonder: *Is there really more grace than fury?* Because sometimes it sure seems like there's too much fury, too much sadness, to go around.

"You know that kid you brought in a few weeks ago—ATV accident—he's still here," Nurse Groucho adds.

"You're kidding," I say. "What's going on with him?"

"Don't know," she adds, handing Tracey the paperwork, so we can sign off and leave. "They've got him sedated still. Trying to get his brain to stop swelling."

"That's awful," I say.

"What isn't awful in this line of work?" she grumbles, turning to the PICU. "His mother's been driving up here every day, sleeping over on weekends. Those kids need to get off the dang motorbikes or ATVs or whatever. Those businesses should be illegal."

And then she's gone. Through the double doors.

Tracey folds the paperwork as we walk out to the landing pad. "She is *not* my favorite."

"I can't believe that kid is still here," I say. "His poor mama."

Tracey nods.

Once back in the helicopter, I lean my head against the window, my helmet tip tapping any time we hit a pop of turbulence.

"You know there's plenty of good in this line of work," Tracey says through our headsets.

I nod, without lifting my head. Sure there is. That's why I'm here, right? It's just that sometimes, some days, it's really hard to see it.

THE NEXT MORNING, I get a text from Andy, inviting me to the soft opening of his rifle range.

Another dangerous business. In more ways than one. He doesn't call it a date, just an invitation. But still…

I hover over the phone, nearly deleting the message, his number, everything. Ready—almost— to forget about Andy and his wet t-shirts and his ATVs and the kid at the hospital and this whole messy business.

I hover. But I don't move. Because there's something deep down inside me that needs to find out, that needs to settle whether there's really any grace in this life that feels so full of fury.

And for some insane reason, a soft opening at a rifle range feels like the right place to start.

CHAPTER 26

ANDY

Gretchen calls it a soft opening. But it seems pretty grand to me.

The rifle range, which I'm calling Home On the Range, isn't actually up and running yet, but we figured we could open with the throwing room and make a little money while we finished up the range.

I stand at the makeshift welcome table with fliers and candy, greeting people as they come through the door. All my buddies of course, several of their girlfriends and wives, even a few of their kids. And plenty of other people too, some of whom seem to have crawled out of Kentucky's woodwork (and Kentucky has a lot of woodwork) to see something new, especially if it involves guns.

I'm chatting it up with several old men, showing

them the flier, and pointing out the range. One wears a Vietnam vet hat and is eating butterscotch after butterscotch like it's his job. Which might explain the missing teeth he's also sporting. But he's a fun guy, telling stories, giving me more information about guns than I ever would have asked for.

It's exactly the type of thing that gives rifle ranges a bad name in some circles, but it's the type of thing that I believe feeds a need. People want to get together, to socialize, to share their life's stories. And sometimes to shoot a clay pigeon.

Ned's wife, Nina, is toting their three little kids around, pointing things out and telling them not to touch anything every four seconds. Which is why I'm glad we sprang for the little bounce house outside.

I excuse myself from the circle of older men and make my way over to Nina. "There's a kid area out back."

"Thank the holy heavens," she says. "You're a saint, Andy."

"Just a businessman, ma'am," I say.

"Yeah, I guess that too," she says. "Trying to get 'em young, are you?"

"Mostly just trying to make their parents happy," I say.

"And you sure are good at that," she says, patting

my cheek. "How long do I gotta wait to see you toting around some niños?"

"You sound like my mama," I say.

"Well, your mama is right. A sweet thing like you," she says. "What about that woman at your birthday?"

"Hoping for a second date," I say.

"Well, baby, if that don't work out, I've got a friend. Just broke up with this guy. An absolute jerk…"

Fortunately, before I can find myself on yet another blind date, Gretchen peeks through the back door and waves me in. Which means the food is here.

Nina gives me a nod that says, "Go on then."

And I go. "What we got?" I ask Gretchen.

"Sandwiches, chips, cookies. The basics. And you better refill that candy jar. It's almost empty."

I cast a suspicious look at the old man, who has moved toward the ax throwing room, still talking the ears off of his friends. "On it," I say.

But then I'm not. Because it's at that moment that Madigan walks through the door. "In a minute," I add.

Gretchen rolls her eyes. "I got it," she says. "Just tell me where the candy is."

But I don't really hear her, staring at Madigan who's wearing tight jeans and an oversized t-shirt.

Flat tennis shoes, her hair up in a high ponytail, small golden hoops hanging from her ears.

"Candy," Gretchen prompts.

"Um, storage," I mutter, making my way toward Madigan. She's looking around like, well frankly, she's looking around like a ballerina at a boxing match—all big eyes and tight lips.

"Hey!" I say.

"Oh, hey," she says, clearly relieved to see me, which I consider moderately gratifying. Maybe the secret is to keep exposing her to uncomfortable environments.

"You came." I'm not quite sure what to say after that since I'm trying not to make things weird.

She leans toward me slightly. "I feel like a lost girl at a circus."

"Well, I *did* provide candy," I say.

She laughs just a bit, dare I call it a giggle. Maybe more of a sniggle. "You definitely know how to bring a crowd. Did Gretchen make cake?" she asks hopefully, looking around.

"Ah, I see the real reason you came," I say.

"Can you blame me?" she asks with a cute lopsided smile. "I haven't stopped thinking about that cake."

"We do have cookies. But no cake." I lead her from the entrance to the food table where Gretchen has brought the first installment of snacks.

Somehow she's managed to make it look like a buffet, even with the basic offerings.

"Did Gretchen make the cookies?" Madigan asks.

"Will you leave if I say we bought them?"

"I guess not," she says with an exaggerated sigh. She does give Gretchen a little wave when she sees her, and I'm starting to feel pretty confident about this whole thing. That is, until Tim gets on the intercom to announce that a shooting demo will be beginning at one out on the south lawn. Then Madigan's back to the big ballerina eyes.

"A demo?" she says. "With all these people."

It's meant to be a question, not a judgment, but she doesn't manage to avoid the judgment part.

"It's only on the range," I say. "Nobody allowed past the tape. And only Tim will be shooting. He's been practicing."

"I see you even have ear protection," she says, pointing to a basket of ear plugs, each set wrapped individually in cellophane. Though as she says it, we both notice that almost no one is stopping to take a set.

"Maybe we'll have to make that announcement over the speaker as well," I say. "But not yet. First we'll be doing an ax throwing demo. No ear plugs necessary."

"When is that?" she asks.

"In about five minutes," I say, glancing at the wall clock.

"Guess we should go then, huh?" she says. "You being the boss and all."

The crowd is already beginning to flow toward the ax room, bottlenecking at the door.

Looking at Madigan, I can tell she's wondering if we're violating any fire codes or anything.

I almost make excuses for the crowd, opening my mouth to say that there are two emergency exits inside.

But she speaks first. "Should have brought my dad. This would have been right up his alley."

"I would have loved that," I say, and I mean it.

Which earns me a nice smile.

"Alfie probably could have come too," I say, noting that there are a few dogs in harnesses with their owners.

"Nah," she replies. "Too many loud noises, big smells, and—you know—chocolate chip cookies. I can't have him throwing up all night."

"Fair," I say. "And, except for the cookies, it seems like those other things are tricky for *you* too," I say.

"You have no idea," she replies, looking to the bottleneck of people like she expects to drown in it.

"You up for it?" I ask. "The demo?"

"I guess that's why I'm here."

I look down at her. I might be the only person

more surprised than she is that she *is* here. "I'm really glad you came. But if the crowd's too much, that's okay too."

She squares her shoulders. "I've done crowds before. Let's do this." She takes a cookie and gives me a little smile.

They're like fairy dust, those smiles, weightless and glittered and seemingly scarce.

We head into the mid-sized room, the room next to the one Madigan said could be used to destroy stuff, arriving just in time for the demo.

Tim is positioned in one of the cubbies we've created with nets and strawbale bullseyes. He demonstrates how to hold the ax, how to pull it back, how to let it go. It sails forward into the haybale, almost at the center.

"Now, we've got a little employee wager going," Tim says into his microphone. He's got a big toothy smile, like he should have been working carnivals his whole life. "The one of us who's the best shot wins a free month for a friend."

The audience claps politely as those who will be competing make their way through the crowd.

"Are you going to throw?" Madigan whispers.

"In a minute," I say back.

"But before we get started with the ax throwing contest," Tim continues with his carnie grin, "we've got a little contest for y'all too. See them buckets set up over there. Those are for various charities. Each employee picked a favorite. If you're so inclined, drop a dollar or some spare change into your favorite."

The crowd shifts a bit, their collective gaze settling on the long table of buckets. And then, because no one's moving, I pull out my wallet and make my way to the table myself, dropping a few dollars into each of the buckets. "Ice is broken, folks," I say loudly. "Come on up!"

And they do, wiggling their way through the crowd as I walk back to Madigan.

"This is nice," she says, as the crowd moves like fish through a pond, making their way to the different buckets.

Several of the employee spouses have agreed to supervise the buckets, thanking people and making sure the money all goes in instead of the sneaky handful going out. They stand at a long table that's been decorated for each charity.

"What are the charities?" Madigan asks, craning her neck to try to see over the crowd, and fingering her purse.

"Mostly the basics: Humane Society—that's Tim. Women's Shelter—Sandra's choice. Ronald McDonald House—Ned. He's still mostly at The Molehill, but agreed to help me get this running as well. And the Swallowsville Cancer Clinic. Mahoney

—they took care of his dad real nice a few years ago."

"Those are amazing choices," Madigan says. "But what about yours?"

I shrug, feeling a little embarrassed.

"I mean, if you have one," she says. "I guess I shouldn't have assumed…"

I laugh. "Of course you can assume," I say. "I'm the boss. I should have one. It's just that it's kind of a different one." I glance at the bucket Gretchen agreed to be in charge of, although her spot is empty since she's still dealing with the food.

"Which means?" Madigan presses.

"Well, there's this old church on Panning Street. Real pretty. I went there with Mama when we first moved here. She picked it 'cause she said you could feel the Holy Spirit better in a place with stained glass windows. But a few years ago, they stopped holding services there because it flooded and then there was mold, plus the beams started to rot."

Maddie doesn't say anything, just stares over my shoulder at the lonely-looking bucket without anyone even standing behind it. It's nearly empty, that much is clear. Which means I start rambling in earnest. "They've remedied most of the flood damage and it's just about broken the budget of a little place like that. So now they're talking about selling it or just taking it down, maybe preserving a few of the windows for the historical society. But that breaks my heart. The pastor set up a little fund, and I thought it'd be nice to support that."

Madigan continues to stare, right past my shoulder as a few older gentlemen drop some change into that bucket. I figure that for a dog-loving, feminist, safety-enthusiast, pragmatist like Madigan, it probably feels like a waste of money. What good's an old building anyway?

"You guys should match the funds for the winner," she finally says.

"Why, Miss Madigan, I didn't peg *you* as a gambler."

"I enjoy a good wager here and there," she says. "Especially for good causes."

"It's a fun idea," I say. "But who is the winner? The ax thrower who gets closest or the fund who earns the most?"

She narrows her eyes thoughtfully. "Both," she says, looking at my empty bucket.

I lean toward her. "In the spirit of charity, I'll take your challenge. Let me make the announcement."

"Nice doing business with you," she says. "Now if you'll excuse me, I need to go make some donations."

I watch her walk away—it's a nice walk, with just the right amount of sway—then make my way back to the sound system. "Hey, ladies and gents. To make this contest even more exciting, we've decided to up the ante. Whoever wins at the ax throw, The Range will match that donation."

The audience breaks into a nice applause with a good bit of stomping and whooping.

"I hope y'all have been practicing," I say, looking to the ax throwers. Sandra flexes and I smile. "And not only that," I say into the microphone, "whichever bucket has the most money at the end of the night, we'll double that one too."

The applause turns into a respectable little thunder.

"We'll give you a little more time to make your donations, and then we'll begin the contest."

Madigan wanders back to me, zipping up her purse.

"Did you find a good one?"

"They're all good," she replies.

And maybe she is a gambler, because she's got a right decent poker face. I have no idea where she put her money.

"I reckon Alfie would be voting for the Humane Society," I say.

"He probably would," she says. "But truthfully, he's fairly broke at the moment."

I laugh. "I'm gonna do my best to beat Tim anyway."

"You do that," she answers with an impish smile. Then putting on her best Kentucky accent, which I didn't even know she had, she says, "Now I reckon y'all best get started. Those charities aren't going to double themselves."

I glance at my bucket and then back at the door, looking for Gretchen.

"I'll watch your bucket," Madigan says as though she just read my mind. "Now go on."

So I do.

CHAPTER 27

MADIGAN

As soon as I get behind the church bucket, several men come up to make donations. Yeah, I notice it. At least it's for a good cause. There's this tiny little part of me that wishes Andy were over here to notice it too, but as soon as that thought hits, I do my best to hit it back. That's the last thing I need—to start thinking like a junior high school girl.

Besides, it's not like I need Andy to be jealous or something. I don't need anything from him. I just came today, well, to sort some things out. Call it curiosity.

And I have to say, Andy can throw a party. The charities are a nice touch. I glance into his bucket. Mostly a few bills and some change. To my right, the humane society bucket is already starting to overflow and Tim's wife or girlfriend is fishing around for an empty box to put on the table beside it.

I find one for her, under the table. She throws me a grateful smile and then Tim is back on the mic. The contest is about to begin.

Ax throwing is pretty straightforward. Not subjective like painting or music or literature. Nope. You pull the arm back. And throw. And if the ax hits, they pull it out and mark the spot in chalk. A different color for each contestant.

Two of the employees miss completely, which inspires laughter from the crowd and elaborate bows from the throwers. Sandra hits within the rings. Tim is up next. And he *has* been practicing. His ax lands just inside the bullseye. A beautiful throw.

I see his girlfriend do a little leap.

"Nice," I say, high-fiving her.

"Andy's up," she says, and I try to erase anything from my face, nodding noncommittally.

Andy lifts his arm, the muscles rippling up the forearm and along his triceps. I am *not* the only woman in the room to notice. And then he lets it go —a straight shot through the air, you can almost hear it—as though it was a bullet, not a blade. It lands with a solid thud in the bullseye. Directly opposite Tim's.

"Nice," I murmur under my breath, clapping along with the rest of the crowd.

Tim's girlfriend gives me a little glance. "I'd say those are almost even."

I laugh. "I'd say you're right."

By the bullseye, the two guys are giving it a good inspection, then Andy calls out for a tape measure and someone from the crowd hurries to find one.

"You and Andy dating?" the woman asks. She must have been at his birthday party, though most of the faces from it are a blur to me.

"Oh, um, just friends," I respond.

She smiles. And there's something in it. "Well, he did good, baby."

"He did," I say.

"I'm Dierdra," she says, extending a hand. "People call me Didi."

"Madigan," I say.

"If those are tied, Andy's gonna be doubling three of these pots," Didi says with a laugh as they measure the chalk marks from the center of the bullseye. "The funny thing with Andy is, that might make him even happier."

"Ladies and gentlemen," Tim announces. "It appears that I have beat our fearless leader by about one millimeter. However, to account for the—as he puts it—discrepancies that could be caused by using chalk lines, he plans to give both our charities double the money. And of course, we'll both get to bring a guest for free all month to practice our game. I got you, baby," he says to Didi, kissing two of his fingers and gesturing to her.

She giggles beside me. It's sweet, and something about that makes me a little sad.

"I might call Andy a sore loser, except that it's his money, not mine," Tim continues with a laugh. "Now all y'all go get some sandwiches in the main hall. And remember those buckets will be here all night."

"Told you," Didi says. "That kid likes giving money away. Long as it's a good cause." She glances around at the emptying ax throwing room. "I sure hope this place takes off."

"Yeah," I murmur, looking around at the happy crowd, at the buckets of money, at Andy making his way toward me. "Me too." It's something you probably couldn't have paid me to say a day earlier, but somehow now, it feels oddly true.

THAT NIGHT ANDY TEXTS ME. "You'll never guess which bucket won," he says.

"We had to get an extra box for the humane society," I say, stroking Alfie's fur as he tries to get his entire body to fit into my lap.

"I KNOW," Andy texts in all caps. "But that wasn't it."

"So…?" I text.

"The church!!!" he texts. "Can you believe it?"

"Wow," I reply. "It didn't look that full when I left."

"It wasn't that *full*," he says. "But somebody put several hundred-dollar bills in there. Crazy, right?"

"That's awesome!" I text. "Well, except that now you've got to double it."

"Are you kidding?" he texts. "I can't wait. Pastor Dan is gonna lose it. That'll probably pay for the drywall in the basement. Especially if I double the doubling since it won at both contests. That is so cool. Can't wait to announce it on the website."

"Just don't get in over your head," I text, sounding like—I don't know, like someone's grandma. "Your business isn't exactly profitable yet."

"Oh, it will be," he says, followed by a very happy emoji.

And if I had that much confidence, well, maybe I could rule the world. Or at least find my place in it.

Alfie has settled into sleep, his head tipped to the side, his tongue lolling out of his mouth.

"Hopefully, Alfie isn't too disappointed," Andy texts.

"Oh, I think he'll be alright," I say. "Thanks to

Tim and his ax throwing." I send Andy a laughing emoji, then look down at Alfie.

"We should celebrate," Andy texts. "Both the wins. Wanna get pizza with me next weekend?"

I stare at the text, thinking all the thoughts, grateful we're texting instead of talking so I can pause.

Do I? Do I want to get pizza with Andy next week?

The most surprising thing in the whole wide world is that I realize I do.

But I can't. And that's the thing that just feels too hard to explain. It's been almost four years, but it still feels too soon.

I set my phone to the side, ignoring it for now. "You'll forgive me, won't you, Alfie," I say, changing the subject with myself. "That I gave that old church all my money instead of the animals. I just couldn't bear to think of them tearing it down. Not that one."

And then Alfie startles from his sleep, reaching up to me and giving me three wet kisses. Right cheek, left, then right. Just like the French.

Three. The number of completion, of wholeness. The number of full years that Joshua has been gone.

"But I can't?" I murmur. "Can I?"

Alfie is settling again into my lap, his head bobbing up and down, like a human nod.

And I don't know how many signs a person

needs, but I could honestly do with just one more. Which is when Alfie's paw settles onto the phone.

"Fine," I mutter, scooping up my phone. "It's just pizza, not a betrothal or something."

I take a deep breath, send the text. "Sure. What time?"

Sure. When I am anything but. I click my phone fully off, not ready to make more plans. In fact, I feel exhausted. I nestle into the couch with Alfie, putting my feet up and burrowing into the warm softness that is my dog.

***

When I wake in the morning, my body is a whole web of cricks and cracks. Since when do I sleep the whole night on the couch? And then I realize, since when do I sleep the whole night at all? Especially without a glass or two of wine beforehand. But I did. The first time in three years. The first time since Joshua left.

One solid night's sleep.

I rush to get ready for work, still stunned at the beauty of it, the miracle.

My phone is only at ten percent. I plug it in to charge as I shower. I'll charge it more as I drive.

I pull into the station just two minutes before my shift begins.

"Good glory," Tracey says, looking up from the couch. "I thought you were dead. Did you not see my texts?"

I look down at my phone. "Sorry," I say. "I turned it off because I forgot to charge it last night and I wanted it to get as much as possible while I drove here."

Tracey gives me a weird look. "You forgot to charge your phone?"

"Yeah," I say. "Fell asleep with Alfie on the couch."

"With Alfie?" she says.

"Yeah," I say, not noticing her face.

"Are you hungover?" she asks, stepping closer.

"No," I laugh.

"You don't smell hungover," she says. "And even when you do, you show up for work on time."

"I smell hungover sometimes?" I ask, pausing as I settle into the station.

"Only sometimes," she says. "But yeah."

"It's only a little wine," I mumble. "I'm never hungover. And then, as though to prove it, I add, "And I didn't have anything last night. Just fell asleep. Tired, I guess."

"You're always tired," she says.

"Well, I feel great today," I say.

"I can tell," she replies.

Matt comes in with a coffee. "Holy highness," he says. "She has arrived."

"Oh my gosh, you guys. I'm not even late." I'm starting to feel just a little annoyed.

"You've gotten here at the same time for the last two years," Matt says. "On the dot."

"How do you even know?" I ask. "Either of you. I'm always here before both of you."

"Blue shift was freaked out," he says. "And that freaked us out."

"Well, stop freaking," I say. "I'm fine." I've gotten a little edge to my voice.

"Ah, there she is," Tracey says.

"So I have to be grumpy to be me?" I say, feeling even grumpier.

She does this shrug thing that I think is supposed to be funny, but I only find it annoying.

"Anyway, I'm here," I say. "So let's get everything inspected and stop—"

And just then the tones go off.

"Thank goodness," I reply. "Something to do."

CHAPTER 28

ANDY

I fully charged my phone. I've been doing it since the night I asked Madigan out for pizza—charged it while I waited for her response.

Which didn't come until a full twenty-six minutes later, even though we'd been having a whole text conversation.

I spent those minutes reminding myself that she's got a wacky schedule. And that she works a lot, picking up extra shifts—maybe she'd had to go in suddenly. Reminding myself there are other fish in the sea. Reminding myself about a lot of things, though none of my reminding really helped.

By the time she finally texted me back, I was ready for a full shut-down. I had to read the text twice to realize she'd actually accepted my invitation instead of rejecting it.

And now, finally, tonight's the night. I'm determined this time to get to know Madigan better. And to pick her up instead of meeting her there. I'm determined to buy her flowers, to start to make this a thing. It's more determined than I've felt about a woman in a long time. Scratch that. It's more determined than I've felt about a woman ever.

"Our boy's got it bad," Ned says, clocking in on his phone. It's the first official week The Range is up and running and we've got a bachelor's party coming in for ax throwing at 1:00.

"Don't he though?" Tim says without even looking up.

"What are you two yammering about?" I ask.

"You look like crap," Tim says. "Welcome to the club."

I look down at myself. T-shirt and shorts. "I look the same as always."

"Well, you don't always *not* look like crap," Ned says. "But what Tim means is that you've got dark circles under your eyes, your hair's a mess, and your socks don't match."

"They do too," I say, though as I look down, I realize they don't. One is slightly darker than the other. "Or not. I just didn't sleep well last night."

"Exactly," Tim says. "And since when do you not sleep like an absolute baby?"

"Well, since this week, I'd say, which is reasonable with the new business and all."

"And I'd say you've got it bad." Tim adds. "But she's cute. Seems nice too. Didi liked her."

"Nina likes her too," Ned chimes in. "Seems a little uppity to me though."

"She's not uppity," I say. "She's just…precise."

"Sounds like the same thing," Ned says.

"It's not," I say, and realize that it really isn't. Although precise women are not usually my game.

"Well, if she's 'precise,'" Ned says, "you better show up tonight with socks that are the same color."

"Noted," I say.

WE'RE LAYING out the last few throwing knives when men start arriving for the bachelor's party. They're laughing and shoving and they've got the groom decked out in a black suit jacket.

"I assume you're the lucky guy," I say, coming up and shaking his hand.

"Lucky?!?" one of the other guys shouts.

"That coat's for his funeral," another one chimes in and they all laugh.

Sure is different than the women Gretchen gets at The Cottage for the bridal showers who are all pink and roses and wine glasses and weepy happiness.

Don't get me wrong, this is happiness too. There's just a lot more shoving involved.

As I look around at the group, I hope everyone's sober. I assume that's why they set the time for 1:00, so they could have their fun here, before hitting up the bars this evening.

Even so, I lean over to Ned. "You got all the release forms signed, right?"

"Every one," he whispers back.

I nod.

"Well, gentlemen," I begin. "Tim here is gonna get you all started." I have to bite back a lecture about how we all want to have fun, but these are still real axes and knives and to use caution. I figure Tim will get to it in his spiel, but we haven't had such a big group, much less such a rowdy one. And it's making me nervous. Maybe Madigan's *preciseness* is rubbing off on me.

Tim goes through the instructions, the warnings, the coaching, not missing a thing. The guys line up at the cubbies, still joking, still teasing, booing when one of their buddies misses completely. And it's just what I wanted. A whole lot of fun.

A little bit of the tension eases out of my shoulders and I have a quick look at my phone. I have to admit that ever since we got this date set, I've been worried Madigan would cancel it. But so far, we're good to go.

The axes hit in a fairly steady rhythm, some sinking softly into the straw walls, others pinging against the wood. Hooting and cursing and high-fiving and back slapping and the occasional bet (and the occasional lost bet). And lots and lots of laughter.

Until there isn't.

I hear it as a gasp, then a hiss, then a moment of perfect silence.

A terrible sound.

Tim's feet slapping the ground.

A growing, growling murmur of worried men. It's different than the murmur of worried women—not calmer, not even quieter, but more foreboding somehow.

I trot out from behind my makeshift desk to the group that has huddled around one of the guys. The one in the black suit coat. The groom.

For the second time this summer, I find myself on the phone with 911.

For the second time this summer, an ambulance chugs up the road, sirens blaring.

For the second time this summer, I face Madigan in uniform. Guess she'd picked up a ground shift.

I admit I'm relieved to see her. At this point, we're looking at a lot of blood. One of the guys nearly fainted and another retched into a nearby trashcan. So, yeah, we're not doing great as a collective.

From the chaotic shouted stories, I've gathered this. The groom had thrown his ax—a decent shot that had hit an outer ring—apparently his first hit. He'd gone to retrieve his ax, stepping to the side as the next guy stepped up for his throw. But too many people were doing too many things at once. Someone had shouted for the groom to pose for a picture. He had, reaching his hand out and pointing to show the divet where his ax had hit, just as the next guy had thrown his ax. An unfortunately exact throw that had hit two of the groom's fingertips. At least I hoped they were fingertips.

It's hard to tell in the chaos. There are no fingers lying on the floor, at any rate. Which I consider a good thing.

The groom sits on the floor—pale, but calm. Tim has wrapped his hand with gauze, though the tip is already soaked with bright red blood.

The sea of men parts for Madigan and her partner, a burly man almost a head taller than she is.

"Can you walk?" she asks softly, stooping down to examine the gauze, though she doesn't remove it. "Or you feeling woozy?"

"I'm okay," he says.

Madigan nods, taking one of the groom's elbows as her partner takes the other, helping the groom up.

"You good?" she asks again.

He nods and walks to the door where the cot waits. I trail after them.

The groomsmen cheer and the groom smiles, waving at them with the middle finger of his good hand. That feels like a pretty good sign.

I stand to the side, watching as Madigan helps him onto the cot and the burly guy pulls a couple bars out of the ambulance. The cot lifts, connected to the bars, and slides into the ambulance.

"Wow," the groom says to Madigan. "High tech."

"We aim to please," she replies, throwing him a small smile, then looking to the sky.

Low clouds are gathering and a few fat raindrops pelt the ground.

"At least we don't need a helicopter this time," I say.

Madigan pinches her face together in a look that's difficult to interpret. It's not a mean look, though it doesn't look like a good look, and it's definitely not a relaxed look.

"Right?" I whisper, stepping close to Madigan. "You don't need a helicopter."

"Depends on the state of those fingers," she says quietly enough that the groom won't hear.

I feel my body tighten, my heart speed up. Unfortunately, we don't have time for questions.

Madigan tries to give me a comforting smile, but I'm struggling to grab onto it.

I step away from the ambulance, from her, my own face flat as the muscles in my back and neck tie into knots.

Madigan hops into the back of the ambulance, one quick step. Her partner's already up front, buckling in.

I nod as she closes the doors. Normally, I'd go for a little repartee, something along the lines of, "Guess you might be late for dinner." But somehow right now, I can't find the energy for that.

And then they're gone.

The rain is picking up, darkening the cement where I'm standing, pelting my shoulders and hair. I turn around and look into the building. The groomsmen are milling around, texting, talking.

Ned comes outside, wiping his forehead with a handkerchief. "So maybe the date is off, no?" he says.

But I'm not really in the mood. "Did Tim find the cleaning supplies?"

"He's already on it," Ned says.

"Wearing gloves?"

"Double," Ned answers.

"Good," I say. "It's about time we took some care around here."

But it's not what I mean. What I mean—what I

really mean—is, *It's about time I took some care around here. It's about time I grew up.*

Ned puts a hand on my shoulder. "We got this. Why don't you head home?"

I shake my head. "Close this place up, Ned. Close it for the rest of the day."

———

I'M GETTING DRESSED when the text comes in. I've been waiting.

"Can't make it," Madigan texts. "I'm really sorry, but that guy lopped off more than his fingertips. One of those fingers was just dangling. Normally the helicopter would have taken him from Midvale Hospital to Louisville. But with the weather, they couldn't fly. So we drove him. We're headed back now, but we won't be there in time."

Obviously.

Honestly, I'm impressed she bothered to text me instead of just standing me up. I'm not sure I would have done the same for me.

I pick up my phone, planning to text her back. But instead, I pull up Uber Eats, put in my order, and call it a night.

CHAPTER 29

MADIGAN

I'm expecting a follow-up to the text I send Andy. A *How about dessert?* Something.

But my phone is silent for the rest of the night.

The rain has settled by the time I get home. I take Alfie for a quick walk, stopping at the church on Panning Street. The renovations are clipping along—new door, repaired stairs and walls, most of the scaffolding gone, except at the south side, where they've just installed a long window, though I can't see what it looks like in the dark.

I wonder, staring at the fresh repairs, how much Andy ended up donating, and if it had an impact on such a big project.

Does any of the small stuff we do have an impact? I sure hope so.

The man in the ambulance, the one getting married, his name was Jeremy.

Two hours is a long time to drive to the hospital. Especially when you've got fingers that need care. Especially when you're getting married the next day.

He'd asked me, "Do you think I'll make it to my wedding tomorrow?"

"I think you're headed in for surgery," I'd said. No reason to beat around the bush.

"So," he'd asked. "Will I make it? To the wedding, I mean—not, you know, will I make it make it—I'm assuming that's a 'yes.'"

"That's probably a yes," I'd said with a wink. "You can be grateful you got hit by an ax, not a truck."

"Not sure Amelia is going to see it that way, if I don't show up to my own wedding," he'd said with a laugh.

I'd laughed with him. What else was there to do? "Well, tell her a few fingers are nothing in the larger scheme of things."

"You married?" he'd asked, his voice growing a little groggy from the painkillers I'd given him. "It's a big day."

I'd patted his arm and looked away. The conversation is a little too close to home for me. "You should call your fiancée. I'm sure she's been told and is on her way, but you should still call her."

"Do you think she'll kill me?" he'd asked, holding his phone with his good hand.

"Not while you're at the hospital."

He'd laughed. He had a nice laugh, one he wasn't afraid to use.

"I'm really sorry," I'd said.

"Not your fault, now, is it?" he'd replied.

"Never is," I'd answered. "But it doesn't make me any less sorry. Morning or evening wedding?"

"Afternoon," he'd said.

"Well, maybe you can move it back to the evening. If everything goes well at the hospital." Though by 'well' I meant 'perfect' and I wasn't really expecting that.

"Probably won't be any more foggy-headed than if I was hungover, huh?" he'd said.

"Maybe not."

He'd called her then, and I could hear her crying on the other end. I didn't blame her. On any count. Her wedding day. Her fiancé going in for surgery. The whole deal.

"This is going to set back my schooling a bit," he'd said when he was off the phone.

"What are you in school for?" I'd asked.

"Dentistry," he'd answered.

"Oh, I think you'll be alright," I'd replied. "They'll get you fixed up real pretty and you can go back."

"Not just dentistry," he'd said, resting his phone on his chest. I had his injured hand propped on a small pillow. "Surgery. Oral surgery."

"Mmm," I'd said. "That *is* a little different."

"Think they can save my fingers?"

"I think they're gonna do their darndest to try."

He'd settled into a silence, his eyes growing heavy. "Thanks."

He'd slipped into sleep after that, the sweet little drip of morphine doing its job.

And I'd counted the fingers on his healthy hand.

Five. The number of balance and equilibrium.

The fifth element—ether—if you asked the Greeks, the purest form of existence.

God's grace and favor if you went Biblical.

The universe of the gods if you studied the Egyptians.

A good number all around.

How would it feel to have such a lovely number robbed of two of its parts? The remaining three fingers would not be complete, no matter what three usually meant. And why, why did things always have to get taken away?

He'd stirred in his sleep, humming and smiling. Even when his hand had just been ruined. And I'd wondered, in that smile, if it was just the morphine working, or if it was time to for me to figure out how to hunt down the grace in the fury.

Jeremy's phone had slipped off of his chest and I'd caught it, tucking it into the bag with his other personal things.

I take out my own phone now, as Alfie and I walk past the fresh, new church, and pull up Andy's number.

CHAPTER 30

ANDY

Is it a superpower to be able to turn off your phone? Maybe sometimes, but not for me, not today. Right now, it's more like my version of getting drunk. My version of checking out. Which doesn't quite feel like a superpower when you think too hard about it.

I don't.

It's charging now, on the three-hour drive up to Indy. I'm not looking at it though.

I'm going to see that kid—Saul—see how he's doing, see if he's awake.

Because that's the other thing I'd done on my ruined date night—a little sleuthing to figure out if that kid was still up there. He is and—per the gossip Gretchen heard at The Cottage—still unconscious.

Because I was dumb enough to leave the keys in the ATVs at work.

After all, you can't really blame ten-year-olds for being dumb. They're just built that way. But me—a twenty-seven-year-old man who owns his own business—two businesses. That man should know better.

Just like I should know better than to let a bunch of potentially beer-in-the-morning groomsmen throw axes. Even if they did sign releases. Even if they are grown men. I should have followed my gut, asked a few questions, made sure everyone was sober as a newborn baby—and if they were, I should have made sure they were following all the rules anyway.

I glance at my phone, wonder if there's an update about the groom, though I don't pick it up to check.

I make most of the drive in silence, only turning my GPS on at the end so I can find the hospital. I have the boy's name written on a small slip of paper tucked into my pocket. Saul Reneau. Room 203.

I find a parking spot in the shade far away from most of the rest of the cars. Sit with a little prayer in my heart like Mama taught me. Then open my door.

The hospital is homier than I expected. Warm brick that gives it a friendly look.

I make my way in and wait at the information desk for the older lady in front of me to finish asking questions to the receptionist. I don't really expect them to let a non-related guy in to sit with an unconscious kid. In fact, standing there while the old woman in front of me asks another question, I'm not sure what I expected, period. I suddenly feel ridiculous, stupid even. And, trust me, I've *been* ridiculous and stupid many, many times in my life, but me *feeling* it—that's something new.

I turn, a quick 180, ready to go back to my car. But there, just feet from me, is the boy's mother. "Andy Putman."

"Yes, ma'am," I answer.

"What are you doing here?" It's blunt, but not exactly mean.

"Well, to be honest, I was hoping I could see your son. I'm really sorry about what happened."

She looks down at the floor for a moment, then meets my eyes. "Truthfully, there's not a whole lot to see. They've got him on a medicine that keeps him in a coma. His brain swelled a lot and they're wanting that to go down and for him to rest and heal, in order to reduce as much trauma to his brain as possible."

"I'm so sorry," I repeat.

"Well now, it ain't just you to blame, is it?"

I don't answer.

"Don't get me wrong," she says. "I one hundred percent blamed you for everything at first, thought about suing."

I swallow, but don't speak.

"Guess that's a stage of grief," she says. "Suing people. But then the other stages kick in. *Not* suing people, crying a lot, sleeping too much, then sitting with him, watching him, staring at that little face and thinking about all the great things about him. Eventually I got to some semblance of acceptance. And I remembered that I was the mother of the little delinquent who thought it was okay to steal an ATV. And that I was literally standing in the room when it happened—*not* keeping very close tabs on my son. Neither was my brother. And you weren't even there."

I look at the floor. "I did leave the keys in, ma'am. That couldn't have helped."

"Call me Shannon," she says. "And it did make the boys' job easier. But that's just it, it was still their choice, a thing they did. And I was their mama and aunt. Right there. And I bet you don't leave the keys in anymore."

"No, ma'... uh, Shannon, no, not anymore."

"Good," she says. "Well, then I suppose you might as well come up. They tell us to talk to him as much as possible. You good at talking, Andy?"

"Most times," I say. "Though this place has me all tongue-tied."

She laughs as we step into the elevator. "You got that right. My boyfriend usually just brings his guitar. And Saul's dad comes up most Sundays. They try to miss each other."

"Fair enough," I say. The elevator opens and we walk down a wide hall, squeaky clean, though not with the sterile feeling that adult hospitals give. They're trying to keep it cozy with carpet and plush chairs and pictures.

Shannon stops at a door. "Get your conversation on, Andy. Here we go."

I've been in hospitals before. They're not great, but you know, they are what they are. Still, it takes me back a little to see this thin little body hooked up to monitors and drips and other hospital-y stuff. I stop just past the door, my throat feeling thick and choked. Not the best conversation throat.

"You alright?" she asks.

I step farther into the room and she motions to a seat. She leans over, kisses Saul's forehead. "Hey sweetie," she says to the sleeping boy. "I brought you a guest. Mr. Putman. You're just lucky he's not mad you ruined his ATV."

"Not mad at all," I hop in, clearing my throat. "That was quite the run you took with it actually. Something a lot like what I would have done at your age."

And then it's the weirdest thing. Because I talk and talk and talk, almost like I can't stop. Yammering at this little boy who can't see me, doesn't answer me back. But he's breathing, steady and calm, his face tranquil.

After I've blabbered on for at least an hour, I finally lean back. "Thanks for letting me come," I say to Shannon.

"You *are* good at talking," she replies. "I'm impressed. And Saul looks happy."

I look at his face and can't tell the difference. "I'd love to come up another time if it's okay with you."

"I'm here every Friday and Saturday," she answers. "Lots of other days too. Text me first next time. But, sure, the more guests the better. That's what I figure."

"I really appreciate it, ma'am."

She lifts an eyebrow.

"Um, I mean, Shannon."

"I appreciate it too," she answers. "And I'm really glad I didn't sue you."

"Me too," I answer, though an uncomfortable little thought is tip-tapping against my brain, wondering how many people have thought about suing. Wondering how many chances I'll get until someone actually does. Wondering how the groom is doing, and hoping he's standing in a church somewhere with a bandaged hand, exchanging vows.

WHEN I GET into the car, and finally look at my phone, I see that a bunch of people called me last night.

I ignore almost all of them. Except Madigan. Her number I click, hoping for a little information about the groom.

The trick is getting Madigan to answer.

She doesn't on the first try. I wait two minutes and call again. Not usually my style, but I figure that knowing is worth one annoying double call.

"Andy!" she says, a question in her voice.

"You busy?" I ask.

"I'm taking Alfie for a walk. Are you okay?"

"Yeah, I'm good," I say, staring at the straight road ahead of me, corn rising up on either side as I drive through southern Indiana. "I was just wondering how the groom is doing."

"The groom," she says. "The guy from yesterday?"

"Yeah," I say. "How is he?"

She pauses before answering. "I don't really know."

"But you took him in. To the hospital," I say.

"Yeah," she answers. "I took him *in.* That's what I do—*take* people to the hospital. Make sure they're as stable as I can get them, and then drop them off with doctors and surgeons and state-of-the-art equipment. Then I leave. And that's it. We're not exactly important enough for the doctors to be calling us and giving reports on the patients we bring."

"Oh," I say. "I guess I hadn't really thought about it."

Madigan is gracious enough not to make a snide comment about that. Instead, she says, "Honestly, I rarely even know if most of my patients live or die. Of course, in this case, he most likely lived, but who knows if he made it to his wedding. I'd guess not, if you were asking me. At least not today."

"Is there any way for you to find out?" I ask, desperation dripping from my voice.

She pauses and I hear her make the clicking noise to Alfie—the one that tells him to come sit by her heel. "I doubt the hospital will be willing to give me any information about his personal life. They would probably tell me if he's still in the hospital, and that's it. But do you know who *could* get the information?"

I literally lean toward my phone. "Who?" I ask.

"Someone with more connections than me," she says. "Someone who has every single number of every single groomsman who was at your business on that day at that time."

I lean back, realizing what she's saying. "You mean the guy with a bunch of names and numbers on release forms?" I ask.

"Yup," she says. "That guy."

I take a hand off the steering wheel and run it

through my hair, thinking. "If they are at the wedding, they probably won't answer," I murmur, thinking aloud.

"The wedding was supposed to be this afternoon," she says. "Jeremy was hoping he could make it, or at least just bump it to the evening."

"Jeremy?" I ask.

"The groom," she says.

"Oh."

"So, yes, if you call and no one answers, that's a good sign," she clarifies.

"And if I call and someone does answer…"

"Then at least you can ask how Jeremy's doing, if he had to go in for surgery, how it went, all that," she says.

"Yeah," I murmur. And truthfully, it sounds really uncomfortable. Truthfully, I realize that I called Madigan hoping she could give me information and reassure me and I could let it go. Truthfully, I'd been trying to sidestep adulthood yet again.

I sigh.

"You don't *have* to call anyone," she says, misunderstanding my sigh. "I mean, it might be nice, but they also might, um, they might not want to talk."

"Why wouldn't they want to talk?" I ask, veering toward the exit, my focus on the road.

Once again, she doesn't answer right away, and I

realize I'm missing some crucial subtext that I can't seem to catch between the lines.

"The guy was going to be a dentist," she says. "An oral surgeon."

"Cool," I say. "I wonder if he knows my mom."

More silence. Another little click to Alfie. "Surgery requires a lot of fine motor skills," she says.

And slowly, like my brain is made of molasses, I put it together. "You think he might want to sue me too," I mutter.

"Too?" she asks.

"Never mind," I say.

"Truly, he didn't seem like the suing type," she says. "He was really nice and upbeat. Of course," she mutters almost to herself. "Who knows when it's the pain meds talking or the real person." I hear Alfie barking at something. "And the bride was really upset when he called." She clears her throat and says more loudly, "But he seemed like a nice guy."

Nice guys can sue too, I almost say, but don't because Madigan's not one to tell a pretty lie. And I don't want to hear her say the truth—that, yeah, nice guys sue too. Especially if your business has robbed them of the livelihood they'd been investing in via several years of expensive schooling.

And suddenly I don't have the energy to say anything more. For the second day in a row, all I want to do is go home, let my phone die, and crash into bed.

"Andy," she says, breaking into my thoughts. "I know it can be hard, but…"

"Thanks, Madigan," I say, interrupting. I don't tell her where I spent the day, don't tell her that I just talked for an hour to a boy who couldn't hear a word, who hasn't opened his eyes for weeks. "Sorry to call and pester you."

"No, it's okay," she says. "It's good. I—"

"I better let you go now," I interrupt. "I expect you've got things to do."

"Well, I…" she begins, but I mutter goodbye and hang up the phone.

I'm not winning at adulting. Not today. But I know I need to call. Even if they are planning to sue. With any luck, no one will answer. With any luck, they're all at a chapel somewhere decked out in tuxedos. But I'm not so sure.

"Hey Ned," I voice text into my phone. "Look up the name of whoever booked the ax event for the bachelor's party."

"Jeremy Schmidt?" he replies in seconds.

"Nah," I voice text. "Send me the name of one of his buddies."

CHAPTER 31

MADIGAN

The weirdness of the last two days doesn't stop with my phone call with Andy.

When we get to the church on Panning, Alfie just stops, sits right in front of the door to the little prayer chapel, and refuses to move.

"I don't think it's open," I say, gently tugging on his leash when my normal clicks don't work. "And if it was, I'm not sure they'd allow dogs inside."

"On the contrary, my dear," a voice says from behind me. A man in jeans, a black shirt, and a clerical collar is walking to the steps, keys jangling in one hand, dog on a leash in the other. "Natasha and I were just coming to check on its progress. Would you like to come inside?"

"Oh, you don't have to worry about me," I stammer, still trying to get Alfie to move, though that's become even harder as he seems quite smitten by Natasha, the flaxen goldendoodle at the pastor's side.

"Nonsense," he says. "Natahsa wouldn't have it any other way."

Natasha gives Alfie a delicate sniff, which he enthusiastically returns.

"I believe I recognize you," he says. "Have you been to my services before?"

I squint at him, trying to picture him in full clerical robes. "I…" I begin.

"It's okay if you haven't," he replies with a laugh, misreading my hesitation. I let it drop. The person who used to frequent this little chapel with Joshua—that was an old me anyway.

He gazes at me for another moment before unlocking the chapel and flicking on some lights. "I didn't expect this little chapel to be done so soon, but we've gotten a lot of support from the community, including a wonderful bonus donation recently from a new business in town, and *voila*."

Voila indeed. The room is still small, but it smells of new wood and new paint. Red velvet padding adorns the antique wooden pews, each row dotted with small white Bibles for anyone who wants to read or pray. Most notably, the once-plain exterior wall sports a long, thin stained-glass window, which runs from end to end, depicting scenes from Jesus' life. Ending with three days in the tomb, and then Easter morning.

Pastor Dan arranges the Bibles so they look like humongous marshmallows on the red pews.

"You're not worried those Bibles will walk off?" I ask before my brain can stop my mouth.

"I suppose if someone needs them more than we do, they might," Pastor Dan says in the most cliché pastor-y way possible.

I manage to clip my lips together and not respond.

Three candles at the altar up front. Three panels of decorative wood behind it. Three scenes from the life of Christ on the wood.

Threes.

All over the room. In a painting with Peter, James, and John. In the Father, the Son, and the Holy Ghost. Even in the three Marys visiting the tomb. And of course there's the tomb itself, at the end of the stained-glass—three suns signifying the three days Jesus waited for his resurrection.

Joshua once explained that in ancient Jewry around Jesus' time, they didn't consider a person fully dead until the fourth day. That deadly number four. And Christ beat it. In three. The number of completion.

"It's beautiful," I murmur, tearing myself from my thoughts.

"Smells better too," Dan says with a laugh, and I can't help but smile. "Have a seat," he says, lighting candles.

"Oh, I don't want to impose," I say.

"Impose? On a pastor at a church. I'm happy to have someone finally here. We've been shut for far too long. Please," he says, gesturing to the bench.

Alfie and I sit. Natasha does too, right next to Alfie.

Pastor Dan waves to an unfinished window above the entrance. "We just had a donation fall through for that one. I might have to drywall it, but for now I'm waiting to see if something else comes through. Trying to have a little faith, though sometimes it sounds foolish when I say it out loud. Maybe I should just finish it up."

"No," I say. "Give it some time. You've got nothing to lose by waiting for a bit."

"No," he says. "I don't suppose I do. I guess you're a bit of a believer too then?" He smiles.

"'Believer' feels like a strong word," I answer. And then don't say any more.

We sit in silence and I pick up a white Bible, thumb through the pages, all of them fresh, untouched, straight from the printer. The words so old—some scholars dating the priestly blessings from the Old Testament as early as 7th century BCE

—but the pages all new. I hold it in my lap, that old-new thing.

I'm glad the chapel is different. I'm glad that I'm on red velvet instead of hard wood, that I'm looking through stained glass instead of at the original wood walls. I'm glad that I can try to forget that Joshua once sat here on these same seats. With me.

The scent of the wax catches my nose and I lower my head, not to pray, but to try to keep myself under control.

Control.

Lately I've felt it slipping through my hands. And the craziest thing is, I was kind of okay with it, kind of ready to let it slide, maybe even relieved.

A man who asked me out when I didn't want to go, an accidental acceptance, a date where he rescued me at the end. Truth is, it's the beginning of a great plot. But then, right at that point of slipping, of turning, right at that moment when maybe I was ready for a yes instead of a no, right then, he slid away instead. A twist. Just when I wasn't ready for it.

"Have you ever been to Home on the Range, my dear?" the pastor asks. "The new rifle range in town."

Like he was reading my thoughts. "Yes, actually," I reply.

"That's how we could afford the pews and Bibles. Andrew gave us the money."

So he has been called Andrew by more than his kindergarten teacher.

"Yes," I say, looking down, suddenly devoted to the Bible in my hands. "I saw that it was one of the charities during the soft opening. I'm really glad you won."

"Won?" he asks.

"Um, yes," I say. "All the charities got money, but the one with the most money got it doubled. And then I think—um, the owner—doubled it again because he hit a bullseye or something."

For a second, I wonder if I've said too much, if Pastor Dan is going to be abhorred that he got his new pretty pews from some type of gamble. But then he throws his head back and laughs.

Natasha looks up with a bark. Alfie joins her.

So that I'm the only one in the room still looking serious. Per my usual, I guess.

"Wonderful child, that boy. Makes it fun, giving."

"Yeah," I say, my face still looking down at the Bible, "he does."

"You seem enthralled," Dan says. "Why don't you take that one home?"

"Oh, no, I couldn't," I reply. "It should be for someone who needs it."

"It is," he says, in his second super pastor-y comment of the night. Though his smile is almost impish. "Please," he says.

"Of course," I reply, tucking the Bible into my bag. "And thank you for letting us come in. It's been wonderful."

"It has," he says. "Come again. I'll be posting open hours above the door."

I nod, clicking for Alfie, who reluctantly rises from his place by Natasha and joins me at the door. Fresh varnish, new hardware. But underneath, I can smell it, the old wood, that place that was me and Joshua. When we didn't know there would be a before and after.

Another twist I wasn't ready for.

CHAPTER 32

The best man picks up on the second ring. When he should be at a wedding. Shoot.

"Oh, hi," I say, as awkward as a tween girl. "This is Andy Putman, owner at Home On the Range. I was just calling to see how the groom is doing. No wedding today, I'm guessing."

"Nah," the best man says, all good humor. "He's in surgery right now, actually. Amelia went out to be with him. We're just chilling at the church and trying to do damage control for the people who didn't get the memo."

"Oh, wow," I say. "That sounds really awful."

"It's not the worst," he answers. "Wish we were at a wedding, but what do you do? Guess we manifested it or something with all that talk about him getting trapped. He sure showed us."

"Man, I'm so sorry," I say.

"Not your fault," he replies. The second time today I've heard that and not quite believed it.

I resist the urge to joke back with a *Can I get that in writing?* Doesn't seem like the right time.

"So is it, uh, postponed?" I ask, reaching for the right words.

"We were trying to get the church for tomorrow night," he says. "But it's a no go. Apparently, churches book up in the summer, least in a small town like this. And that's assuming Jeremy will be feeling up to it. We have no idea how the pain will be. Honestly, Jeremy and Amelia might just tie the knot at the hospital chapel tomorrow and then do a big reception Sunday or something. If he's up for it. Probably in somebody's back yard, because—yeah— same problem with the reception hall. That way the guests who flew in will still get to be here for part of it."

"The hospital, huh? Bet the bride is disap- pointed."

"Probably. My girlfriend told me if I ever pull a stunt like that, she'll leave me for the mailman, so…"

I open my mouth to say 'I'm sorry' again and stop myself. "Gretchen," I murmur.

"Excuse me," the best man says.

"I was just wondering about my sister. She owns The Cottage here in town. I wonder if she's booked up this weekend. Maybe she could get them in."

"I mean, there's still no guarantee this weekend will even work," he says. "Jeremy could be in loads of pain. Who knows? But, yeah, if you could check, that'd be great."

"Tell you what," I say, taking yet another gamble. "Let's plan on it. I'll talk to her. I'd bet a million bucks we can work something out."

"You sure?" the best man says.

I mean, absolutely not, but surely once Gretchen understands, we'll be able to work *something* out.

WE ARE *NOT* able to work something out.

"Andy," Gretchen says, drawing out my name. "You can't be serious."

I respond by not answering.

"I've got a huge reception tomorrow night. One of the biggest of the year. Some rich family from Louisville is coming all the way here. In fact, the bridesmaids *are* already here, staying in the guest rooms at The Cottage, eating, drinking, gossiping, and—I don't know—making sure every detail is in place."

I vaguely remember that a group from Louisville

also booked some ATVs at The Molehill, but fortunately Ned's taking care of it.

"You don't think there's any way you can work something out?" I ask. "Maybe find some time after the big rich wedding?"

"The one that ends at eight?" Gretchen says. "And is fancy. And catered. And that I hired a huge team to clean up."

"It *sounds* like you're trying to say 'no,' but I really want you to say 'yes.'"

"But I'm saying 'no,'" Gretchen says. "Time isn't something that can be found. It has to be made. And this time, I don't think I can do it."

"Sunday?" I ask.

"A local church is having a big meeting or gala or something."

"Can you…?"

"I'm not cancelling it, Andy."

I sigh into the phone.

Gretchen does too. "Look, Andy. I appreciate what you're trying to do for the groom, and for the bride, because my guess is that the groom is…less concerned. It's sweet. But it's not something I can do tomorrow. Or this weekend. We might be able to wiggle in a booking during the week sometime. Maybe on a Thursday."

"The out-of-town guests will probably be gone by then," I answer.

"Yeah," she says. "I'm sorry. I really am."

"I know," I reply. "You know, while the bridesmaids are living it up in The Cottage, the groomsmen might, in fact, be riding through mud at The Molehill."

"Well, just make sure nobody chops off a hand or has to get Lifelighted to the hospital."

It's meant to be funny, not to hit a nerve. But it definitely hits a nerve.

"Okay," I say. "Well, I better go make sure no one's dying. Have fun with the reception thing."

"Andy," Gretchen says, cutting me off right before I hang up.

I almost pretend I don't hear and hang up anyway, but I've never been great at that sort of thing. "Yeah?"

"The Molehill."

"Yeah," I say. "We got a group booking from Louisville. Guessing it's the same group."

"No," she says. "I mean…The Molehill. Isn't it closed on Sunday?"

"Yup," I say. "Everyone deserves a day of rest. That's what Mama tells me, anyway."

"Plus you like the day off," she says.

"Not gonna apologize for that," I reply. "Jesus gave that day to me."

"And you've got that great big beautiful property,"

she says, ignoring me. "Lake in the background. The woods, the creeks. Gorgeous this time of year."

"You don't mean?" I ask.

"I could probably spare some tables," she interrupts.

I take a deep breath, letting it sink in. "The Molehill, huh?"

"You've just got to pretty it up."

"We've got some things left over from the soft opening," I murmur. "Tablecloths, chairs."

"That should work," she says. "I'll bring the lights we used for your birthday."

"Yeah, okay," I say, nodding into the phone. "I'll give them a call, offer it up. I'm no good for food or anything, but it's something."

"It's definitely something," she says. "Good luck. And, hey, how'd your date go with Madigan?"

"It didn't," I answer. "She was the one on the ambulance."

"Again?" Madigan asks.

"She works a lot," I say.

"I'm sorry," Gretchen says and I realize I made it sound like Madigan was avoiding me.

Which I guess she is. Unless. Unless I'm the one avoiding her.

Which maybe, just maybe, I am.

Because I don't want Madigan to be right. Not

about The Molehill. Not about The Range. Not about me.

One of the many reasons to pull off a nice country wedding at The Molehill.

And make things right.

MADIGAN

I go home, take down a glass for wine like I do most every night, then wander to my bedroom and pause at my desk. A huge piece of furniture. Too big to move to storage with my books, especially when my dad was the entire moving committee.

Though he might not have moved it even if he could.

I drop the white Bible onto the desk.

And realize that, in almost four years, that Bible is the only thing to change about the desk.

Everything else—the pens in the drawer, note-books piled on a shelf beneath, even my old paper planner from years ago, story ideas and all, none of them any good now—it's all still there, still untouched.

Like if I used it or changed it, something in my heart might have broken open that I could never fix.

———

WE MET ON AN AIRPLANE. Joshua and I. I was reading a book. Up to that point, I'd never actually watched a movie in an airplane. Why would I when I had that delicious time alone to sit with my thoughts or a good book or my notebook?

Though I have to admit that that day, I wasn't sitting with my book very much and my thoughts were a little over-focused on the passenger beside me. Dark hair, dark eyes, nice jaw outlined in the dying sun from the window. I'll always remember him like that—face lined in orange as he focused on his screen, sometimes smiling, sometimes frowning —caught up in the storyline of his movie.

I caught myself glancing over to him more and more, and catching glimpses of his in-flight movie. Some war movie with two brothers, who also seemed to be in their own sibling war. The more I looked at him, the more I caught the line of his movie. He'd jump when there was an explosion, breathe heavier when the action got intense, soften when the love interest came onto the screen. I liked the softening the best, the way his lips would turn up just a little. They were full lips, with a tiny scar at the bottom right.

And then, just as the movie was nearing its finish, the flight ended, the screen turned off. We hadn't said two words to each other. To be honest, I wasn't even quite sure we were the same age. Or the same… anything. He'd been watching a war movie, after all. When I was more of a romcom girl.

Yeah, romcoms. It seems impossible now. But that was a different life.

He picked up his backpack, put away his water bottle, collected his trash. Maybe that's what did it— that he cared enough not to leave his spot a mess for the stewards. It was enough, at least, for me to open my mouth—a bold move for a safe girl like me. "You know how the movie's going to end?" I asked, moving into the aisle to retrieve my overhead bag.

He looked at me like he hadn't known a woman had been sitting beside him for the last two hours— not the most flattering thing in the world—but he smiled and answered, "Not a clue. Kind of annoying actually. I've never had a flight stop right before the end of a movie."

I smiled, lowering my bag. "My guess would be that the injured brother—the one who's the bully— he's going to save his brother in some gallant way. Like, by shooting the enemy right before he dies himself. Something like that."

"You've seen the movie before?" he asked, like I'd just intentionally spoiled it.

"Nah, I'm just a writer and that'd be my guess." I'd paused, the two of us looking at each other. And I know it's cliché, but there was just this charge—like it felt like a literal thing going between us. Otherwise, I never would have had the courage to do what I did next. I gave him my card. "After you finish it, let me know if I'm right."

He'd glanced at my card with my number, a list of my socials, any way in the whole world a person could find me if they wanted to. But before he could say anything, I got a nudge from someone behind me—people were moving through the plane, that flood of bodies and hard luggage.

"Thanks," he'd said, but the river was sweeping me down the aisle.

I hadn't really expected a call.

He seemed out of my league, like one of the cool kids, not some quiet nerdy girl who didn't watch movies on airplanes because she liked the pocket of time to think or read. I mean, who even does that?

But he did call. After he'd finished the movie. "How'd you know?" he'd asked. "The ending? You called it exactly. Like some sort of movie psychic."

"I'm just the kind of girl who knows things," I'd said, which wasn't my best line. But it must have been good enough, because after that, he'd invited me to dinner. Not coffee or a movie. But dinner. Like proper grownups.

And I thought I'd know the ending to all our stories.

For a while I was right.

Boy meets girl, fall in love, plan a life together, get married, love each other even more than seems possible.

It doesn't stop there, only getting better. Two good careers. The struggling writer starts to make a little money. The ancient studies scholar starts to make waves in academia. They buy a house, redesign the kitchen, order matching couches. Talk about getting a cat. Talk about making a baby.

The story's on the right track. First comes love, then comes marriage, then comes...

One rainy night, riding home on his motorcycle after giving a lecture at the college. He'd slid, skidding into and then over the guardrail—dead before his body had hit the ground. At least that's what the doctor had told me, though now, knowing what I know, they wouldn't have known that—not exactly. It was just a guess, and the best the doctor could do to comfort me when I worried about Joshua dying slowly and in pain.

I hadn't seen that ending of that story coming.

Not even a little.

Me being a writer, it hadn't saved him, not on

any level. Because it turns out that reading and writing don't save people. They don't help you predict the endings either—not in real life. In fact, they're not much good at all in the large and long scheme of things.

After Joshua died, I let my dad pack my books and journals, tight and deep into eight big tote boxes —that's how much I had. Until the day that my dad carted them off to a storage unit somewhere.

After that, I started studying things that might benefit the world.

Two months later, I was an EMT, a year after that, a paramedic, and another fourteen months later, I was on the helicopter. I figured those would be the patients with the most intense injuries—the place where I could contribute the most to people who needed it. And something as different from writing as could be.

CHAPTER 34

ANDY

*H*ere's to making things right.

The Molehill is going to work out. Bride and groom are both thrilled to have a place to host a wedding. Gretchen gives up her one morning off to come over and help me organize.

We stack tables in the storage room, untangle lights, which I'm going to string from the trees, tie bows like it's our job (I guess it IS one of Gretchen's jobs), count utensils and napkins and white dinner plates.

"You better spray the lawn for mosquitoes," she says. "Before you set out the tablecloths and stuff to eat on."

"You really think we'll need the spray?" I ask.

"Andy," she says, in that big sister voice like she'd been doing the big-sister gig her whole life, not since we discovered each other a few years ago. "It's deep summer. In Kentucky."

At that moment, a mosquito bites my ankle. Twice. "Fine," I say. "Just not a huge fan of pesticides."

"Trust me," Gretchen says. "Not to put too fine a point on it, but if that bride or her mother or basically any woman at this event gets a cluster of mosquitoes or chiggers up her dress, the mosquitoes won't be the only ones out for blood. And you'll be wishing you let the happy couple get married at the hospital."

"Okay, okay," I say. "I'm on it." I open the box with the fogger kit in it, take it out, and turn it upside down to have a good look. "I'll take this out to the lawn."

"Actually," Gretchen says, reading the paper instructions. "You're supposed to wait till a couple hours before the event. So let's just be sure you've got everything ready to go. That way, you can set up when the time comes. Do you have anyone helping you?"

"Ned'll be here," I grumble, putting the fogger back in the box.

"That all?" she asks.

"Do I really need more?" I snap.

Gretchen pinches her lips together. "Look, it wasn't my idea to host a make-up wedding."

I blow out a breath. "Sorry, Gretch. It's just stressful stuff."

"I *know*," she says. "And the less prepared you are, the more stressful it will be. Which is why I'm trying to help. But I can't help tomorrow. And the closer and crunchier things become, the more stressful it all gets. So be prepared. You'll need a little more help. Pay them if you don't have any favors to call in. And you should probably get out a piece of paper and write down the to-dos in order. Like: fog, set tables, flowers—"

"Flowers?" I ask.

"Or not," she says, glancing around the sparse storage room.

"I'll order some today," I say, pulling out my phone so I can write it down.

"It's a nice thing you're doing, Andy," she says. "A really nice thing. But if it's a disaster, then it will just be a disaster. And not really very nice at all. I don't say that to be mean, just honest."

"I know," I say. "Writing a list. Texting my friends. I got this." I look up from my phone. "Thank you."

"You're welcome, kiddo," she says, wrapping an arm over my shoulder. "And it's gonna be great."

"I don't suppose Jackson is off work tomorrow night? Would he want to come over and help with set up?" I pause. "I would pay him."

"He wouldn't take pay even if you offered," she

says. "Text him. It's worth an ask. And Tim, Didi. Who else in this world owes you a last-minute favor? Surely you've earned a few."

I sure hope so, because Jackson has already messaged me back. He'll be at work Sunday night. Tim's text comes in next. He and Didi are in Lexington for the weekend. I roll my shoulders, shake it off. I've got a whole list.

A WHOLE LIST of people who are not available to help me Sunday night. Guess that's what happens when you desperately need help the day before an event.

Gretchen left an hour ago and I'm still scrolling through my phone, hovering over names, thinking.

I hit the section of 'M' names. Pause on Maddie's name.

She's usually so busy. And she definitely doesn't owe me any kind of a favor. And I never even tried to make up our date, though maybe she's been too busy to notice. Or maybe she doesn't care anyway.

But desperate times call for desperate measures. Plus, she knows the groom—they spent a couple hours in an ambulance together.

I click on her name and send a text. "I've got a weird request. You up for being my plus one at an event at The Molehill?"

"An event?" she messages back.

"It's cool if you've got work or something," I continue. Ugh, nothing worse than a text ramble, but I can't seem to stop myself. "But I could use a bit of help if you've got the night off."

"Help?" she asks.

"Yeah, with some set up. It's really last minute and most of my normal guys are busy."

"I do have the night off," she texts. "What time would you need me?"

"Six-ish," I say. "After set up, there'll be some finger foods, so dinner's free. Plus I'd be happy to pay you."

"Free food is good enough for me," she says.

"I will pay you," I text.

"Please don't," she replies. "I'm happy to help."

I send a smiling emoji.

"When should I plan to be done?" she asks.

"Not quite sure. Maybe six to ten," I text. "That'll give us set up; we can hopefully relax in the middle; then a little time at the end to take down. Is that too long? Any amount you could help would be good."

"It's not too long," she says. "See you at six."

"It's a date," I text, not thinking about it.

CHAPTER 35

MADIGAN

$\mathcal{I}$ arrive in jeans and an old t-shirt from a library fundraiser that says, "Get your lit together." Ready to help, ready to get to know Andy a little bit better, ready to take a plunge.

Though Andy's in a suit. Well, he's not quite in a suit yet—just the suit pants and a button up shirt, but I can see the jacket hanging over the back of a chair behind the desk.

"What's going on?" I ask. Whether I mean it in a general sense or a why-are-you-dressed-up sense, I'm not sure, but he answers the first.

"I set the fogger up a couple hours ago," he says, looking around like he's crazy distracted. "So we should be good to go out and start on the tables."

"Okay," I say, following him into the storage room. It's smaller than the one at the rifle range, and packed to the hilt with tables, chairs, and decorations.

"I ordered flowers, which should be arriving really soon," he says, wiping sweat off his forehead. "Wish I'd dressed like you at first. I don't know how Gretchen does this day in and day out."

He grabs a table before I can ask any questions and hurries outside. I take another table and drag it, following.

"Why *aren't* you dressed more like me?" I ask.

"Thought I'd be saving myself some time," he responds. "Though in reality it looks like I'm going to have to go home and change shirts."

I nod. He really might. His shirt is darkening with sweat in the August heat. "So what is the event?" I ask.

He looks at his watch, then cracks his neck. "Two hours," he mumbles. "It doesn't seem like enough time. Ned should be here soon."

Right on cue, Ned pops his head out the door.

"Thank goodness," Andy grumbles and I'm not sure if I should feel insulted or not. At any rate, I'm relieved to see that Ned is dressed more like me.

"What are you wearing, dude?" Ned asks. "It looks like you jumped in the pool."

"I'll run home and change once we're set up," he says. "It was a lapse in judgment."

Ned goes inside and comes back out, lugging a

table in each arm, which is impressive. "I'll be heading out at eight," he says. "Nina needs me to help put the kiddos to bed. I'll be back to help you break it down."

Andy nods, just as the bell at the front of the office rings. "Flowers!" he says. "Maddie, can you help me get them?"

"Sure," I say. "What are they for anyway? What kind of event is this? It looks a lot different than your Friday Night Food Trucks."

"Yeah, well, I definitely wish I'd gone with that theme," he says. "It would have been so much easier, and I wouldn't be wearing this stupid suit."

He flings open the door and a delivery kid is standing there with ten matching bouquets in vases. Pinks and dusty purples. Lots of white. A sticky feeling creeps up my neck.

"What did you say the event was?" I ask again, taking a box with five of the vases as Andy pays the guy.

"The family will be here in about thirty minutes," he says by way of an answer.

A shot of adrenaline dumps itself into my stomach. "It's not that kid, is it?" I ask. "Did something happen?"

"What kid?" he asks, distractedly taking the other box from the deliveryman. "We'll put one vase on each table. But I've got to get the tablecloths out of the storage room. Oh no," he says suddenly. "They're probably supposed to be ironed or something."

"Andy," I say sharply. "Is this a memorial service?"

He stops, looks at me like I've gone clinically insane. "No, of course not." He glances down at the flowers in his box. "And please, please, please don't tell me that these look like funeral flowers. Please."

"Well, no," I say. "When I first saw them, I actually thought they looked like—" I stop talking as all the pieces click together, just like a good plot twist in a story. I swallow, praying Andy is going to tell me I'm wrong. "—like a wedding."

He releases this relieved sigh. "Hallelujah," he says.

"Andy," I say, holding the box against my hip and standing directly in his way so he has to answer me. "What. Is. This. Event?"

He squints at me, like I'm speaking a foreign language. "It's a wedding. For that groom, Jeremy. And his bride-to-be, Amelia. Like I told you. She'll be here in thirty minutes. Probably more like twenty now. Hey, do you happen to have a steamer or something we could use for the tablecloths?"

The rage bubbles up all the way from my feet. "You did *not* tell me this was a wedding."

He opens the storage door with his foot. "Sure I did," he says. "In that text. I asked if you could be my plus one."

"You asked if I could be your plus one for an *event*," I say. "And that you needed help setting up. You never said this was a wedding."

"I'm sure I said it was a wedding," he says.

"You *didn't!*" I reply, my voice rising. "I'm really sorry, Andy, but I—"

We hear a little shuffle outside the front door. Voices.

"Shoot, they're early. Do you have a steamer?" he whispers to me.

"I do not," I reply with as much ice in my voice as I can possibly muster. "Nor do I have linens that would require steaming."

"Man, I feel that," he says, completely missing the ice, still smiling in that happy-go-lucky way—a look that has completely missed that everything inside of me is collapsing into a puddle since he's trapped me in my worst nightmare.

If the bride hadn't stepped through the door at that exact moment, I would have taken that box of flowers and thrown them straight at his chest—before storming out the door.

But she does enter at that exact moment, all nervous laughter and chatter, her dress wrapped in a huge dry-cleaning bag, the petticoat hanging beside it.

"Hey!" Andy says, stepping toward her. "So good to meet you. The groom, of course, I know."

Jeremy laughs, shaking Andy's hand with his good hand—the left one. The right is wrapped tight in a bandage, up past his wrist. He gives me a quick glance, then does a double take. But he can't quite place me, so his attention goes back to Andy. "Thanks so much for doing this for us. You have no idea how much it means."

"Aww, it's nothing," Andy says like the countriest country boy in all of country-dom. "We've got one of the back rooms set up for the bride. She can change and do her makeup and whatever else she needs. There's even a bottle of champagne or sparkling cider or something. Gretchen added that."

He's leading them down the hall as he talks. "Much smaller room for the groom. Sorry, bro. But I figured you could deal with it. And no bottle of booze either."

"That's alright. I'm not allowed to drink with my pain meds anyway. So I guess I'm high enough as it is."

The front door is right there, still open. The mother-of-the bride and a few bridesmaids chatting beside it. No one notices me. All I have to do is casually make my way to the door, walk out, get in my car, block Andy and his stupid phone number, and move on with my life.

Except that at that moment, Ned pops in. "Hey Madigan. Could you give me a hand with some of these lights? Andy said we're supposed to string them up across the trees. And making things pretty isn't exactly my forte."

I wish I could shove those lights down Andy's stupid, clueless throat, but then I remember the sound of the bride's nervous laughter, her cheeks flushed, her hands shaking a bit as she held the dress. And I remember that feeling—that sweet fear and anticipation, that day most women look forward to for much of their lives. And here it is—*her* big day, her family still in town, her soon-to-be-husband healing and happy.

"Sure," I say, clamping my teeth against each other. After all, it's not Ned's fault that I'm here. "I'd be happy to help you out." I take the lights out of his hands. "I don't suppose you have a steamer. Andy's worried about the tablecloths."

Ned rolls his eyes, which I thoroughly appreciate. "I'll call Nina."

WE GET the set up done in just over an hour. I string the lights, climbing Andy's short ladder or straddling low branches to get it done. It's the most I've climbed trees since I was a kid and it's honestly kind of fun. Ned gets stuck steaming the tablecloths. Caterers bring little plates of finger foods, which are easy enough to arrange. This is good, since neither Ned nor I are incredibly inclined toward design.

Andy pops in and out. A small band is setting up in the corner. He talks to them, then runs inside, then chats with Nina, thanking her for the steamer. He tosses us a few smiles, but I turn, not wanting to catch a single one.

"When exactly does the wedding begin?" I ask Ned.

"7:30, I think," he says. "Guests should be arriving soon, which means it's almost time for me to get out of here. I ain't dressed for no wedding."

"Me either," I say, adjusting a crooked napkin. "I'll just follow you out. Where'd Andy go anyway?" I ask, not because I want to see him, but because I want to avoid him as completely as possible.

"Who knows? He likes to chat it up with everyone. That's one of his superpowers."

Everyone but me, whom he can't bother to call for a new date or to adequately communicate with about a *wedding*.

"Or maybe he went to change his shirt. Dude was practically dripping."

Perfect. If he's gone, it will be even easier for me to leave. And, honestly, just like Ned, I couldn't stay in this outfit even if I was dying to go to a wedding. I look awful, and Andy isn't the only one who is dripping on this humid August evening.

The band starts up with a warm-up. It's the perfect cue.

I wave to Ned, slip into the building, and make a beeline for the front door. None of the women are in the hall—probably all with the bride in her changing room. A few of the groomsmen are milling around, fidgeting with their hands like they wish they were holding a drink. They're not the only ones.

The first thing I'm going to do when I get home is pour myself a really tall glass of wine.

I wrap my fingers around the doorknob, practically smelling the sweet freedom ahead of me, when I feel a hand on my shoulder. I jump slightly, turning quickly, expecting to see Andy's face. But it's Jeremy, the groom.

"I *knew* I recognized you," he says, pulling me just slightly away from the door. "You're the EMT."

"Paramedic," I correct, casting a quick glance backwards at the door.

"You know Andy?" he asks, gently drawing me farther away from the exit.

I pinch back a snarky comment about Andy and settle for a simple nod.

"Real nice of him to do this for us. I can't thank him enough."

Another quick nod. Another glance at the door.

"You're not thinking of sneaking away," Jeremy says, noticing.

"Oh," I stammer. "I just came to help with set up. I couldn't possibly impose on your wedding."

"Are you kidding?" he says. "You saved me."

"I didn't save you," I say with a smile. "I just took you to a hospital. With some nice pain meds. As quickly as possible."

"And that speed may have saved the nerves of my hand," he says. "Thank you."

As he talks, he's steering me farther and farther from the door, from my escape. I see Andy walk back in through the door, no longer sweating, hair wavy and freshly-washed, suit jacket on over his broad back, trim waist. I turn quickly back to Jeremy, let my steps fall in line with his.

"I would love for you to stay," he's saying. "And Amelia would love to meet you."

"Oh no," I begin. "I'm just... I couldn't... I'm not even dressed for it." I wipe the sweat from my forehead for emphasis.

"Aww, don't be silly. I guarantee Millie has at least ten outfits in that dressing room of hers. You two are about the same size."

"Oh, she's thinner than me," I stutter, but he's leading me down the hall, tapping on Amelia's door.

"Millie," he says.

"Don't you dare come in," she shouts through the door. "You can't see me in my dress before the wedding."

And once again, I can't help but be touched that Andy did this for them, offered them a chance to have a normal wedding instead of having to tie the knot in the sterile walls of a hospital in a totally different city.

"I found us an extra guest," he says. "But she needs a dress. The EMT, uh, paramedic who took me to the hospital was here helping set up."

"Are you serious?" the bride says from the other room. "She's *here?*"

"In the flesh."

I hear the bride unlocking the door.

"I really don't need to stay," I say. "It's so much trouble."

"I know you've got an extra dress, or five, in there," Jeremy says through the door. "Think you can spare one?"

The bride peeks out, her hair up in a silky wrap, her body hidden behind the door. "Girl, get in here," she says, her teeth flashing as white as the sun at noon.

"No, really, I..." But she pulls me in.

She's still wearing a robe, although she shakes her hair out of the scarf, letting the curls tumble to her shoulders. Several other women are in the room, too —her mother, a few bridesmaids who are doing the hair and makeup, and a flower girl. The girl's face is tipped up at a blonde woman who is dabbing a bit of blush onto her cheeks. And I can't help it—I choke up. Joshua's little niece did that, and I remember that same gaze—that sweet look as my best friend wove pearls into her hair.

"I'm so sorry," I stammer. "I really shouldn't be here."

"Of course you should," Amelia says. "You saved my darling idiot of a fiancé when he went and mauled his own hand. We invited the surgeon too. I hope he can make it." She pauses as though something just crossed her mind, but she brushes it away and gets back to business. "Now let's see what we've got." She rummages through a stack of dresses in a little suitcase.

"Are these for your honeymoon?" I ask, stepping back like the suitcase is going to bite me.

"Oh, baby," she says with a wicked smile. "It's not like I'm planning on wearing a lot on my honeymoon anyway."

A few of the bridesmaids giggle. I force a smile.

"Now how about this one?" she says.

She holds up a pale pink sundress with slim cap sleeves.

"Oh, you're definitely going to want that one," I say, trying to back up. "I couldn't possibly take it."

"That's why I'm *giving* it to you," she says with a laugh. "I really won't need it. We were planning to go to the Florida Keys, but now we're just going to

Lexington because Jeremy can't travel far with that stupid hand." She sighs.

I want to tell her that I'm sorry, that it's okay, because a hand injury is just a hand and there are things that could be so much worse. But before I can get my mouth to work right, Amelia holds the dress up to me and clucks approvingly. "Now tell me that dress won't kill with your dark hair and those eyes. Go on, girl. Try it on."

All of the women do this communal woman pause, look at me. At this point, I either have to put the dress on, or make an absolute jail-break-esque run for the exit.

I take the dress.

"Merry's on makeup and hair," Amelia says. "She'll get you done up real good."

"Thank you," I say, looking around for a corner that might offer a drop of privacy. There isn't one. The room is stuffed with women, stuffed with lace, with beads, with pearls. Stuffed with wedding.

I close my eyes and slip out of my jeans.

ONCE DRESSED, made-up, and sprayed with about forty gallons of perfume, I'm not quite sure what to do. I don't belong with the bridal party. I don't belong with the other guests. I don't belong with

Andy. I don't belong with anyone. And the truth is, I don't really need to *belong.* I just wish there was something else to *do.* Doing is what I'm best at.

Which is why it's nice when one of the bridesmaids tears the hem of her dress with her stiletto heel. There's a little cursing, some near weeping. Until I say, "I can hem it."

Somewhere in my car, I've got a little sewing kit my Aunt Nellie taught me to use when I was a teenager. I wasn't a prime student, but I wasn't the worst either. "Let me grab my stuff," I say.

"Is there anything you can't do?" Amelia—Millie —asks.

"Plenty," I reply. "I just try to hide it from everyone."

That gets a few laughs, though there's nothing truer.

I go to my car, get the sewing kit and my phone.

Back in the room with the bridesmaids, I send a quick text to my dad asking him to let Alfie out for a little walk since I got stuck somewhere and won't be home for a few hours.

"Where are you, sweetie?" he replies. "Do you need a rescue? It's not that guy from the fire station, is it?" That reminds me for just a sec of Andy saving me from Terry.

"Even weirder," I reply, not wanting to go into it.

"No rescue needed?" he asks.

"Nope."

"Okay. Alfie and I will just spend the evening alone like proper bachelors."

I glance at the bridesmaids, feeling strange not telling my dad where I am, but I could barely make it through Nellie's bridal shower (and that not sober). How can I tell him I'm at a near-stranger's wedding?

I thread the needle with a bit of purple, sit near the bridesmaid, and begin to stitch.

CHAPTER 36

ANDY

Ned's gone. Madigan is…missing. Probably also gone. I scroll through my phone, reading the text thread I sent to Madigan. And she's right. I didn't say it was a wedding, just an event.

Which probably explains why she's gone.

I shove my phone into my pocket, smiling at a cluster of guests, and showing them to the seating outside.

I'd been trying not to notice Madigan all evening, trying not to think about how nice she looked in the tight jeans, holes along the thighs, t-shirt hugging her as she'd hung the lights. I'd tried to stay busy, to show her that I was, in fact, a fully functioning adult.

Guess that backfired.

I paste on a smile, lead more guests to the chairs out back. The band is playing a series of soft, slow love songs, which lowers my mood even more.

Another glued smile as I retreat back inside to wait for more guests.

A man walks through the door, hair graying just above his ears, designer suit. He looks around as though struggling to get his bearings. I wave him over. "Right through here."

He gives me an expensive white smile.

"You here with the groom or bride's family?" I ask.

"Both, I suppose," he says. "I operated on Jeremy's hand and they invited me. I was going to be a witness if they married at the hospital. When that wasn't necessary, they invited me here." He gives an awkward shrug.

As we walk through the door, the groom waves him over. I see the man glance at the bandaged hand.

"You're over here, Dr. Niels," Jeremy says, coming over to him. "Millie and I wanted to have you meet our family."

I drift away as Jeremy leads him to the front row.

And then there she is, coming through the door. Madigan. A soft, pink dress, the sleeves slipping off her shoulders, accentuating the olive skin, the near-black hair, those eyes.

She must have gone home to change.

I stare for a second.

She doesn't notice. She's too busy looking like a lost puppy. Which is beautiful too.

I move toward her, about to invite her to sit with me near the back when Jeremy pops up again. "Madigan!" he says, taking her arm with his good hand. "Glad Millie could find something for you to wear!"

"I still feel a little guilty," I hear her murmur.

"Don't," Jeremy whispers. "If I had my way, I'd have her give you all the clothes from her suitcase so she never had anything to wear."

He laughs, leading Madigan to the front row. Right next to the mother-of-the-bride, and that surgeon. A spot of honor. I guess that's the difference between being the person who saves someone and the person who owns the business that might ruin his career.

"Dr. Niels," Jeremy says. "Here's someone I want you to meet. Our other savior. This is the paramedic who brought me to the hospital. Madigan."

The surgeon shakes her hand, giving her that bright white smile, along with his first name. "Oliver," he says. "Nice to meet you."

She nods, a pretty tip of the head, granting him her own beautiful smile. And then they're seated. Next to each other. On the front row.

And it's me who's left being the lost puppy.

Fortunately, at that moment, someone taps me on the shoulder, whispering about a problem with the sound system. And I'm off to find an extension cord.

276

MADIGAN

The speakers are acting up, which means that the guests are starting to shift and chatter while we wait. Fortunately, the surgeon—Dr. Niels, or Oliver, as he's asked me to call him (though I seem to be the only one doing so)—can talk about anything from politics to Oprah's Book of the Month, which I didn't even realize was still a thing. He's a little starched around the edges, both literally with his suit and figuratively with everything else. Though, to be fair, he knows about as many people as I do and he's probably a little uncomfortable too. Which somehow makes me more comfortable. We talk about our work, emergencies we've seen, how different they are from my end to his. It's nice, honestly, having someone who kind of understands.

He asks me how long I've been in my field.

"Close to four years," I answer.

"Wonderful. Headed for the skies as soon as you could, it seems."

I nod. "Seemed like the place where I could do the most good." I'm not sure I've ever said this aloud and that feels nice too.

"And before that, before your work in EMS, what did you do?"

I've been asked it before, in every job interview I've attended, by some of my partners in the different crews I've worked for. But rarely by someone outside of my field, much less at a social event. And never at a wedding.

I clear my throat.

Over by the homemade stage, a group of groomsmen is fiddling with the sound system, trying to get it to work.

"I was self-employed," I reply to Oliver. "I worked from home."

"Well, that's about as different as possible," he says.

I nod, smiling too brightly—glad that when he's about to ask the obvious follow-up question about what I did while sitting at home and working—the speaker by the stage crackles angrily, distracting any further attention from me as we all look to the malfunctioning sound system.

A few babies whimper at the noise and the pastor gives the sound system a stern look.

Both the pastor and the groom are standing at the front, underneath a flowery arch, which was surely provided by Gretchen and set up by Ned. The flower girl is at the back, basket of petals in hand, along with a little boy—maybe two years old—who is holding his mother's hand along with a little box. The ring-bearer. Everyone in place. Everyone ready. Everyone waiting.

Until Andy hurries out with another large speaker and a bright orange extension cord. He kneels near the little band, digging around in the grass, trying to get things plugged in until finally, there's a much more gentle crackle and the sound comes back on.

Several people clap and a couple groomsmen whoop. Andy stands up and dusts dirt off his knees. I watch the simple, non-assuming way he does it. Like, of course he would kneel down in the dirt and get this taken care of to make things go smoothly. Never mind his suit. Never mind the sweat, the drycleaning, the trouble.

The band starts to play, the guests settling into their spots, bridal party making its way down the aisle. I almost forget to watch, so caught up in Andy —the way he smiles at the groom, the way he sways to the music, the way he seems like he belongs exactly wherever he is.

In fact, I almost can't stop staring.

At least until the bride steps through the door, her hand trembling on her father's arm.

With it, I feel my own trembles, though for entirely different reasons.

My stomach lurches with each step they take and when the tears come—like they do to so many other of the guests—they're not exactly there for the same reason.

But at least I blend in.

"You get emotional at weddings?" the surgeon asks me.

I blink at him. "Yes." And then I blink toward the bride and groom, as they exchange their vows, their promises, their hearts. *Three*. Bride, groom, pastor in between. *Completion*.

Two. They lean toward each other, share a kiss. *Balance, duality, partnership*.

One hundred. The crowd explodes in clapping, laughter. Ten—*perfection*—multiplied by itself.

I feel wobbly as we all stand, as though I tossed down a thousand champagne toasts. I wish I had. Especially since I know that soon the dancing will begin.

Andy is looking at me. One. *Origin*. I look away. The loneliest number. I can't quite hold it right now.

So when the chairs are cleared, creating a makeshift dance floor and Oliver nods to me, asking, "May I have the honor?" I practically thrust my hand into his.

HE'S A GOOD DANCER. I get the impression he's good at a lot of things. He tells me he likes to paint on the weekends, asks if I ever go to museums or shows. I think of Joshua in Paris, Joshua in Amsterdam, Joshua in London. "I've been a few places," I say. "Nothing recent though."

He sways, pressing me on the back to cue me to the moves. "Well, perhaps we should remedy that. I've heard rumors they've got some of Salvador Dali's art coming to Newfields in Indy."

I don't commit with a reply.

"Or perhaps Dali isn't your thing," he says, misinterpreting my silence. "Besides work, what do you do with your free time?"

"I...," I say, stepping left at the slight press of his fingertips. "I guess I try not to have any free time." It's not what I mean to say. What I mean to say is that I rather like Dali and I'd love to see some of his art just a few hours from home. But for some reason, my struggling mouth cannot seem to produce these words, even though they're true. Or they were once.

He laughs, moving me easily around the dance floor. It's a nice laugh, if a bit stiff.

"I work a lot," I say. "Stay pretty busy with that. You wouldn't believe how understaffed we are sometimes."

"Oh, I would," he says. "And I'm so sorry."

A few more turns on the dance floor. "Surely there's something you like to do for fun though?" he asks again. "Even if you don't have much time."

"Well, I do have a dog. He takes the rest of my time, I guess. We walk. So maybe that's what I'd call my biggest hobby these days. Walking my dog."

"Walking your dog is good," he says. "Good for the body. Good for the heart." Then he adds, "'In art, the hand can never execute anything higher than the heart can imagine.'"

"Emerson," I murmur.

"Ah, so you must like to read at least a bit," he says, looking down into my eyes.

I don't answer immediately, watching the band through the light. Andy is no longer there, helping. He's now dancing with one of the bridesmaids, talking and laughing. I can tell that he's in the middle of some elaborate story— probably about some kind of joyride or something.

"I read less now than I used to," I say. "At least for pleasure. Though I do keep a fat anatomy book on my shelf." We turn and Andy is lost from my view. "What about you? What do you read?"

"Little of everything," he answers. "I even went through a Sylvia Plath stage about a year ago."

"Did you combat it with a Sophie Kinsella stage?" I ask, referring to the rom-com author.

He laughs his pretty laugh. "Not this time, though if that's a recommendation, I'll take it."

"Just a little something to combat Ms. Plath."

"I'm not sure she needs combatting," he says.

I don't argue. Her poetry, after all, was beautiful. Though her life was troubled enough to lead to her death. It's not a thought I want to sit on.

"Do you live in Louisville then?" I ask, changing the subject.

"For now," he answers. "My ex-wife and I had settled there, so I'm stuck for the time being."

"Oh," I answer, not quite sure what else to say. "I'm sorry."

"Don't be," he responds. "We were never quite right for each other anyway. I'm a bit of a workaholic—I don't actually just read and paint." He laughs again. "And surgery is a stressful job, requiring huge chunks of time, absolute concentration, study, disappointment. And my wife, understandably, needed more from me than that. Fortunately, things ended amicably."

What a strange word—amicably. A word that

implies harmony, but is often used in regard to divorce. I wish I could think up a joke about the word, but I can't. Which is probably for the best.

"What about you?" he says, breaking into my thoughts. "Have you been married before?"

I reply by tripping over my own feet. "Oh, uh, yes actually."

"Divorce is a beast isn't it," he goes on. "I'm just glad I get the kids every other weekend."

I nod, absorbing the information.

"What about you?" he asks. "Any kids?"

"Um, no," I say, looking down. "We didn't exactly get that far."

"I wouldn't trade my girls for anything," he says. "Not even a job in a different city. That's the thing about kids. They hold you down—and I mean that in a good way. Even when it means you have to hang out in a city with your former spouse."

"Um," I say, swaying. "I feel a little light-headed. Do you mind if I get something from the bar?"

"Oh, I'll help you," he says, taking me by the hand.

"No, really," I say. "It's okay."

But he's already leading me to the bar. "Seltzer water," he says, holding up an authoritative finger.

Seltzer water is *not* what I was going for, and it doesn't even do the trick of giving me a few minutes' break from talking, since Oliver—sweet, well-read, artistic, over-working, former-spouse Oliver—is hovering next to me, in a way that barely lets me breathe.

"You do look pale," he says.

I sip delicately, fanning my face. "Just a little hot," I say, giving my best please-step-back hint with my eyes.

"At least you've got a dress instead of a suit," he says with a smile, his eyes flicking to my body, which makes me feel self-conscious.

"You okay?" Andy asks, coming over to me.

"She got a little overheated," Oliver says. I gaze longingly at the wineglasses at the makeshift bar.

"I'm fine," I say, not loving the way Oliver spoke for me.

"Why don't you come inside?" Andy says. "It's air conditioned in there."

"No, really," I say. "I'm fine. Just need a little drink."

At that moment, a new song starts up, some kind of line dance.

"Ooooh, I love this one," Andy says, giving me a look. "You really okay?" he asks.

I wave him away. "Go dance," I say.

"You know each other?" Oliver asks.

"I helped set up," I answer. "Andy hired me."

"They don't pay medics nearly enough," Oliver says. "Having to pick up side hustles like that." And I appreciate it. Minus the slightly condescending tone when he says 'side hustles.'

It reminds me of the way some of Joshua's professors used to talk about my writing, even though I was earning a full-time income with my work. As though teaching in academia had more sway over the world than sending love stories out into it. As though you had to attain a certain level of genius (or at least boring academic research) before your work could count.

Not Joshua though. It was one of his arguments for getting a motorcycle—he wanted to feel the air, to stay down to earth, humble, in the moment. That's how he said it. Even with everything that happened after, I smile to think of it—Joshua's words always more poetry than research.

I'm startled from my thoughts by the feeling of Oliver's fingers winding around mine.

I turn, slow motion, toward him. "I'm feeling a lot better," I say, retrieving my hand. "I must have just been a bit dehydrated. Maybe we should dance."

"Oh, I can't do this sort of thing," he says, gesturing to the lines of people hopping in unison.

And neither can I, but what better way to make a brief escape, from both Oliver and my own thoughts. I stand up. "A little blood moving through my limbs might be just the thing for me."

"Are you sure?" he asks. "It might heat you up again."

"I think I just needed some water," I say, casting him a smile as I walk to the lawn-now-dance-floor.

Dozens of happy feet tramp down the grass. Tap, kick, some kind of shuffle.

I step into the messy lines of dancing. And really regret not getting that glass of wine. At least then, if I made a fool of myself, I wouldn't care as much.

Now I wonder if I've jumped from the frying pan of former spouse conversations into the flame of looking like an idiot.

And I'm not sure which is worse.

Andy shuffles his way to me, laughing. Always laughing. "You getting it?"

I want to ask, "Does it look like I'm getting it?" But I'm struggling way too hard at the moment for snark.

"Tap tap, right leg, left," he says, walking me through the moves. "Then shuffle shuffle shuffle, turn."

I almost get the turn, but not quite, and bump into him. He takes my shoulders, orienting me in the correct direction, and we do it again. Tap tap, right, left, shuffle shuffle shuffle, turn.

"You got it!" he says.

Without thinking I laugh. "'Got it' feels generous," I say, shuffle shuffle shuffling. "But at least I ended up looking in the right direction."

The sweat is pricking along my forehead, but I don't care. In fact, I barely notice. It really is kind of fun. The bride and flower girl shuffle along beside me, the bride reaching out for my hand. "Come on, Andy," she says. "Join in."

He takes my other hand, both of us sweaty, but laughing. Until, almost too soon, the music ends. I steal a quick glance at the table where Oliver is sitting. Except he's no longer sitting, because he's stood up and is beginning to walk my way. Andy still has my hand and he doesn't seem to notice Oliver at all. Instead, Andy says, "Care to dance?"

My stomach flip flops and I almost turn him down, but Oliver is heading my way and my brain goes into some type of freeze mode. "Sure," I say.

Andy, not missing a beat (literally or figuratively) pulls me in, right in time with the music, then wraps his other hand behind my waist.

Oliver sees us and I give him my best innocent shrug. He nods, walking back to the bar and ordering himself a drink.

I relax, softening into Andy's arms before I fully realize whose arms I'm softening into. But it's too late.

He pulls me in a little closer, moving me effortlessly over the grassy dance floor. I'd kicked off my borrowed sandals during the line dance and now the soft, cool grass presses my feet and tickles my ankles as we swirl through it, neither of us talking.

The music is a soft sway, a gentle violin playing the melody line of a popular song. I feel that violin as it arches over the guitar and piano, the delicate line above a bigger noise. I lean into that line, finding my footing as Andy moves us around.

"You're quiet," he says.

"Just enjoying the music," I answer.

"Me too," he says, looking down at me. His green eyes match the late summer leaves and I glance away. "So I checked my texts," he says. "And, you were right, I didn't say it was a wedding. I'm sorry. I know you—"

"It's okay," I say, cutting him off. "It's worked out just fine."

"Where'd you get the dress?" he says.

"Oh, I just stole it from the bride's honeymoon stash," I say.

"Wait. What?"

"Jeremy recognized me from the ambulance and insisted I stay. Millie insisted too."

"Who's Millie?"

"The bride. Amelia," I say.

"Wow, nickname basis," he says, lifting me over a cord in the lawn so that I swirl and land like a butterfly.

"The nickname feels less committal than the honeymoon dress," I say.

"I guess that explains why it looks so sexy," he says.

We both sort of pause, and then he lifts me again, though this time there's no cord, just gratuitous swirling.

"You weren't going to stay?" he asks after a few more moments.

"In my 'get your lit together' t-shirt?" I say. "No."

"I mean, it's a good message," he says, not missing a beat. Because—again—Andy never misses a beat. "We could all stand to get our lit together a bit more. Especially me."

"You've done pretty well with this wedding," I say. "Careful or you'll give Gretchen a run for her money."

He laughs at that, big and out loud. "No danger of that, that's for sure. I almost died of stress from all of this."

"Died of stress?" I say. "When you run an ATV park and a rifle range. Those sound way more stressful, and deadly." I realize after I say it that it's a little rude, but he doesn't seem to notice.

"Nah," he says. "Those are just fun." He pauses. "Well, usually."

We drift again into a silence—a silence that should be uncomfortable, but somehow isn't with him swaying me back and forth gently to the music, his arms tightening around my waist, my hands soft on his neck.

"I'm glad you stayed," he says, looking down at me.

I'm surprised to find that I'm looking back up—at his sharp cheeks haloed against the twinkling lights, at his bright eyes, twinkling because that's what they do, at his lips soft and—for once—serious. Without thinking, I touch my thumb to his jawline, feel the faintest beginnings of scruff and the soft of his skin underneath it—the boy still under the man. I press my hand to his cheek, and he takes my hand, cupping it in his.

And in that moment, everything around me falls away—the sound of the music, the touch of the grass, the chatter of the crowd. For that one moment, it's just him and me, suspended in the universe.

I know that feeling, though for that brief moment, it still feels like something new.

Andy pulls me closer so that there's no room left between the two of us, no sliver of light, no breath, no air.

Just the two of us. Two. Duality.

Or division.

The music ends. The clapping of the crowd breaking me from the spell. And then I'm just a sweaty girl in another woman's dress, standing bare-foot on the lawn.

I pull back, self-conscious. "Whew, sweaty," I say.

"We're dancing," he says, the lips laughing. "Not posing for a portrait."

It reminds me of something Joshua used to say. "We're living. And that's just the thing we need to be doing." But then he'd gone and stopped living. And here I was, droopy and clammy and caught in a crowd. Not two people at all, or even a lonely one, but one among dozens. What is the meaning of a dozen? I can't remember, can't think at all. Except for how ridiculous this is, how embarrassing.

Andy's phone buzzes. A woman's name, Shannon, popping up on the screen. "Oh, hang on," he says, a line forming on his brow.

He texts something quickly. I can't see exactly what, but something about seeing her in Indy.

"I really don't feel well," I say. "I think I need to go."

"Oh," he says. "I'm sorry. I thought you were doing better."

"For a minute I did too," I say. "But I think I must be just a little sick. I don't think I can help with the clean-up. I'm really sorry."

"It's okay," he says, the laughter gone from his lips, like I took it from them. But that's not something I can worry about right now.

"Please tell Oliver I had to go," I say.

"Oliver?" he asks.

"The surgeon."

And then like Cinderella—if Cinderella forgot both her shoes and left at nine o'clock and not midnight and had sweat dripping down her back—I excuse myself from the ball—if the ball were a replacement wedding on the cool lawn of an ATV park on a Sunday night with a couple of finger foods.

Either way, the clock is striking and I flee from the scene.

CHAPTER 38

MADIGAN

When I get home, my dad is chilling on the couch, Alfie's head on his lap, like they're on a date and I'm interrupting.

"Where were you?" he asks when I open the door, my pink dress drooping.

"I got stuck somewhere," I say, heading into the kitchen and rummaging through the cupboards.

"Yes," Dad says, creaking up from the couch. I hear Alfie's soft yip of protest. "But where?"

I sigh, jerking a glass down. "The Molehill."

"The ATV park?" he asks, settling onto a kitchen chair and lifting an eyebrow at my outfit. Alfie, on the other hand, is standing in the doorway, staring at me accusingly.

"Hey, buddy," I say, squatting down and reaching out my arms.

Alfie is not great at holding grudges. He runs toward me, tail wagging, licking my arms up and down. "Okay, boy," I say, hoping my dad has forgotten the question. But his memory is longer than Alfie's.

"The Molehill," he presses. "That's a strange clothing choice for an ATV park. And I didn't even think it was open on Sundays."

"It's not usually," I reply, popping the cork of a bottle of white wine. "It was a special event."

My dad leans back in his chair, like this conversation is a special event. "What kind?" he asks. "Didn't they just do a soft opening for that other business? How many special events can they have?"

"It wasn't an opening," I say. "It was just an event. For a couple."

He squints at me.

I pour the wine. "You gonna stop looking at me like that?"

"You gonna tell me where you were that's got you so upset?"

"Upset?" I ask.

"Yes," he says.

I turn to him, feel the tears pushing against my eyes—that hot, swelling feeling—though I don't know where they're coming from, or why. "It was a wedding," I say. "A weird make-up wedding. But I didn't know that. I thought I was just helping set up for something, so I agreed and then I got sort of roped into attending and at first it wasn't so bad. It was even nice. And then, well, I left."

"A wedding?" my dad says, like he didn't get past the first phrase. He looks at me, sniffing. "And you're still sober."

"Hoping to remedy that," I say, lifting my glass.

"Oh, honey," he says and that is all and I don't know what else to say so I take a swig of wine and then start to cry like I'm really not sober at all.

My dad comes over, wraps his arms around me.

"I didn't know," I say, all blubbery.

"That's okay," he says. "Look. Why don't you put that down and just come watch a movie with me and Alfie. He's been waiting for you."

I let my dad persuade me to set the glass down. I can always come back for it later.

He leads me, Alfie at my heels, into the living room. "What were they doing having a wedding at The Molehill anyway?" he asks. "That's not a normal thing."

"I know, right?!?" I say. "This guy—this groom—got hurt at the rifle range during his bachelor party and the owner—Andy—he was trying to make it up to him, and it was nice and stuff, but I wasn't prepared for it or anything."

"He didn't tell you?" Dad says, patting a spot on the couch. Alfie jumps on instead of me, and I laugh.

"He thought he did," I say. "But he just said 'event.'"

"Why is he asking you for help with an event anyway?" Dad asks, settling down.

"He, well, I don't know," I say, flustered as I sit next to my father. Alfie somehow manages to crawl over both of our laps, spreading out his limbs.

"And how well do you know this Andy guy?" Dad asks.

I shrug.

"Well enough for him to ask a favor, I guess," Dad says.

"I guess," I answer.

"Is he a friend?" Dad asks.

"Sure, yeah," I say, like a teenager avoiding her prying father.

"Does he want to be more?" Dad presses, like the dad of a teenager-who-is-avoiding-her-prying-father.

I pick up the remote. "Don't make me regret leaving my glass of wine on the counter." I click the TV on. "What were you and Alfie watching?"

"You know Alfie," Dad says. "He prefers comedies to dramas."

"Well, that makes two of us," I mutter, scrolling down the screen. "*Dumb and Dumber*, Alfie?" I say, noticing their watch history. "That feels low, even for you."

Alfie lifts his head in response, though I can tell he doesn't regret it.

"We should finish it," Dad says. "Remember when you and your friends did a remake of it in high school?"

I snort. "Yeah, well *that* was a work of genius."

"Perfect," Dad says. "Then you can relive the glory days."

I click the movie on to where they left off and lean my head onto my father's shoulder. Alfie, in turn, leans his head onto my lap.

Threes. They really are complete.

And I'm asleep in minutes.

AND YOU KNOW WHEN, sometimes, it feels like everything was wrong with the world, but then you found a safe place and everything got right again. Your dad's there and your dog. And that's not quite how fairytales end, but it's something you can work with.

Until you wake up alone on the couch. Your dad has covered you with a blanket, but of course he's long gone. But your dog—where is he? Because he always wakes up with you. Well, with me. Because that's who we're really talking about.

I check the foot of my bed, the kitchen where I

keep his food, the back door in case he had to go potty and is waiting patiently. And too quietly.

But he's not in any of those spots.

I panic for a minute, worried that Dad left the door open and Alfie got out. But the whole house is locked up tight and perfectly quiet.

Also odd. Because the only thing more reliable than Alfie sleeping at the foot of my bed is Alfie coming for me, leash in mouth, in the morning when I wake up.

"Alfie!" I call, my voice rising, getting more and more hysterical. "Alfie!"

I open every door of the house, searching every room, under the bed, inside the closets. I even check the bathtub. He's gone. Like someone snuck into my house and stole my dog.

Which is impossible.

And then I laugh. Of course, it's impossible. Which means that my dad probably took him home with him. He knew I had to work later today. He knew I was upset. He knew I was exhausted.

And he takes Alfie all the time.

Though I would have expected a note or a text or something.

I send him a quick message. Check the table, the refrigerator, steal another look at my phone. Maybe he scheduled a text so that it wouldn't wake me too early.

I roll my shoulders, give my dad a call. He doesn't pick up.

I grab a cup of coffee, noticing that my wine glass from the night before is empty. Dad must have poured it out. I hope he's corked the bottle and put it away as well.

I put my hand on the pantry door, which isn't latched all the way shut. And doesn't smell quite right. Details I don't fully process until I swing the door open.

It's then that I find Alfie, curled into a limp little ball on the floor of the pantry closet.

I try to process the image along with the nauseating smell that hits me in the face. Poop and vomit.

"Alfie," I murmur, squatting down to look at him.

His side is moving up and down, and I release a tight breath. He's alive at least. "Oh, little boy, did you eat something naughty?"

I scour the pantry quickly, looking to see if he got into the chocolate chips or something else, but don't see anything at first glance.

I call my vet and tell her I'm coming over. I message my dad that Alfie is sick, that it looks like he got into some food he shouldn't have. It's then that I remember the empty wine glass. "Oh, Alfie, you didn't, did you?"

I find an old towel, wrap it around him, and scoop him into my arms.

He's absolutely limp, and something about that feels bad. Like, shouldn't he just throw up and then start to recover? I'll look up alcohol poisoning and dogs when we get there.

Fortunately, the vet is a quick ride away. And it won't take long to get him taken care of. Andy owes me a favor (or a few) and he adores Alfie, so I'm gambling that he'll be able to help out with some dog sitting tonight when I go to work.

I don't remember until later why I'm not a gambling woman.

CHAPTER 39

ANDY

’m humming when I walk into the Riley in Indy. I left bright and early (as in before the summer sunrise) this morning, so I could be there for Saul’s first rehab. Shannon invited me.

She said that they decided Saul was doing well enough to wake up, and that he’s been wanting to see me and apologize for wrecking the ATV. I told her I couldn’t think of anywhere else I’d rather be.

I stop off at the gift shop to buy a balloon. It feels like one of those feel-good movies where somebody got hurt, but everything is going to be alright.

A text from Madigan beeps just as I enter the room, but—yeah—it’s going to have to get ignored for now. Because it’s all I can do to keep from choking up when I see this kid.

He’s skinny as a rail. I mean, I assume he was

skinny beforehand, but after several weeks of being in a drug-induced coma and just being fed through an IV, the kid looks positively gaunt. He's not paralyzed—a thing for which I've literally been thanking God every day, but between the concussion, a little swelling in his brain, and one small stable fracture in his back, which has been healing, well, I'm just glad to see him.

They put him into a wheelchair and we all head to the rehab area together. A nurse has tied the balloon I brought to the wheelchair and I have to admit that, trailing behind Mom and Dad (or maybe boyfriend) as well as the nurse and physical therapist, I feel a little silly.

Like, do I even really belong here? Nope.

I figure out that I'm walking alongside Saul's bio dad when he turns to me with a smirk and asks, "You the newest guy, then?"

And I admit I'm a little slow. I'm not sure what he's talking about until Shannon turns around and hisses, "Grow up, Dale. We're not dating. He's the guy from the ATV park and he was nice enough to visit. Saul even remembered it, even though he was really out of it, so just shut up."

A smile does not seem appropriate right here. Truth be told, I'm not exactly sure which facial expression would be appropriate, so I settle for something I hope looks neutral. Which is when the guy leans over and says, still with a smirk, "Sorry, I had you pegged for the new boyfriend. But I guess you're really the guy I'm probably going to be suing."

I have a feeling I'm going to get lots of practice with my neutral face, though fortunately at that moment, we arrive at rehab and a group of specialists greet Saul with squeals and confetti. Sometimes it's a little shocking how different the kids' hospitals are from the adult ones.

They wheel him in and get him all set up with different colored bands to stretch and work his atrophied muscles and other stuff I don't know anything about.

They stretch him out and work him hard. Sometimes his parents are asked to help. Me, I just stand there, tossing out a smile or a thumbs-up whenever Saul seems to need it. Which is a lot. He's close to tears after the first few minutes, his face red, sweaty.

Mom and Dad are not doing the most amazing job in the world at presenting a united front as Dale keeps making sideways comments about Shannon's very recent breakup until finally one of the nurses asks him to stop.

It's at that point that he tells Saul he needs a little smoke break and storms out.

The nurse rolls her eyes and then her gaze lands on me. She's one of those no-nonsense nurses who is about fifty years old, and has heard every single thing ever in the world that could come from a patient or parent. And she's clearly over it. She waves me over and gives me Saul's foot. "Okay," she says. "You're going to help stretch him out."

"Me?" I croak.

"You're the boyfriend, right?" she asks.

"Um, no, I'm just a…friend," I say.

Another eye roll from the nurse. "Well, let's use some of that friendship and get this sweet kid's leg stretched out." She does manage to smile at Saul.

Shannon has the other leg, and together we stretch while the nurse talks us through it.

"You know," I say to Saul, unable—as usual—to keep from talking when I'm nervous. "I had to do a bunch of rehab once when I broke my leg."

"Nobody has to do rehab for a broken leg," Saul grumbles, his eyes watering from the pain.

"I did," I say. "Broke my femur. Riding a four-wheeler just like you. And just like you, it was when I shouldn't have been—right at the beginning of a big storm. I hit a house. And broke my femur. You know what bone that is?"

All Saul has for me is a grunt. We're helping him with a deeper stretch and let's just say you can tell the kid hasn't been doing yoga for the past few weeks.

"It's the thigh bone," I say. "They had to do surgery. Weeks of recovery, just like for you. But I got better," I say, as I watch a tear drip onto the blue vinyl of the table. "And you will too. It's a beast right now though, huh?"

He nods, not seeming to trust himself to speak.

"Was for me too," I say. "I cried like a baby the first session."

"You did not," Saul says.

"I did," I say. "My mama was right there—different exercise than this. But the nurse moved my leg and it hurt so bad. I just couldn't help myself."

We release his legs and he sighs in relief.

"You're doing better than me," I say as the nurse presses gently on his feet, testing them. "You're younger and more pliable. Plus, you got a nicer nurse."

He glances at his nurse, unconvinced. But she seems to appreciate the compliment and gives him a big smile.

Dale comes back in, smelling like a pack of cigarettes.

I step away. "You know what I'm gonna do," I say. "I'm gonna go get y'all a box of donuts. Then when you're done, you can celebrate."

Dale sits down in a puff of cigarette smell and I scurry through the doors. I know there's a spot down the street. And I figure donuts will make everyone happy.

It's not until later that evening when I finally remember my phone. I'm turning into a little truck stop to grab some dinner. Naturally, I'd let my phone die during the therapy session, so it's been charging in the brief ride to the truck stop.

Looking at it, I wish I'd let it stay dead.

Several messages from Gretchen about the grand opening, which is supposed to happen in two Saturdays. I scroll past those. I'll read them more closely when I've got time. Or just give her a call to see what I should be doing for it.

Two from Ned about him having a flat tire and getting into work late. Whoops. That would have been good to tell Gretchen, who is covering for me.

And then that one from Madigan. "Alfie is really sick. Taking him to the vet right now. Can you watch him tonight? I've got to go in to work."

I glance at the time. Nearly five. I'm not sure I'll be back in time. It's over three and a half hours. "Um, when do you leave?" I text. "I'll be home around nine tonight."

Nothing comes back through. Which isn't a surprise. I think she starts work at six, so I'm behind. Hopefully she found someone who could do it.

CHAPTER 40

MADIGAN

 go through every single contact on my phone for the thousandth time. Granted, there aren't a lot. I'm me, after all, but I go through every single one.

It's five o'clock. My shift starts in one hour. And Alfie is still groggy and droopy from his stomach pumping this morning at the vet.

I need someone to watch him.

But my dad is halfway to Illinois. He's driving there to pick up Grams so she can be here for a few weeks before Nellie's wedding.

Now *that's* a reasonable excuse. As opposed to Andy's vague 'I'll be home at nine tonight.' Of course. It seems that he's always ready to help everyone *except* me.

Which is fine. Definitely fine. Because at this

point, I'm probably better off without receiving help from him anyway.

I stroke Alfie's back as we sit on the couch. I've only got one more name on my list—one Santos gave me, though he advised me not to call. "But if you get desperate," he'd said. And seeing the way Alfie barely has the energy to lift his head, I feel pretty desperate.

"Terry asked me to give you his number," Santos had said. "I never did, 'cause that guy's not my favorite. But I guarantee he'd do a favor for you."

I can guarantee it too.

I could just take the night off work. But I doubt they'll be able to fill my shift with such late notice, which means the helicopter will be grounded. Which means someone might not be able to get to a hospital quickly. Which means…

I sigh, gripping my phone, then tapping out the words before I can second-think it. "It's Madigan. Not sure if you're up for me to call in a favor you don't owe me." It's not the best way to begin, but I don't know that yet. "But my dog was sick today. I was wondering if you could stay with him for a few hours till my dad gets home. We'll be at his house."

His text comes back lightning fast, which is gratifying after a day of striking out. "Sure, Mads. What's up?"

It's a nice response, legitimately nice.

"My dog is sick," I repeat. "You up for some doggie daycare?"

"Of course," he responds.

Again, super nice.

I realize as my fingers fly over the phone that I'm kind of inviting this guy I've been avoiding for over a year into a really vulnerable moment in my life. But looking at Alfie limp on the couch, I don't know what else to do. "My dad will be back around 8:00 and he'll take over from there."

"I gotcha," he says. "Just let me know where to meet you and tell me what you need me to do."

And I almost want to cry with relief.

CHAPTER 41

ANDY

*M*adigan does not return my texts.

I send one a day, hoping not to overwhelm her.

Way more than my lucky four. One every day for a week and a half. At this point, it's looking like she's blocked me. If she hasn't, maybe she should. Because it's definitely time for me to stop.

I hover over her name once again, but this time, I turn my phone off.

Instead, I head over to The Molehill for some mud therapy. Except when I get there, I can't find the key for Rico, my favorite four-wheeler. It's not in the vehicle, because I'm now a responsible adult. But it's not in the correct envelope either, because apparently I'm not a responsible adult at all.

As I dig through envelopes, some of it keys and

some of it actual mail that I'm supposed to go through, I find a thick legal envelope. Smith and Smithson, Attorneys at Law.

I slip my finger under the flap, opening it.

Letterhead paper. Official gobbledy-gook. Though I think I get the gist of it. If I don't settle for $100,000 in damages, I'll face an official lawsuit from a Mr. Dale Reneau. Saul's father. Well, he said he was gonna sue. And I guess he is.

I make a note on the desk for Ned that we need to find the key and that we need to go over the numbers together as soon as he can. And I make a mental note to call my own lawyer and have him interpret the letter. Just to be sure I understand.

Then take another key for a teeny little ATV that'll do for now. I guess.

It stutters as I start it, and I realize that I haven't had some of these things tuned up recently. Another thing to add to my growing list of must-be-dones.

Even so, I get it running and eventually I make it to my favorite path, then up the hill where we found the boys all those weeks ago. I stay in tight on the path, not wanting to see the spots where they were, though I can't help thinking about them anyway, as we crest the hill where the helicopter landed and Madigan jumped out.

I shake it off, catching just a bit of air as I descend. At least Saul is doing well. Walking, stretching, laughing. Shannon says he'll be back to school soon.

I hit a sharp curve. This part of the path is clear. Hot. Sunny.

Sweat pricks up all over my face, the sun battering my neck. And I like it. I love it.

I pull back as I round down, coming up on the fence around the lake, the fence that separates one property from another, the fence I was planning to take down.

I'm not sure I will now. I'm not sure of anything. The Range is set for its grand opening this weekend. But I've been thinking. Just like I thought the last time I drove out here, only opposite. I've been thinking that maybe I should just sell the thing. What is it anyway, except one more big liability? And right now, my life feels like it has enough liabilities.

If I sell it, that'll be one less thing attached to my LLC that Dale Reneau can take from me.

RIDING BACK TO THE MOLEHILL, I feel more clear-headed than I have in weeks. I'll cancel the grand opening, sell the property, and hopefully recoup that cost.

When I get back to my office, I text Gretchen and

message Ned that we need to get the grand opening cancelled, and then call my lawyer. *My lawyer.* Yeah, at what point did a job where I have to have my very own lawyer sound like a good idea to me? Anyway, I call my lawyer and set up an appointment to go over the letter.

To celebrate, or maybe commiserate, I stop at Mom's office. She, at least, will let me take her to dinner.

"Hey, hon," she says, when I peek into her little office. "How was your day?"

"You up for dinner?" I say without answering her question.

She throws me a quick glance. "Looks like you've been riding."

"Helps me think," I say.

She spins around in her chair. "Let me finish a little bit of paperwork. Give me…ten minutes or so. How does pizza sound?"

"Pizza always sounds good," I say.

She spins back. "Oh!" she says, as she flips open her laptop. "You'll never believe who I met today!"

"Ghandi," I say dryly.

"Close," she answers. "Okay, not close. But a guy named Jeremy Schmidt. Ring a bell?"

"Yeah," I answer, furrowing my forehead. "What was he in here for?"

"Looking for a job," she answers. "And I could

absolutely use another dentist in the office. I've been drowning for the better part of a year, ever since Dr. Thims retired."

"I know," I murmur.

"What's wrong?" she asks. "Is something wrong with him? I got the impression you two were friends. He said *you* gave him my number. And that you hosted a wedding for him?" Her voice is full of a thousand questions at the last bit.

"Only because his hand got hurt at The Range so he couldn't get married when he was supposed to. So I opened up The Molehill so they could use it. Gretchen helped, of course. Lots of other people too."

"Oh, honey, that's the sweetest. No wonder he came in singing your praises."

"So he's not…" I begin. "…he's not going back to finish his training in surgery?" I ask. I hadn't realized when he'd asked for my mom's number that it's because he was looking for a *job*.

"I don't know," she says. "We just had a short conversation. He'll be coming for a more official interview next week. But what do you mean?"

"He was going to become an oral surgeon," I say miserably. "Before his hand."

My mama looks at me, a bit of understanding dawning. "Yeah, his hand was still bandaged. You're worried it's not doing well."

"If he's looking for dentistry gigs, I'm almost sure it's not doing well," I mutter, flopping criss-cross onto the floor like a little kid.

"He seemed—I mean—he seemed really happy," she says.

"He's a good guy," I reply. "A good sport."

"Hmmm," she murmurs, shutting her laptop again. "How about instead of you taking me out to eat, we go home and I'll make us something. Meatballs still your favorite?"

"Forevermore," I reply with a smile, "but you don't have to make me supper. Though I don't really feel like going out. I'll pick something up for us."

Mama pinches her lips together. "Hon," she begins.

"Take your ten minutes," I answer. "When you're done, I'll be standing here with food and we'll go to your house to eat it."

I STOP at Abuela's Bar and Grill. And, yes, it's just like it sounds. A little bit of everything. It's also the closest decent restaurant to Mama's dentistry. I order a couple of tacos and some pizza bites, along with a Caesar salad because I know Mama will want something green.

I can see Abuela herself (I'm not sure anyone

knows her real name) behind the bar, shuffling around and getting drinks.

And then, a familiar profile—the dark hair, the small sharp nose.

I open my mouth, Madigan's name on my lips, just as the hulking firefighter plops down beside her. I'm about to walk over, do my due diligence to rescue her—again. From this guy who won't leave her alone—again.

Except that she turns to him, pushing over a plate of appetizers so he can take one. I stop. Take in the scene. They're dipping slivers of tortilla in various sauces, sipping their drinks, talking.

It's the weirdest thing to realize that now you're the one with the unanswered texts; you're the one who won't leave her alone. It's you.

I blink like maybe I'm on one of those hidden camera shows, confused and trying to put the pieces together. Then, I turn back to the take-out area and ask the guy if he knows how long the food is going to be. I'm just glad it's Wednesday so they're not busy.

"Probably another ten minutes," the kid says.

There's a hard plastic chair to the left. A lonely thing. I'm about to retreat there when I feel someone bump my shoulder.

I turn to say "Excuse me" like any decent human and then realize it's the firefighter. What was his name? Larry or Terry or something. "Oh, sorry," I say.

He gives me a quick glance and doesn't respond. "You got any napkins?" he asks the kid behind the counter. "My *date* just spilled a bit of her drink."

I throw a quick glance in Madigan's direction and it's true that she's using a small square of a napkin to sop up a mess.

"Oh, here," I say, grabbing a bunch from a place on the counter to my left.

Terry ignores me and the napkins dangle in my hand. The kid behind the counter gives both of us a weird look and then takes some napkins from the exact same place I did and holds them out for Terry to take.

Terry grabs them.

"Need any more help?" I ask. Because I'm a glutton for punishment and because—whatever—I guess I enjoy annoying this guy.

"Oh, trying to be helpful now?" he asks.

The kid behind the counter is watching us a bit warily. He's got a hand on his phone in his pocket.

"Yeeesss," I say.

"I bet you are," he replies, wadding the napkins into a ball in his enormous fist. The kid behind the counter is also observing the size of Terry's fist.

"Look, I don't have any beef with you," I say. And then I hold out my non-wadded stack of napkins.

He literally swats them away. "You might not have any beef with me, but she's got beef with you."

I don't have an answer to that, and I admit that I'm not thrilled she's been sharing whatever beef she has about me with this guy instead of talking to me about it.

"She knows who she can count on now, at any rate," he adds. And I swear he puffs out his chest, just like a rooster. "Too bad you weren't around to help with her dog."

"Alfie?" I say, letting my guard down for just a second. "Is he okay?"

Terry grumbles, "He's fine. But he *was* sick and Mads needed help. She called me."

I think of the day I spent in Indy with Saul, the text I got from her at the truck stop. The way she hasn't texted me since.

And for once I don't have anything snarky to say to this guy. It's weird when the villain winds up as the hero. But not quite as weird as when you wind up as the villain.

Terry takes another chunk of napkins from the dispenser and turns, almost bumping into Madigan, who's come up behind him.

"Oh, hey, Andy!" Madigan says, looking moderately awkward, which I slightly appreciate. She turns to the kid behind the counter. "Do you have any napkins? I'm so sorry, but I spilled my drink."

The kid—that poor sixteen-year-old—he takes the last few from the stack Terry and I have depleted and hands them to her.

"I hope Alfie's doing better now. I'm really sorry he was sick."

She turns to me, throwing a quick glance at Terry. "Yeah, it was a rough night."

"But we got it taken care of," Terry says, stepping closer to her. She eases, very subtly, away.

"I'm glad," I say earnestly. "And I'm really sorry he was sick." *And that I wasn't there.* But I don't add that last part.

"He's a trooper," she replies.

Mercifully, another guy comes up to the counter with my food, bagged and ready, so I can finally escape.

"Well, you guys have a fun night," I say.

She glances at my food. Two drinks.

"You too," she replies. "Do you have a date?"

Terry smirks.

"Sweet night at home with my mama," I reply. "She's had a long day." I don't add that I have too and that it keeps getting longer.

Terry smirks harder.

"Anyway, see you guys around." *Except hopefully never ever again.*

WHEN I GET out to my car, I delete Madigan's name from my phone. I don't block her. It's not that bad. After all, it's not her fault her dog got sick and Terry had to help out. It's not her fault I've been MIA, but it's pretty clear that we're just not right for each other on any level.

It's also pretty clear that she goes out with people who do her favors. I was one of those people and I got a favor date. Fair enough. But not what I'm looking for in a relationship.

I had thought for a minute—longer than a minute—that we might have something, a little spark, an attraction of opposites, that maybe we could be each other's complement—my calm yin to her intense yang.

But really I just need to grow up. And she needs to let go.

And neither of us is being epic at that.

By the time I get back to Mama's office, she's had more than enough time to finish her paperwork and is standing out on the sidewalk, checking messages on her phone.

I pull up like an Uber guy. It's what I feel like lately. And, hey, maybe if everything else in my life doesn't work out, which seems to be the current theme, it's something I could do.

CHAPTER 42

Grams is rolling out dough for an apple pie.

And trying to teach me how. "You've got to get the butter frozen, before you work it in. That way you get that delicious flakey crust."

Her hands are shaking and I take the rolling pin from her, working it over the dough, though it begins to take on an oblong shape instead of a circle.

"Don't forget the east to west, honey," she tells me, her accent still dripping Kentucky even though she moved up north over twenty years ago for Gramp's job. Now he's gone, but she's still there. I've heard Dad and Nellie talking about bringing her back, now that she's slowing down.

She takes the rolling pin from me, and even with her hands paper thin, arthritis swollen, and shaking like two leaves, she manages a beautiful circle with the dough. "This is your heritage, honey," she says. "Even those French ladies can't make an apple pie as good as this."

Of course, French ladies don't look quite the same round donut shape as Grams either, though I don't point that part out.

"Now who's your date going to be for the wedding?" she says, sprinkling extra sugar on the apples.

"You are, Grams," I say.

"Well, that will never do," she replies. "And don't tell me you just need that dog. Every woman needs more than that."

Not me. But I don't say this either. I just heap sugared apples into the pie crust, letting my thoughts wander. I notice they head in Andy's direction, just as Grams says, "No nice men at work?"

I clear my throat.

Calling Terry had been a mistake. Capital 'M.' Mistake. I should have called in to work and taken the night off, should have gone and begged help from the neighbors I barely know. Should have done literally anything else.

"Not really, Grams, no."

Terry had tried to get me to drink too much on our date the night before. Yeah, I'd noticed it. The way he sat us at the bar, the way he ordered drinks for me. I guess I'd been prepared for it. I managed to spill the first drink. And then, Diet Coke all night long, thank you very much. Even when he pressured me to try the margaritas, even when I wanted to. Because, don't get me wrong, I would have loved to drink too much on that date, would have loved to go all fuzzy so I didn't have to listen to him talk about himself and then talk about Andy and then talk about a bunch of other people—none of it nice. Yeah, I would have loved to black all of that out. But I've seen fuzzy women with guys they don't like. And it doesn't usually end in the woman's favor.

"Surely there's someone," Grams says. And for one second, Andy's face flashes into my mind. But Andy is definitely not the man for the job. Not the job of watching my dog. And not the job of caring about me. He's a guy for fun, for crowds, for ease. And that's just not me.

As soon as Dad walks into the room, Grams says, "How we gonna get this one to catch the bouquet?"

"Ah, Mama, she'll catch it when she's ready."

"Oh, sweetie," she says to me. "Your first wedding was so lovely. With that handsome boy." She sighs, not saying anything else.

Dad looks at me over Grams' head. *Sorry,* he mouths. But we both know when women hit a certain age, they say what they want, and Grams is definitely at that age, plus a few years.

"I'm sure you've got loads of men interested in you, especially with that job of yours," Grams says. "Why don't you just bring one?"

Terry had hinted and practically begged me to be my plus one as soon as he'd heard about the wedding. That was a big fat no.

Ever since our date, he'd been calling me every day. And last night at work, he'd swatted my butt at the station. No. Nope. Helping me with my dog does not mean I get to be harassed at work. Or anywhere else. I was calling HR if it happened again, though at this point I wasn't planning to take any more shifts at that station as long as Terry was there.

"Our pilots at work are both married," I say to Grams, as sweetly as possible. "And my partner is a woman."

Grams taps her hip, like she's going through a rolodex of potential mates in her mind and coming up blank. "We'll find you someone, honey. Now place the top crust on the pie and give it some pretty slits. That way all the steam can come out."

I obey.

"Aw, sweetie, that one looks like a heart," Grams says, pointing at a sloppy slit. "A heritage of love."

And it's gonna be more of that all weekend. Every cousin, every great-aunt, every everyone.

So maybe it's good that I'm going to the wedding alone. Because I might have made it through a near-stranger's wedding sober, but I'm not sure I'm going to make it through one with my family—every single one of them talking about dating and love and Joshua. At least dateless I can have a few drinks, go a little blank, and not worry about it.

CHAPTER 43

ANDY

The grand opening was set to happen tomorrow night. *Was.* But I'd enlisted Gretchen's help in cancelling it.

"You can't," she'd said when I asked.

"I'm gonna," I'd replied. "I'm planning to sell it. You were right, and I got in too deep. And we both know a grand opening on a place I'm gonna sell is ridiculous."

"I don't know anything," she'd said. "Besides, these places take time to sell. At least if some knucklehead kid doesn't come along and buy it right away."

"I'll cut the price way down if I have to," I'd said. "I need it gone."

I hadn't told her about the letter from the attorneys at law, nothing like that.

Gretchen had sighed. "Andy…" Then stopped, thought. "Look, I can't stop you from selling it. But do this for me. Promise me you won't make any decisions this week or next."

"I don't know, Gretch," I'd said.

"Promise me," she said. "And I'll take care of the headache of cancelling the grand opening. Newspaper, billboard, phone calls. You won't have to lift a finger."

Now, that was a deal too good to refuse. So Gretchen had taken care of all the cancellations, or—as she liked to call them—postponements. And here I was—am—with nothing to do this weekend, except think about stuff.

I pass the church on Panning. Brand new hours are posted on a brand new copper plate screwed to the door. Mama would like that. We could try out a service one of these days.

Beneath the copper plate is a little note: Dogs welcome during prayer hours. Please be sure they're on a leash.

Alfie would have liked that. Not that Madigan was the type to go in for something like prayer hours, so Alfie was out of luck.

I pause to look at the new stained glass, to admire the fresh smell of wood, to wonder for half a second if the donations from The Range had even made that big of a difference. Likely not.

I hurry away from the church, turning down the old street where Mama's first dental office used to be—way back when I was a kid. Her building is some sort of internet café now—a place where business people rent office space for short periods of time.

Through the large glass window, I see two guys sitting at laptops with ignored coffees resting beside them. So different from the life I've chosen for myself. For half a second, I imagine Madigan's husband in there, doing business, making loads of money. We never talked about him, but that seems like the type of dude she would have married.

Pushing the thought away, I plow down the street into a much older business. The library.

And I'll be darned if it doesn't smell just exactly like it did all those years ago—paper and industrial carpet, and a little air freshener behind the desk. Lavender. Nellie's favorite.

"Well, ma'am," I say, walking to the desk. "I'm surprised to see you here. I understand you have a big weekend ahead of you."

"I'd understood the same thing about you, Andy, though I saw in the paper it's no longer true."

"Sometimes you gotta pivot," I say. "But why aren't you getting ready for a wedding?"

"I am," she says, holding up the book she's been reading.

"Spanish primer, huh?"

"Learning a few phrases of Español for the honeymoon. Now I know I can find a bathroom, no matter what." She smiles.

"You know they have apps for that?"

"You know I'm sixty-one, right?"

We both laugh. "Sixty-one ain't too old for an app, Miss Nellie."

"Maybe not," she says, "but I still prefer a book. What about you? Still interested in sharks?"

"Eh," I say. "I've kind of had enough bites in my life lately."

Nellie lifts a gray eyebrow. "Books on business?"

"Maybe next time," I say. "What else you got?"

She presses her lips together, looking me up and down. Cargo shorts, old blue t-shirt. Hiking boots though I'm not hiking. "There is this one story," she says. "You remind me of one of the characters. It's not the usual thing I give you," she says. "Not the usual at all."

She steps from behind the desk, heading to the fiction books lined up alphabetically by author. "It's been a hot minute since I've seen you in here."

"Yeah, I reckon it's been a few years."

"Well, then," she says, heading down the row of Ms, "maybe it's perfect since it's a little more grown up. But not too much." She stops in front of a shelf of books with spines beat up from being read a lot.

"Not sure as a romance novel is right up my alley at the moment," I say, noticing some of the titles.

"A romance novel should always be up a young man's alley," Nellie says, plucking a book from the shelves.

I have to admit it doesn't look quite as bad as the others. It's not pink at any rate. And there's no woman with only half a dress on the cover.

"Are there sharks?" I ask.

"Only metaphorically," she says.

"I really don't know if it's a good fit," I say, wondering why I'm pushing so hard, why I don't just take the book home and not read it and then return it. Easy enough.

"You know my niece will be at the wedding," Nellie adds with all the subtlety of a peacock.

"I figured," I say.

"Couldn't get her to bring a plus one."

Now it's my turn to lift my eyebrows. "Miss Nellie."

"Oh, I know," she says, turning back to the books. "It's just too bad that youth is wasted on the young."

"I tried not to waste it," I grumble.

"She's a tough nut to crack," Nellie says, her gaze on the spines like they're the most interesting things in the world.

"No," I say. "Honestly, *I* blew it. I brushed her off

when she needed me, even though she was there for me when I needed her."

"Go on," she says.

And I do. I can't seem to stop myself or shut my mouth. I tell her everything—or at least I hit the main points. "And then I wasn't there for her the night Alfie got sick. And I don't think she's forgiven me."

"Maybe it's not as much about forgiveness as general confusion, longing, missteps. Just like a romance novel, if you ask me."

I hold out my hand to take the book she's still cradling.

"This one is packed with surprises," she says.

"Happy endings?" I ask.

"Always," she says. "You don't really think I'd recommend a book for you without a happy ending."

And sometimes with Nellie it's tough to know if we're talking about books or other stuff.

"I'll read it this weekend," I say.

"I recommend you start tonight," she chirps.

"Well, I don't have any other plans," I mutter.

"Good," she says.

Which is how I leave the library with my first ever romance novel tucked under my arm.

I MAKE it to The Molehill for my shift just after six. I've barely worked in the last few weeks, but Ned needed the night off. And I owe him one. Well, I owe him a hundred, but for now, one will have to do.

We don't usually have a ton of customers at this time of day anyway—I'm mostly waiting for people already out to get back and return their keys. Which means I might have to settle in with the book Nellie gave me, just to pass the time.

Though as I'm skimming the back cover, the door swings open.

I look up, surprised to see Shannon and Saul walking up to the desk. "Oh, hey," I say, standing.

"Two ATVs," Shannon says brightly. "Unless it's too late."

"Nah," I reply, looking from Saul to his mother. "Though I admit that I'm surprised to see you here."

"Well, I promised Saul that as soon as he got cleared for it, we would get back on the proverbial horse, if you know what I mean," she says. "This time with an adult. And a helmet. And a non-stolen vehicle."

I nod, fiddling with the drawer that holds the keys. "I guess just with your, um, ex-husband's letter and all."

I watch Shannon freeze—her face and body turned to straight stone. "Saul, honey," she says, "why don't you head into the room for the safety video while Mr. Putman gets me the keys."

I open the door for Saul. "Let's get this going and then I'll get you suited up," I say, setting up the YouTube channel with our video.

As soon as I go back out, Shannon hisses, "What exactly did Dale send you?"

I clear my throat. "A letter," I reply, figuring I've got nothing to lose from telling her. "From his lawyer."

"He's got no more lawyer than I do a yacht," she says.

"I mean, it looked real official," I say.

She holds out her hand, in a very mother-of-boys way that doesn't expect any back talk.

I dig into the drawer and hand the letter over.

She opens it, the paper snapping from the crispness of her movement.

"Hmph," she says, looking down her nose at it. "Yeah, his friend Jim surely made that. Don't pay it no mind. If Dale was going to sue, it'd be for more than $100,000."

I take it from her, looking at the thick paper, the gold letterhead. I'm not quite sure Dale's friend Jim could have managed something of this caliber, but I'm not about to argue with Shannon.

I clear my throat. "At any rate, it's good to see the two of you here."

"It's good to be here," she says warmly. "And thank you. For all you did for Saul. He was so excited to come here. I wish someone else was working so you could ride with us."

I wish it too, mostly so I can make sure they're both safe. "Are you sure he's ready?"

"Yes," she says, and it's not the kind of yes you argue with.

This time I make sure to get the release forms signed before the kid heads out on a vehicle.

CHAPTER 44

MADIGAN

From the front door to my seat in the church—already three people have asked me if I'll be the next bride they see up there.

I have no intention of making the mistake of getting through this wedding sober.

Honestly, if I had a flask hidden in my dress, I'd be chugging at it right here in the pew. As it is, all I have is my father's hand, protectively resting on my forearm. And, for now, that's good enough.

Though it's only for now. Since Gramps is gone, Dad is going to be the one giving Nellie away.

I pat his hand as the church fills, as the voices grow louder, people hugging and kissing.

Then breathe out through my teeth when he squeezes my hand and stands to leave the room. If only Alfie was here.

Grams is already sniffling beside me, a lace hand-kerchief in her hand.

I settle for patting her arm just like Dad had done with mine. And, you know, it kind of helps. At least until Grams says, "Next I'll be seeing you up there again."

My teeth click together and I try to smile, but don't succeed.

Fortunately, at that moment, the pastor walks to the front, followed by the groom. Normally, the groomsmen and bridesmaids would follow, but apparently it's different when you marry older—a little more laid back. The wedding party seems to consist primarily of a flower girl (a second cousin of some sort) throwing petals around like it's the thing she was born to do. Everybody else gets to watch instead of participate and, looking around, people seem honestly, genuinely happy. Nellie knew just about everyone in this town and at least half of them have turned up, ready to celebrate her big moment when she's spent a whole lifetime celebrating theirs.

Something about that fills me with a sweet warmth as the music starts and I hear the back of the chapel open. I take a deep breath, placing my hand on Grams'—this time for my own support, not hers, though she doesn't know that.

The wedding march begins—played on the organ —traditional, beautiful, the sun reaching through the stained-glass window above the pastor's head. Daddy and Aunt Nellie working their way in rhythm down the aisle littered with petals.

One of Nellie's friends lets out an irreverent whoop as Dad settles Nellie into place across from her groom.

I want to look away, but can't seem to tear my eyes off of the smiling couple gazing into each other's eyes. In fact, I'm not sure I even blink for the entire service, through the short ceremony, the precious vows, the kiss to seal it all.

Grams squeezes my hand as we all stand, clapping, and I beat the tears from my eyes. The groom sweeps Nellie up into his arms, carrying her out of the church, as though they were thirty years younger than they are, and I have to admit I'm glad I didn't have a flask hidden in my dress, glad I didn't go fuzzy, glad I got to be fully here in this moment for Nellie.

Now if only I can make it through the reception.

———

SHANNON AND SAUL stay out nearly as long as they can. Which, admittedly, makes me sweat a little. More than a little. I pace a bit, plunk into the seat, flip open the library book, shut it, read the back for the thousandth time, then finally open it to the first page. A dedication, a quote about true love, chapter one.

Which is when, mercifully, I hear the four-wheelers pull in and the sound of a young boy whooping as he dismounts.

I slam the book shut, sinking back into my chair with relief. Reason 765 that I should be selling the rifle range and, heck, maybe this place too.

They come into my office, keys jingling, Saul smiling from ear to ear—everybody in one piece.

"You made it," I say, trying to sound casual.

"That was so cool," Saul says. Then, "Thanks."

It's a nice thing to hear, especially in the last few weeks, and I wonder if Shannon schooled him a bit on what and what not to say when he came back.

"Thank you," Shannon adds, handing me the keys. "I hope we're not late."

"Not at all," I say. "In fact, you're four minutes early."

I slide the keys into the final envelope, filing it into the cabinet as Shannon glances down at my desk. "Ooooh, that's a good one."

I shoot a look at my desk, slightly embarrassed to see the romance novel still sitting there. I clear my throat, but Shannon has lifted the book up. "I read this about five years ago. I'd forgotten all about it."

"Nellie recommended it to me," I say. "I figured

she just had a wedding on her mind. It's not my usual type of reading."

"Aw, now, nothing wrong with a little romantic read," Shannon says. "I'm sure your girlfriend appreciates it."

I give Saul a little shrug and he smiles.

"It's got a good ending. I bet Nellie gave it to you because it's written by some local author."

"Really?" I say. "I didn't know we had any local authors in Midvale."

"They probably hide in the woodwork thinking big thoughts. Or, well, thinking of kissing scenes."

I laugh. "Do you want to borrow it?" I ask. "Not sure I'll get to it. I've been distracted this weekend. A lot to do."

"No, you read it," she says. "Every guy should be required to read at least one romance novel in his life before going on his first date."

"I don't know. What do you think about that?" I say to Saul.

He scrunches up his nose.

"That's cuz he ain't ready for no date yet," Shannon says. "But when the time comes…"

"Can we come back Monday?" Saul says, ignoring his mother's discussion of dating.

"Probably not," she says. "But maybe once a month if you get your chores done every day."

I nod, giving Saul my best conspirator smile.

"Maybe if you'd give me better jobs," Saul grumbles.

Shannon pushes him gently toward the door. "You'll know why if you don't see us," she says. "And get to reading. That book's a good education for a man."

"Yes, ma'am," I say, gathering the book up with my other things. I'd hate for Ned to come in and see it on my desk. Might never live that one down.

I balance the numbers for the day's business, count the cash and prepare it to be deposited, double check the keys in their envelopes, and then head home for the night.

It's not even nine o'clock. No plans, no date, no prospects for anything at all. Maybe I really do need an education on love.

I settle onto my couch and open the book, flipping through the pages to see how many there are—an old habit from childhood.

Only when I get to the end, to the About the Author section, there's a little headshot. Black and white, younger, different hair, dark lips, but still unmistakable.

I turn back to the front, Madigan Morrison. Maybe her maiden name? A pen name? A dedication "To Joshua." A quote from Shakespeare from *A Midsummer Night's Dream.* "The course of true love never did run smooth."

Nellie, you rascal.

And then the story—yes, I start to read it. And I keep reading it. It's good—loads of funny scenes, but also kind of poignant and beautiful. I'm about a hundred pages in when I realize something. I need to apologize to Madigan. Apologize for not being there when she needed help, even though she was there when I needed help.

She can accept my apology or not, but sometimes things just need saying, regardless of the result.

I leave the book face down on my coffee table and grab my keys.

It's after nine when I show up at her door, later than is polite. Though I don't have much time to overthink that choice, because she answers the door within seconds, practically throwing it open.

"I just wanted to say," I begin, "that I'm really sorry."

She interrupts. "I don't need your sorry right now." I can smell a touch of wine on her breath.

"No, I really am," I say. "About everything. The way I treated you, the—"

She starts to cry. "No," she says. "I need you to help me. To take me and Alfie to the emergency clinic up in Swallowsville. He's sick, Andy. Please."

"Alfie?" I say. "Again?"

"He hasn't been himself since the last time, but I

thought he was just recovering—his stomach and all, but…please…he's almost all I have."

"Of course, I'll take him. And you."

"He's not doing well," she says. "And he keeps barfing." She steps aside, and then I see Alfie lying, like a puddle, in the middle of the hall floor. He looks like all his bones melted away, leaving him skin and fur. He doesn't even lift his head when I walk in, though his eyes flick up at me, just for a moment.

Madigan is kind of in a puddle herself, sitting slumped next to him, stroking his back, her cheeks wet, eyeliner smudged. She's dressed in a shiny blue dress, matching shoes slipped off and resting next to her.

"The wedding," I say, putting everything together. "That was tonight."

"Yeah," she mutters miserably, "and I should have taken a page from your book and gone at it dry, but at the reception, everyone kept asking when it was going to be me walking down the aisle, and I just couldn't do it all night."

"It's okay," I say, wishing I could just give everyone a hug and make both of these problems better. Instead, I look around for some kind of carrier.

Madigan points to a bedroom. Her bedroom.

I stand and push the door open gently, doing my

best not to look around at her personal space, while also trying to look around at her personal space in order to find the carrier.

"By the closet," she says from the hallway, and I can hear her starting to get up.

"Found it," I call, so she can stay near Alfie. I move a pair of shoes out of the way and retrieve the carrier, noticing the makeup strewn on the dresser, the tightly-made bed. Then I make a beeline for the door.

She's tucking a blanket around Alfie when I get back. "I got him," I say, crouching down and maneuvering my arms under his body. He's heavy, dead weight, but his eyes open and I feel like he's thanking me. I look into those sugar brown eyes and when I do, I try to communicate that he really needs to pull through for Madigan. Though I guess he knows that; dogs always know that.

Madigan is tearing up again, seeing him in his crate.

"Don't worry," I say. "I know someone, up in Swallowsville. One of my sister's best friends used to work for a vet up there. I'll make a call."

"That would be great," she murmurs.

"Where's your dad?" I ask, carrying Alfie as Madigan locks the front door behind her.

"I was about to call him," she says. "Right before you showed up, but it might have taken too long anyway. He had to take Grams home tonight and get her to bed. She struggles on her own. And I wasn't the only one who had a little wine—Grams did too—so that makes it harder."

I nod, stopping abruptly at Madigan's car. "Do you have your keys?"

She pats her dress, like she might have pockets in it (she doesn't), checks her shoulder for her purse, and then lets out a faint curse.

"It's okay," I say, turning back to the locked house. I tilt my head to the side, cracking it. "Do you have a hidden key anywhere, so we can get back into your house?"

In answer, she closes her eyes and tears stream down her face in a silent cry.

"A neighbor?" I ask gently.

She shakes her head.

I look from her car, to my Jeep.

"Madigan," I say. "I know you don't like my vehicle, but we would all wear seatbelts, and I could belt Alfie's carrier in real good."

With every part of her face drooping downward, she waves her hand toward the Jeep. "It's okay," she whispers.

And then I know, really know, just how desperate she is.

CHAPTER 45

ANDY

The dog lives. Bells, whistles, happy endings.

It feels like a cheat to skip over it like that—as though there should have been an action scene—a team of doctors rushing out and calling 'Clear' as they resuscitate Alfie and he revives.

Instead, Madigan and I sit together in the waiting room—too awkward for me to even hold her hand. Most of the time, she leans over, her head against her fists.

Once I pat her back.

And then, just before midnight, I go to a gas station down the street and get her a coffee.

She rewards that with a lopsided smile.

"Nothing for you?" she asks.

"They didn't have any milkshakes," I respond and

she bumps her shoulder against mine. It's a nice bump.

"Thanks," she says.

"Any time," I answer.

And right at that moment, when maybe it seems that we'll be able to talk, an aid comes out, beaming from ear to ear.

That's a good thing.

Dr. Reynolds follows. "Well, Alfie is a very lucky little soldier. Seems he's been fighting a nasty infection. We've got him on an antibiotic, which should clear things up. I think he's going to be just fine."

Maddie jumps up.

And then we have a sedated-but-getting-better Alfie buckled into my Jeep. It's nearly 2:00 in the morning when we get home.

Does she invite me in? Do I sleep on her couch? Do we fall asleep together holding hands? Nope. Nope. And definitely nope.

Instead, when I take her hand and say, "Maybe we can grab a late breakfast tomorrow morning," she pulls her hand away, takes a deep breath. "I really appreciate what you did for me and Alfie tonight. I really do. I appreciate your friendship—probably more than you will appreciate what I'm about to say. But I've realized I'm not up for dating, not right now, maybe not ever."

It's not the best thing to hear at 2:00 in the morning.

Although it gives me some time to think.

I spend the rest of the weekend finishing her book. It's gushy, mushy, and strangely beautiful. Something that's hard to imagine her having written.

I wonder what it takes to get a woman from there to here, to the middle-of-the-night rejection. From love story to sob story. Not that she'd ever want it phrased that way. From our first coffee non-date to, well, to a bunch of other avoided half-dates, so I guess that part makes sense.

I read the dedication again. *Joshua.*

And suddenly I'm anxious for Nellie to get back from her honeymoon so I can return the book.

CHAPTER 46

MADIGAN

The first thing I do in the morning is give Alfie his medicine. The second thing I do is dump out every bottle of wine and liquor I've got in the house. Yeah, it feels like a bit of an extreme measure. It's not like I'm an alcoholic or something. But it's a measure I take. Because my dog got sick from drinking it. Which masked some other symptoms he had that I should have noticed. And because, just last night, my dog almost died and I wasn't sober enough to take care of it alone. And, well, enough is enough.

I'd had to ask someone for help, someone I didn't want to ask. Again.

One thing I've realized about being the damsel in distress is that I hate it. I hate being needy. I hate grand gestures—the same ones I used to write about in my dumb books.

I just want to live my life with my dog and the few people I care about. Without needing other people who I don't even want in my life to have to be there, picking up the slack.

As I rinse the last drops down the drain, I think about something Dr. Reynolds said when she spoke with me. "He's not going to live forever, but we'll get him to live a little longer."

I'd tossed all night thinking of that little phrase— a little longer. What did it mean? And how could I stop it? How could I stop losing the things that mattered to me most?

Step one. Take care of myself.

I set the empty bottles in the recycling, then open the windows, even though it's hot, in order to air out the house.

"It's a new day, Alfie. And a new us."

Next on the agenda. Return Millie's dress so I can stop looking at it, stop remembering the way Andy's arms felt on my waist as he swirled me over the grass.

CHAPTER 47

ANDY

Gretchen arrives right on time, which is very Gretchen of her.

What is not very Gretchen is the way she begins without letting me get a word in edgewise. "I really don't think you should sell, Andy."

I wrinkle my forehead at her. "Why, when you didn't think I should buy either?" I ask.

"Because I went to your soft opening. And because it was awesome. Because people love you and because it's a nice thing for this community."

"I can't keep doing it," I say. "I can't keep taking risks that hurt other people."

"What if those same risks help them too?" she asks. "I mean, isn't that the nature of risk?"

"I'm thinking of selling The Molehill too," I say, ignoring her philosophical question.

"No," she says. "I've got a half share of that, and I say 'no.'"

"Gretchen," I say. "You have to understand. I'm just sitting here, waiting to be sued. Like, literally—by Saul's father. And if not him, then someone else is eventually going to come along. I've let you down, Ned down, Saul down, Jeremy down, even Mad—well, I've let everyone down."

"You've visited a sick kid in the hospital," she counters. "Threw a wedding for a guy who almost didn't have one. And that's not all. Remember how when we first opened, you gave Ned a job even though he had a criminal record, gave him a job when no one in this town would—a job that has allowed him to support his family. And me—you could never let me down. As for Madigan—if she can't see what I do, then maybe she's the wrong girl for you."

"Nah," I say. "I'm just the wrong guy for her. And there's a difference. Did you know that she was a writer before? A romance writer? But not cheesy stuff—nice stuff, beautiful stuff. She doesn't do it anymore, since her husband died."

"Well, maybe she needs a good reason to."

"That's sweet, Gretchen. But I am not that reason."

"Andy, if anyone is the reason for someone to start feeling better, it's you."

I give her a long hug, but not a response. Lately I haven't been the best guy for making anybody's life feel better.

"And what would you do if you gave all of this up?" she asks.

"Iron Fit downtown is looking for a new manager."

"The gym?" she asks in what can only be described as a condescending tone.

"I'd be good at managing it," I say defensively.

"That's not the issue," she replies. "You'd be too good. You *are* too good. That's why you should be here. With this business. With what you love."

"What about when things I love hurt other people?"

"What about when things you love help other people?" she counters. "The wedding, the hospital."

"Those are all things I did because I hurt them FIRST," I say, my voice rising.

"Those are all things you did because you cared," she counters. "And that matters."

"I do care," I say. "Which is why I'm selling The Range and why I think we should consider getting rid of The Molehill as well. It'd be in good hands."

"You do *not* know that," she says.

"Well, why don't we do an experiment," I say. "I put the rifle range up for sale, see if we get any bites. And I promote Ned to general manager—see how he would do managing for someone from afar. I'd only sell The Molehill if the guy was willing to continue with Ned."

Gretchen's face goes tight. "And you would apply for this other job?"

"I *already* applied for the job at the gym," I say. "So I'll see how it goes stepping back myself. If I miss it too much, well, then we'll know."

She folds her hands across her chest. "You're stubborn as a mule," she says.

"I come by it honestly," I retort.

Then she laughs. "That you do. Daddy was the stubbornest man in the world. So if you want to call that honestly, then fine."

"Daddy isn't the only stubborn relative I have," I say.

"You're right," she replies. "And I hope you remember that."

CHAPTER 48

MADIGAN

I pick the dress up from the dry cleaner, still in the bag, looking beautiful and sterile, not like something a woman swirled around in under the stars. No, definitely not something like that.

When Millie opens the front door of their little house, she is glowing, and I almost don't dare cross the threshold. It feels like taking a step into my own happy past, and I don't want to go there.

So I hold out the dress. "Got it cleaned for you," I say.

"Girl, you did *not* have to do that. I was honestly hoping you would keep it. Looked better on you than me anyway."

"I seriously doubt that," I say, still holding out the limp dress, which Millie hasn't yet taken.

"Why don't you come in for a coffee or something?" she asks, stepping back to let me in. "Don't mind the mess. We're still unpacking and getting settled."

"I really should be going," I say, trying to back away, but Millie isn't having it. She's already halfway down the hall, expecting me to follow.

I step in, still holding the dress. So far, I've not succeeded at my goal of returning it or getting out of here quickly.

"How do you take your coffee?"

"With caffeine," I answer, thinking of Andy for a moment when I say it.

Millie laughs. "Well, I'm adding cream and sugar to mine."

"Where should I set this?" I ask, nodding to the dress still draped in my arms.

"Back in your car," Millie says. "I really want you to keep it."

I really don't, but I go for a smile.

"You do be needing some caffeine," Millie says, looking at my fake smile.

I change the subject. "So how's Jeremy doing?"

"Great!" she answers.

I don't know why I wasn't expecting that, but I wasn't. "I'm so glad to hear that. His hand is healing up nicely then?"

"Eh," Millie says. "It's healing, but not responding quite as well as the therapists had hoped."

I take the mug Millie hands me, but don't drink it. I don't even look at it. "What's going on with it?"

"He's just having trouble getting some of those fine motor movements back. He's still in physical therapy for it, but it's not looking awesome. I mean, to the naked eye, his hand is healing great. He can do all the normal stuff. It's just, well, he might have to drop out of surgery. In fact, he's planning on it."

I set down the mug. "Oh, Millie, I'm so sorry. I didn't know."

"Don't be sorry," Millie says. "The truth is—the honest truth—he hated surgery. Man, it feels good to say those words. We've been dancing around them for a year, gritting our teeth and muscling through and pretending it was for the best and all. But, yeah, he hated it. He was doing it to make his mama happy, and now he doesn't have to. He can do what he wanted to do the whole time, which was be a dentist."

"Still," I say. "The money, the investment of time."

"Opportunity costs that are being lopped off after one year instead of four. He was *miserable.* But with his mama and—yeah—what we'd invested, we just couldn't take the plunge and pull out. Now we can. This injury has been the most freeing thing of Jeremy's life. Isn't that weird?"

"Yes," I say. "Yes, it is."

"Plus," she adds. "I was wanting to start our family sooner rather than later, but that didn't seem possible with all the school and debt. Not finishing will cut that by a quarter. He's already talking about working just four days a week once we have kids. Normal hours, no obligation to be on call. How dreamy is that?"

I sip my coffee to avoid answering. But, yes, fairly dreamy.

"And… you'll never believe who connected us to Dr. Putman in town."

But I have a guess.

"Andy gave us all the contact information for his mom. She's been needing a partner ever since the last dentist retired. And if we'd waited another three years, well, that spot in town might have been filled. The timing, Maddie girl, it's nothing less than serendipity."

I still have a hard time wrapping my head around the idea that a terrible accident could be called serendipity, but Millie is smiling and glowing. She hasn't even touched her coffee and she still looks happy.

"Which reminds me," Millie says, interrupting my thoughts. "I heard a rumor you and Andy were dating."

"Dating?" I ask, my voice practically a squeak.

Millie narrows her eyes.

"We're friends," I say. "More of acquaintances, actually."

"Hmm," she murmurs, finally picking up her mug. "'Cause when I saw you two dancing at the wedding, I thought that maybe we'd tried to set you up with the wrong guy. I don't suppose that you and Dr. Niels are dating either."

It takes a moment for me to place the name of the surgeon—Oliver. "No, not dating him either."

"Well, that part isn't a surprise," she says. "You ever thought about Andy as more than a friend?"

The coffee tastes bitter in my mouth. And then, I do something I've never done before. I blurt. "I'm a widow. My husband died four years ago. I just don't think I'm ready."

And then, before my brain can catch up with any other parts of my body, I start to cry. I have never cried about Joshua in front of anyone other than Alfie and my family, and now I can't seem to stop.

Millie doesn't say another word, just sets down her mug and wraps her arms around me, rocking side to side and occasionally murmuring 'shhh,' though she doesn't mean for me to be quiet at all. It's just a sound, a womanly sound, a sound as old as grief itself.

"It's okay, baby. Get it out," she says.

"Everyone's always wanting to set me up," I blubber, not even thinking that this might hurt Millie's feelings. It doesn't. "And then I wind up drinking a little more than I should or not sleeping, or both."

"I know, baby. I know," she says.

I sniffle.

Millie shifts back, holding both my shoulders. "You just take your time, move at your own pace. You don't need to ever find someone else if you don't want to."

I nod, my brain starting to catch up, starting to be mortified. But Millie's eyes are glistening with tears just like mine, and that makes me feel better.

"You'll know what you need, baby. And when you need it. Don't let other people dictate that. That's what had started to happen with me and Jeremy. And it took this accident to shake us out of it, wake us up. If you want to be just you, you just be you."

It's a big concept, and one that maybe no one else has ever told me, that I can just be me, that I'm big enough alone to just be me. Something about the idea is so freeing. If I can just be me, then I can do what I want. And if I can do what I want, well, then, all I have to do is figure out what that is.

Because—truthfully—I'm not sure I know. I've been so busy avoiding what other people wanted for me that I haven't really taken the time to figure out what *I* want for me. It's not to be sad for the rest of my life, that's for sure. But what is it? And what will it look like?

WHEN I GET HOME, I do something I haven't done in years. I sit down at my desk. And begin to write. It's not the next great American novel. Or even the next great American romcom—definitely not that.

Instead, I settle in and jot down some of my thoughts—a long stream of them that probably don't make any sense. I write down what Millie said, what I might want. I realize, when I'm done, that I've written a journal entry. So I plop a date at the top of it.

I realize something else too. I never returned the dress. Somehow it never left my arms and I returned home with it. It's lying, draped over my bed, right now.

I slide out of my jeans and t-shirt and slip the dress over my head.

That's the first thing I want. To look pretty today.

I'll take Alfie for his walk, and we'll get a sandwich, or stop at the church and look at the sun through the stained-glass windows. Or maybe we'll get all crazy and do all three. It is, after all, the number of perfection.

CHAPTER 49

ANDY

They make me the night manager, which feels like a weird slap in the face. Like, they didn't feel like I could handle the busyness of a day shift. I know somewhere deep inside that that isn't true, that they just had a night shift open because night shifts would be harder to fill. Plus, it pays more and there is absolutely *nothing* to do, since we only get a few patrons during my shift—some true night owls until one or sometimes two in the morning, and some true early birds starting around 4:00am. But in those hours in between, well, it's hard to stay awake.

I do my own workout then. It wakes me up at least. But there's always more time to kill. I try listening to podcasts, which puts me to sleep, watching a show on my phone, which puts me to sleep, audiobooks, which put me to sleep.

Finally, one night, I take a page out of Madigan's book (figuratively, not literally—I still need to return the literal book to the library), and bring a notebook with me to work.

I start writing about the night that I hit Gretchen's memaw's house, about the pain I was in with my broken leg, about the healing process, about the time it gave me to think about my business, about Gretchen coming into my life, our business collaboration, our friendship and sibling-hood. About all the good things that came from one bad thing.

It takes me several nights to get it all out and I never once fall asleep.

By the weekend, I've got my story down. I don't know why, or what good it will do me or anyone else, but it's there and I feel pretty good about that.

Except there's nothing left to do except check my email.

Though tonight that keeps me awake too because there, amid all the junk and coupons, is an offer for The Molehill—an offer that is three times what I actually believe the business is worth.

I check the name at the bottom of the email, wondering if it's spam. It's not. It's a name that tip taps against my brain, something familiar that takes me a moment to place. Dr. Oliver Niels, the surgeon from the wedding. He wants to take my business here in town.

I press my lips together, thinking. I wasn't even sure if I'd wanted to sell The Molehill and if I did, I'd wanted it to go to someone local, though the good news is that with someone distant, he'll probably want to keep Ned on as the manager. Right? Ned with his criminal record.

I chew my bottom lip, forwarding the email to my real estate agent and Gretchen. We can discuss it more on Monday. But three times. Three times. That is an offer that is hard to refuse.

CHAPTER 50

Tracey looks up from the couch when I come into work. She's got a funny look on her face and I realize that I've been humming.

"You're later than usual," she says.

"But still solidly on time," I reply.

"Solidly," she says, staring at my hair. I realize I've braided it in a little crown around my head instead of my usual ponytail. And I'm wearing blush.

I take my duffel bag into my room. When I come out, Tracey is whispering with Matt, who's just arrived.

I lift an eyebrow.

"I'm just gonna say it," Tracey says. "Either you've been taken over by an alien. Or you've fallen in love. I can't decide which is less likely."

"Neither," I reply with an eyeroll. "I've just had a

really good week and have been thinking about some stuff."

"Well, keep thinking," Tracey says. "Because you look great."

Matt wanders to the landing pad to inspect the helicopter for the start of our shift. It's a good thing too, because within twenty minutes we've got our first call.

"At least it's not a kid this time," Tracey says.

"Right?!?" I say, adjusting my helmet. "But it's kind of weird to be going to Amish country."

"They pay in cash," Matt says through his headset. "I've been there once before. Nasty farming accident. The guy lost his arm. This one sounds easier."

<hr>

THE PATIENT HAS A SHATTERED limb from falling off a ladder, but he really is doing okay, all things considered. We load him onto the litter and then into the small space in the helicopter. Good thing most Amish men are light. And Matt is right, they pay in cash.

Fire and EMS are both on scene. Terry, unfortunately, among them.

He makes a point to stand beside me as we lift the litter into the helicopter. "Heard your 'little friend' was selling that rifle range he just opened," he says in a snide whisper. "Guess he bit off more than he could chew."

"What are you talking about?" I grumble, shifting my weight, so we can get the patient into the smallish door.

"That guy—Andy. He's selling one of his businesses, just a few months after opening. Cheap too. I'm thinking of buying it. Might be a nice place for me and my buddies to camp and shoot when we're off work."

I don't flatter him with an answer, though my head is reeling. Why would Andy be selling the range? Especially after such a successful opening? Especially after everything worked out with Jeremy and his hand? I wonder if something else happened, if someone else got hurt.

"Yeah, heard he was working at a gym—night shift—just managing. Maybe the kid went bankrupt."

"That would be terrible," I say, as we slide the patient in.

"That would be hilarious," Terry replies.

I give him my most solid scowl. I'm sure it's just some nasty rumor.

***

BUT IT ISN'T. When I get home, when Alfie is practically beating at the door, leash in mouth, anxious for his walk, I look it up. Sure enough, the property is listed. Very cheaply. And when I call Iron Fit and ask who the night manager is, the woman at the desk replies, "Some guy named Andy, it looks like. Haven't met him yet though."

I take Alfie's leash, distracted, so much that I nearly forget to clip it to his collar, and wander outside holding the leash, the metal end dragging on the sidewalk. Until Alfie gives me a confused yip. I look back and see him standing in the doorway, like he's the responsible parent and I'm the irresponsible teen. "Oh, sorry," I say, walking back and clipping him on. "Just thinking about things."

And Alfie, he literally nods his head, as though he understands.

I'm meaning to head to the coffee shop, the place I'm beginning to think about as my coffee shop, but when I walk past the church, I see that the lights are on, glowing through the stained glass.

Alfie stops in front of the door, as though he knows exactly what I'm thinking and he's going to help me do it. I stop next to him, then push it open.

It's just me and a few other patrons. Down the hall, I can hear a small choir practicing.

"Alfie," I whisper as though I expect him to answer me. "Is it Sunday?"

The morning light streams through the stained

glass, making rainbows of color on the velvet benches—the ones Andy's donation made possible.

More worshippers are shuffling in and it feels like I can't walk out now. I remember Millie, remember that I can. But then I choose to stay.

Ten minutes till ten. I haven't been to a church service since Joshua died.

Four years. Minus three weeks. Is that four, or three, or seven? Or maybe something else? Unlucky or complete or very complete, or just unknown?

Does it matter, I wonder as a boy wanders down the aisles, lighting candles. I'm here now. And now feels good, now feels better than a number or a symbol.

I settle against the soft pew, listening to the choir as they walk down the hall, their voices increasing in volume, watching the sun through the windows increasing in strength, noticing the people around me increasing in number.

You don't always need a sign, but when you get one, it's kind of nice.

And even before the service starts, I know what I need to do. No, I know what I *want* to do.

CHAPTER 51

ANDY

"Y ou've got a potential buyer," Mrs. Wilson, the real estate agent, says on the other line. Jackson's mother. That's how it goes in small towns. Everybody connected to everybody else. But she doesn't feel like a small town agent—smart as a tack with a huge booming voice.

"For The Molehill, yes, I wanted to talk about that," I say.

"Actually, I meant for the rifle range," she says. "The offer for The Molehill is more complicated. Can you come in sometime?"

I'm dog tired, right after my shift at the gym. And I'd wanted to stop at The Molehill sometime today and at least check in with Ned. "What times you got?" I say.

"Why don't you come in later today?" she says. "Get a bit of rest." So I guess Gretchen has told her about my new gig.

"And the offer," I ask. "What is it?"

"Full price," she answers. "From an LLC called the JM Foundation."

"Any conditions?" I ask.

"Not yet," she says. "Of course, you'd have to accept the offer and then we'd have to get through the inspection and everything. But Andy," she continues. "I know it's for full price and everything, but I think the price is too low. It's less than you even paid for it and *that* was low. I think you should at least try to get your money back."

"I think I really just want the property gone," I counter.

"But do you?" she says in that big voice of hers. I hear what she doesn't say, maybe because it's really my own mind saying it, *Or are you just running away?*

I pause for a moment and she interjects, "Let's discuss it more when you get here. I can show you some comparable prices from nearby towns, and we can see if this is really something you want to accept."

"But I can't really counter with something above what I asked for, can I?"

"Andy, child, you can do whatever you want," she

says. "It's still yours. Personally, I recommend taking it off the market, making a few improvements, and then putting it back on at a higher price. And I can tell you that that sister of yours recommends taking it off the market and not putting it back on again."

Ah, there it is—everyone else's two cents.

"But it's not your job to pay me or even her any mind. What you really need to do is consider what you want from the sale of this property."

"Freedom," I murmur into the phone without realizing I'm saying it out loud.

"Well, if that's what you want and if that's what you expect to get from this sale, then we can consider the offer. Just make sure it's what you want."

And what do I want? For things to go back to feeling simple in my mind. For them to be fun again. The Range doesn't feel that way now, not since Jeremy. But neither does my horrible job at Iron Fit. So what exactly is it that I'm supposed to do to be who I'm really supposed to be?

"I'll meet you today," I say. "At four."

<hr>

I SLEEP for only five hours. It's all I can spare. Before my appointment with Mrs. Wilson, I want to do three things. First, I stop by The Molehill.

"Well, hello stranger," Ned says. "We've missed you around here. Also, you look awful."

"Not getting my usual beauty sleep," I reply.

Ned raises his eyebrows like he thinks I'm an idiot who should come back to The Molehill and get as much sleep as needed at night. "People been asking about The Range," he says. "Everyone's kind of upset."

Well, wait till they learn I might be unloading this place as well.

"Jeremy—that groom—he even stopped by yesterday to talk to you."

"It's just too much," I say. "I'm meeting with the real estate agent today."

"You know what my therapist says," Ned says.

"You have a therapist?" I ask.

"I'm a convicted felon, a recovering addict, and a father of three. Yes, I have a therapist. And she says that one of the key things about dealing with pain is not to be reactive. She always tells me to stop, pause, and think. To consider possible actions and possible outcomes."

"Noted," I say, turning to the door.

"Is it?" Ned asks. "Or are you just determined to go fast, and not think?"

"Two people got hurt at my two businesses within one month," I say.

"And both have been back," he counters.

"But what if something worse happens one day? What if they don't come back, or can't?"

"What if these places build up a community that can deal with that?" Ned counters. "My therapist says to consider possible outcomes. *All* of them. Not just the ones you want to think about right now, because you're dealing with some stuff."

I nod. "Thanks, dude. I'll let you know how the meeting goes."

He makes a sound in his throat. "Nina is worried about my job. She doesn't need to be, right? I mean, it's okay if it is. Just, do me a favor and give me plenty of time to find another one, okay man?"

"You don't need to be worried about your job," I say. "And that's a promise."

I see him sink into the chair a bit, the relief softening him. Then I grab a key from one of the envelopes. "Going on a little ride to see Gretchen."

"That one's reserved tonight," he says.

"I'll be sure to be back by then."

I FIND GRETCHEN IRONING TABLECLOTHS. A lost art, ironing. And one I'm not sure she could pay me to do.

"Whatcha doing?" I ask. "Got an event tonight?"

"Nah," she says. "I'm just thinking and this helps."

"I've been thinking a lot too," I say, handing her a manila envelope.

Her forehead bends into a frown. "What's this?" she asks.

"Not what you think it is," I say, smiling for the first time today. "It's a story, our story. I wrote it down. I wanted to know what you thought of it."

"Oh, Andy, that is the sweetest thing," she says, setting the iron to the side and turning it off.

"Nope," I say, turning toward the door. "I don't want to see you read it. Just text me later. If you want. I just did it for a bit of, I don't know, fun, I guess."

"You're growing up, little brother."

Our eyes meet then and in it, I see a little pride. And a little worry.

NEXT STOP. The library. I pull the book out of a brown sack.

"Did you read it?" Nellie asks, without looking up.

"Every word," I say.

And then she does look up. "And you figured it out?"

"That it's Madigan, yeah," I say. "She's different now, huh?"

"Everyone's different every day," Nellie replies. "But, yes. She's still finding her way back."

"Not sure I can help her do that," I say. "Don't think she wants me to."

"Oh, Andy," Nellie says. "She doesn't need you to help her find her way. You couldn't do that even if she did. She's gonna have to find it. I just wanted her to have some friends on the way."

I nod, don't dare tell Nellie that she's underestimated my ability at being a good friend as well. "Tell me about Joshua," I say abruptly.

She looks straight at me, glasses perched on the tip of her nose—the picture of a stereotypical librarian. "He was wonderful. Handsome, healthy, moving up in his career—smart as a whip, that boy. He studied ancient things, languages and especially numerology."

"Numerology?" I ask.

"Yes," she replies. "Like what numbers represented in ancient cultures."

I must not be doing a good job keeping my expression neutral because she adds, "It sounds boring, but when you were as passionate and intelligent as Joshua, it was infectious. He knew everything about everything. We all loved him, not just Madigan."

"And what happened?" I ask.

"He died in an accident a few months after they

were married. Tragic. It was a rainy night, and he was on a motorcycle."

On the last word, several things shift into place. "He rode a motorcycle?"

"That boy wasn't all numbers," Nellie says. "He liked to feel the wind on his face. They travelled all over the world, the two of them—she writing while he studied. It was a beautiful thing."

"You know Madigan won't get in my Jeep," I say, not mentioning that last desperate time. "She says it's too dangerous."

"She thinks everything is too dangerous these days, Andy. It's understandable."

"Then why did you think we'd be a good match?" I ask, sitting in the chair by her desk.

"Because you like to feel the wind on your face too," she answers. "And I wanted that for Madigan again. And for you. Because she's not such a bad catch herself."

"She's not," I agree. "But she's not in the market for being caught."

"It's not that she's not in the market," Nellie says. "She's just afraid of the market."

"There isn't much of a difference there," I say.

"But there is one," she answers. "And I was hoping you could find it. Tell me you're a boy who doesn't like a challenge."

"Lately most of my challenges have ended in failure."

"Well, that's just how stories work," she says, lifting Madigan's book off her desk and checking it in. "If everything always went well, it wouldn't be very interesting. In fact, it might not be a story at all."

CHAPTER 52

ANDY

Just before I get to Mrs. Wilson's office, I get a text from Gretchen. A bunch of teary emojis. "Baby brother," she says. "It's beautiful. I'll call you later. Meeting with someone in five."

"What'd you think of the writing?" I text back.

"Oh, Andy, it's so sweet. I don't think you should worry about the writing."

I lift an eyebrow at my phone. Apparently, I'm not going to be the next great memoirist, though it still felt good to get all those words out.

Mrs. Wilson has pulled up comps from several different cities in Kentucky—about the size of Midvale. All the properties are priced quite a bit higher than mine.

"But are they the same size?" I ask.

She points to numbers on the piece of paper she's printed out. "And from the looks of the pictures online, yours is a good bit prettier. Look—" She turns her computer to me. "This one's just a mowed over corn field. And they're asking $25K more than you with your pond and those gorgeous woods. Honestly, your property could be a retreat just as much as a rifle range." As she says it, she pinches her lips together, looking at the offer.

"You think someone's going to change it to something else."

"I was just looking at the layout and, well, it'd make a great little place to land a few Airbnb's as well. Just buy some pre-made cabins and…boom."

I tip my head to the side, looking at the property, the pond.

"Could it," I ask. "Could it do that and still be a rifle range?"

"Now *that* I don't know," she says. "It'd depend on the orientation of the range versus the houses. Last thing you want is for some kid on vacation to get shot playing by the lake."

It is the last thing I want. It's the whole reason I'm selling, but I can't seem to stop my brain from spinning through the options. What if the cabins were on the west side in the woods? We could probably fit three or four there, real comfy. They'd be secluded, and have access to both The Molehill and the range? What if that came in as part of the price or an add-on for the rental? What if I oriented the range to the west; would that give it enough room? Though we'd have to be even more careful with families wandering around.

And what am I even thinking? This is exactly why I'm supposed to be selling this thing. Because of the risk. Which I seem determined to create more of, not less. Still, I can't stop seeing those little cabins in the woods. A retreat, that was the word Mrs. Wilson had used. Who doesn't want a retreat sometimes?

"Can I meet with the buyer?" I ask suddenly. "Find out what he wants to do with it?"

"It's kind of unusual," she says. "Usually everything goes through the agents. However, in this case, my office is handling both sides, so maybe it can be arranged."

"Great," I say. "When would that maybe work?"

She glances at the schedule in her paper planner. "You got fifteen minutes?"

I lean back in my chair. "I got more than that."

"Okay, let me have a chat with Mandy—that's the other agent."

Five minutes later, Mrs. Wilson is back, looking a little pinched. "The potential buyer will be here soon, but they're not sure they want a meeting. They just want to know if you'll accept it or not?"

"Well, tell them that it depends entirely on what they plan to do with it."

I can see Mrs. Wilson restrain a sigh. It's a noble effort. "It could break the deal," she says. "Lots of people don't want to disclose this."

"Then let the deal break," I say, my mind still spinning with images of cabins, ATVs, and fun.

Mrs. Wilson sits down, faces me. "Do you want them to make it a rifle range?" she asks. "If so, I don't understand why you're selling, especially so far under value. Or do you want them to do something else?"

Truthfully, I hadn't spent a lot of time thinking about what I wanted with it until right now. "I don't want it plowed down and farmed," I say. "Or plowed down for any other reason either. I want it…" I start. "I want it to be a place for people to connect. With each other. With nature."

Mrs. Wilson leans back in her seat. "So you're hoping it's going to be the next rotary club, are you?"

"If they could use a building, then sure," I respond.

She picks up her phone. "I'll text Mandy and see what we can figure out."

"You got a sketch pad?" I ask.

She pushes one my direction and I sketch out a few cabins in the woods, play with the orientation of the range, text a picture to Gretchen.

Mrs. Wilson's phone dings. "The potential buyer isn't sure," she says. "They need to think about it. I'll keep you posted if we can get you two together for a meeting. Or maybe you can just make it clear what you want with it and we can see if their plans meet your criteria."

WHEN I GO OUT to the parking lot, I see a familiar car. I walk over to it, hoping to see a familiar owner as well, but Madigan isn't there. A towel is on the passenger side. I assume that's usually Alfie's seat and remember that Madigan always brings him in a carrier because she's worried about him getting hurt.

"Andy!" I hear a voice say.

I turn to see her, standing a few spots away.

"Buying a house?" I ask.

"Looking at property," she replies.

We stand there awkwardly. "Where's your Jeep?"

"Brought this instead," I say, tipping my head toward the ATV, which I've parked like it's a real car.

"But how?" she asks. "Surely you don't drive it on the road."

"Nah," I say. "The sheriff would have a fit. But there are back paths from The Molehill to here. And a bunch of other places around town too." I realize then that I'm in jeans and a slightly sweaty t-shirt.

"Guess I better be getting it back. Someone's got it reserved tonight."

"People reserve specific vehicles?" she asks.

"Sometimes," I say. "If they really like one."

"You have a favorite?" she asks.

"I have a few," I respond. "This is my numero uno. I call him Rico. Want a ride?"

It's meant to be a joke. I couldn't even get her to get into the Jeep until her dog was dying. But slowly, she tips her head down into a nod. I assume I've seen wrong. And we just stare at each other for a minute.

"You *do* want a ride?" I ask, this time as a legitimate question.

"Maybe," she says, starting to backpedal, in fact, literally taking a step back. "If you've got enough helmets—one for me and one for you."

"Oh, I'm the helmet king," I say.

"And we won't go too fast," she says.

"I'll drive like your granny if you want," I reply.

"Long as it's my grams now," she says. "Not my grams in her younger years."

"Fair enough," I say, digging out a helmet and handing it to her.

She settles it onto her head, fumbling with the straps.

"Here," I say, reaching over. "You've got to get it tight without choking yourself out. I shorten the straps around her face, moving her hair and tucking it back. I let my hand linger for a second near her cheek, then drop it.

She's looking at the ground like she's regretting this choice.

"Don't worry," I say. I want to reach out, to tip her chin up so she'll look at me. "It'll be just as safe as riding a bike."

"Will it?" she asks.

"Well, an electric bike," I say.

She laughs and the sound wobbles like she might cry.

"Madigan," I say. "You don't have to go," I respond. "Just because you said something in a moment of spontaneity—or for you, clinical insanity—doesn't mean you have to do it."

"I've been trying to do more things that I want to do," she says, looking past me, at the blue sky. "And it's such a nice day."

"It is," I say. "But that doesn't mean you have to take a four-wheeler. You could go for a drive, a walk. Whatever you want."

"I suppose it's different with the wind rushing through your hair."

The third time I've heard that phrase today. "It's the best thing in the world, and that's the truth," I reply. "But that's just me. You can be you."

"Yes," she says. "But the person I am can change too."

I don't dare answer.

"As slow as my grams?" she asks, tightening her strap just a teeny bit more. "She's eighty-six, you know."

"Done," I say, putting on my own helmet. "Now where do you want to go?"

"You choose," she says. "You know these paths. And I clearly don't."

I settle into the seat, motioning behind me.

She sits. I start the ATV. And I can tell she's doing her best not to touch me.

I start intensely slow. Even so, she leans forward, still not putting her arms around me, but I can tell she's ready to.

A younger me, a more flirty me, would have gunned it, so she'd grab my waist. But current me understands that that could be the end of things with Madigan forever and I'm kind of enjoying the warmth of her body behind me, the way she leans forward and I can feel her breath against my neck.

"The Molehill is to the south," I shout. "But we'll head east. I want to have a look at the rifle range."

"The one you're selling," she says.

I'm surprised she's heard, but I give a quick nod.

I've sped up slightly so we can get there sometime within the century, and she reaches out an arm, not for my waist, but for my shoulder.

"That's actually a little more dangerous," I say. "It

affects my steering a little. You can hold my waist if you want to, though you don't have to. I'll go slow."

She puts both hands on the sides of my waist, like a fingertip hug.

"Coming up on a hill," I say, and she tightens, working the hands onto my stomach.

And, I'm not gonna lie, I could have taken a flatter way, but, well, my excuse is that the hill's faster.

"A little acceleration so we've got the speed to make it," I say.

She tightens more.

By the time we make it to the top, she's got her arms around me. Not romantic date style, more like chokehold style. She's shaking a bit.

Until we crest the hill, see the pond through the trees, glistening with the rays of the sun.

At that moment, her arms relax, her body too. And I hear a soft little murmur. "Oh," she says.

"Yeah, you can't get this view from the road," I say back to her. "That's what I love about riding. The things you get to see."

At the sound of our approach, turtles leap from logs into the pond, and just like I planned it a fish arcs out of the waters, snapping up a bug.

"Almost there," I say, taking the path around the pond.

Soon the frogs will start to sing, the lightning

bugs will come out. Of course, that means the mosquitoes will too. But isn't that how life is? You've got to take the good with the bad. Have I lost sight of that?

"Actually, a little detour," I say. "I want to check something out."

I ride through the wooded section, forgetting to go granny speed, though I'm still going plenty slow. This is where I'd envisioned the cabins. There are already natural clearings. It really wouldn't be hard to get some pre-fab cabins in here. But what about the range? I slow the ATV, looking across the pond. It's a good distance, and if they were shooting the other direction. But what about an errant shot, a person who didn't listen to the instructions? What then?

"I didn't know you had so much land," she says, breaking into my thoughts. And this is weird to say, but I'd kind of forgotten she was there.

"Thirty acres," I respond.

"Yeah," she says. "I knew that. I just didn't understand what it looked like."

"You know much about physics?" I ask.

"Only what I've learned from movies and fictional books."

"That's a 'no' then?"

"A hard no," she says.

"Too bad. I'm trying to figure out bullet safety."

"If only I'd read more thrillers," she says. "Might have had to do some research."

I laugh, slowing and then stopping, gazing out over the pond.

"Guess all we need now is sandwiches," she says. "It's the perfect picnic spot."

And even though we've stopped, I notice she still has her arms wrapped around my waist, her head leaning slightly toward my shoulder, not touching it, but hovering there.

I pause, watching the dragonflies swoop.

"I'm the potential buyer," Madigan says suddenly.

"What?" I say, sitting up as her hands fall from my waist.

"I was thinking about buying this place."

"But how?" I ask.

"Well, my Mamie left me some money when Joshua died. She told me to use it for a good cause."

"No," I say. "What I really mean is…why?"

"Because it's a good price," she says slowly. "And because I didn't want anyone else to get it."

"Why?" I repeat.

"I'm not quite sure," she says. "But look at it."

We both pause. The sun is big in the west, preparing for its descent.

"I'm looking," I say, though I'm actually just staring at her. "You were planning to run a rifle range?"

"Not sure I was *planning* anything," she says. "I was just kind of doing."

"Doing?" I ask.

"You shouldn't sell it," she says.

"It's dangerous," I say.

"Is it really more dangerous than anything else in life?" she asks.

"It's definitely more dangerous than reading a book," I say.

"I don't know," she answers. "I met my husband because of books. Well, sort of. And that was dangerous."

"How was it dangerous?" I ask.

"Because I loved him," she says. "And now he's gone. Love is always dangerous."

"I'm sorry," I say.

"Don't be," she replies. "That's what I guess I mean. It's dangerous, but do I wish it had never happened? No. Not at all. You ever been in love?"

"Does my third grade crush count?" I ask. "Because I was devoted to that one. I made her friendship bracelets and everything."

"It can count if you want it to," she says.

"I've never been in love," I respond seriously. "Lots of likes. Never made it to love."

"Well, love is a dangerous place to hang out," she says. "Even more dangerous than this thing." She waves at the ATV.

"But you don't like danger either," I say.

"Yeah," she replies. "Danger involves risk and I'm afraid of it. I became afraid of it when I came up on the short side of risk."

"I get that," I say. "Not as much as you, but I get it. I've been coming up on the short side a lot too."

"But the fact that there's a short side," she says. "Indicates that there's a long side. That's the thing about it. Do we always just want to be in the center, in the safe zone?"

"Maybe not always," I reply. "But nothing wrong with a little safe zone sometimes, right?"

"Sometimes," she says. "But it's easy to get stuck there."

We both look out over the pond. A heron wades in the distance, snapping down to catch a fish.

"You know I was a writer before."

I try to give her my neutral look, but it definitely needs practice.

"You know?" she asks.

"Library," I say.

"Nellie," she grumbles. "Anyway, I became a paramedic so I could help people, so I could make a difference, so I could keep people safe."

I turn to her, listening.

"But I couldn't really keep people safe. In fact, it seemed they insisted on being unsafe a lot of the time. My job was to come in and clean that up, sometimes a little too literally. That made me want to be even safer. But I started to realize something when Alfie almost died. And then after. Nothing is safe, not really. It's an illusion. And it's a dangerous one because it can keep you from the long side of risk. While never actually keeping you safe at all."

"Is that why you want to buy this property?" I ask. "To take a risk?"

"I wanted to buy this property," she says, putting the verb in past tense. "Because I didn't want you to sell it. I knew it was a mistake. See, I was trying to keep you safe too."

"But you can't," I say.

"I have a feeling you resist safety more than most," she says.

"Not lately," I say.

"Don't sell it, Andy," she says.

"When I talked to Mrs. Wilson—the agent—today, she mentioned these cabins and now I can't get them out of my head. I thought about putting a few in this area. But then I don't know if I should have people shooting across the pond. I can't figure it out. Should I do one or the other, or try to do both? Or should I just sell it and let someone else get stuck with the decisions?"

"I like the idea of cabins. People could come here for vacations, honeymoons, writer's retreats. Wow, it'd be a really great writer's retreat."

"You wanna host one?" I say.

"Not today," she answers with a small smile. "Though I guess I owe you something for helping with Alfie."

"You don't owe me anything," I say. "Not now, not ever. I would have helped Alfie no matter what, even if I didn't want to also help you. Which I *did*."

"I know," she murmurs. "And maybe there was something scary to me about that too."

"So that's scary to women?" I ask. "Wanting to help them?"

She laughs. "Only this woman. And it's not because I'm into bad boys. Not at all. Joshua was a total cinnamon roll. He still died on a motorcycle. In the rain. It was terrible. The very shortest side of risk."

She settles down on a rock, watching the sun set across the pond.

"I'm sorry," I say, sitting beside her.

"I know," she says. "At first you didn't remind me of him at all. With your crazy ATV park and your phone that was always dying and your unreliable schedule. Joshua had a PhD in numerology. So…a little different. But then, all of a sudden in certain ways, you started to remind me of him. Not like you were him, but, well, it's hard to describe. And that felt really scary."

"I'm sorry," I say again.

She turns to me, a little smile on her lips. "Nope. You don't get to be sorry about that part."

"I could never be him," I say. "I'm not even actually sure what numerology is."

"That does *not* surprise me," she says. "And you couldn't be him. But your sweetness startled me, your openness, your absolute bigness. That's what was the same."

I look down at my gut.

"Not literally." She smiles, leaning a bit toward me. "But somehow you were bigger than everyone else. When I had gotten stuck at a place in life that felt so small. So I pushed away, using safety as an excuse. Which is maybe what it always was—an excuse to shy away from things that could be amazing. I mean, don't get me wrong, you should still screw your bookshelves into the wall if you have small children who like to climb and you should definitely check your smoke detectors regularly, but you know what I mean."

"Yeah," I say. "I think I do. Though I haven't checked my smoke detectors for, well, ever."

"That should be remedied," she says. "I'll help you. Those are the risks you don't need to take. But the other kind. Like, why didn't you ever charge your phone?" she says.

"I liked the spontaneity," I say.

"Yeah, that sort of thing. How does one manage it?"

"Works out great till—like you say—the short side of risk smacks you in the face."

"It smacks hard," she says.

"You wanna know my latest risk?" I ask.

"You're going to Everest?" she says.

"Nope. I wrote down the story of me and Gretchen. Showed it to her."

"That does take guts," Madigan says. "That type of risk I can understand, or used to. It's hard to show what you've created to someone else. It's hard to risk them hating it. She didn't, did she?"

"Nah," I say. "She got all choked up. But when I asked how the writing was, she did say that it was so sweet I shouldn't worry about the writing."

That gets a straight up belly laugh from Madigan. "Show it to me some time," she says. "I'll help you tighten it up."

"I didn't think you wrote anymore," I say.

"That's not writing; it's editing," she says.

"Uh, considering the state of it, it might be writing," I say. "Re-writing."

"I haven't written anything for a long time, it's true. Recently, I've been trying to invest in a rifle range."

"And I'm currently trying to write my memoirs. How are both of these things going for us?"

She kind of snorts out a giggle.

"Anyway, you'll have to get back to writing for your risk-taking," I say. "Because it turns out I'm going to refuse your offer to buy the range."

"You're taking it off the market?" she says.

"Texting Mrs. Wilson right now. And maybe once I get the cabins up, some writers will come here sometimes for a retreat. And hopefully not get shot from the rednecks across the pond."

"Now that sounds like a wonderful risk," she says, as the sun turns deep orange over the water, as some storm clouds start to come up from the south. "Except the getting shot part. You know if you can't work out the physics of bullets, which I think you probably can, you could always rent it part of the year and use it as a range the other part. Or maybe… you ever thought about paint guns?"

"Hmmm," I say. "I haven't. And it's not a half bad idea. But I guess I always want to do it all."

"Well in that case, you should probably also get a boat. Every pond needs a boat."

"If there was a boat, would you come for a writer's retreat?" I ask.

"Not sure I could resist a boat," she says.

"Turns out you're in luck, because there's an old rowboat somewhere along the shore. No idea if it's watertight, but I know it's there. So now you've got to do a writer's retreat."

"You tricked me," she says.

"Just following my gut," I reply. "Wanna go out in it?"

"The boat that may not be watertight?" she says. "That's been sitting on the shore for who knows how long and may or may not have oars?"

"Yup."

"I'd love to," she says.

I take her hand to pull her up from the rock. Only I pull harder than I mean to and she kind of stumbles into me. Without thinking, I wrap her into my arms, and swirl her around, just like I did at the wedding. I feel her legs tense and I stop, step back—a nice respectful distance, holding both her arms and steadying her. "Sorry about that," I say.

She stares straight into my eyes, not speaking at first, but not moving away either. "I'm a risk too," she says, her voice barely a whisper. "More than a holey boat or a rifle range or a cabin or even an ATV. I'm still a little broken, a little fractured. What if it's too much?"

"What if it's not?" I say, stepping closer. "We'll aim for the long side of risk."

"What if my aim's no good?" she says.

"Then we'll practice," I say, tipping her chin up.

"Practice is good," she murmurs as my lips brush hers, so soft, so warm. I wrap my arms around her, feeling her body melt into mine.

I kiss her cheeks, her forehead, her chin, then press hard against her lips before pulling back. "If this is what risk always felt like, I'd do as much as possible every day," I say.

"If only," she mutters.

Above us a soft patter of rain begins on the upper trees, though the sky over the pond is still blue. "Guess we better hurry to that boat, or we're going to get drenched," I say.

"We could stay here," she says. "It's drier under the trees."

"Trees are nice," I say, reaching down for another kiss, then starting to sway side to side in the beginnings of a dance. Soon, I've got her spinning over the leaves as the water beats down harder, breaking its way through the upper canopy, trickling into her hair.

She wraps her arms tight around my back, burrows her head into my chest, and then the dance slows. "Can we go back through the rain on that thing?" she asks, nodding to the ATV.

"His name is Rico," I say. "And, yes. He loves rain. It just might get a little muddy."

"A little?" she asks.

"Maybe kind of a lot."

"How am I going to explain this to Alfie?" she asks.

"Oh, he's gonna love it, especially the part where you come home all muddy."

"Dogs," she says.

"You know, I've been trying to listen to my gut ever since you got on that ATV," I say. "Get back in tune with my intuition."

"Yes," she says, pulling her wet hair out of her face.

"And you know what my gut's telling me?"

"That it could use a milkshake," she says dryly.

"You DID know," I say, bending down to steal one more kiss. "How about it? My treat this time."

"Do I get to go home and get a shower first?" she says.

"Well, I'm kind of loving your look right now, but I suppose," I answer.

"Then I could probably handle a nice warm drink, maybe even a sandwich."

"No milkshake?" I ask.

"You can keep your sugar bomb," she says. "And you're right. You don't need more caffeine."

"It's a date then."

"Oh, and by the way, I'm driving."

"You don't want to take the Jeep?" I ask.

"There are limits to my risks," she says. "Speaking of, you still owe me a ride on that boat. On another day when we don't risk electrocution from a pop-up storm."

"That's two dates," I say.

This time, it's Madigan who pulls me in for a kiss.

"Sounds like a risk worth taking," she says, pulling back and looking at Rico. "But you're still gonna drive like my grams, right?"

"Yes, as she currently is. Age eighty-two."

"Eighty-six," she corrects.

"Got it," I say.

"Good," she says, climbing onto the ATV, this time wrapping her arms around my waist and snuggling in. "I'm ready."

EPILOGUE

MADIGAN

Four solid nights of sleep in a row. It's still not every night. I'm still me.

Alfie stirs awake at my feet and I know that within minutes he'll have his leash in his mouth and be waiting at the foot of the bed. Some things can be relied on. At least for a time.

Risk. Love. What terrible, beautiful things.

I roll out of bed to get Alfie's meds ready. I wrap the two pills tightly in a piece of ham. I've heard some dogs resist this type of thing, but Alfie always looks at me like this is the best thing I've ever done for him. If anything, he seems to feel betrayed that I haven't been giving him ham-wrapped medicines prior to this.

Within seconds, he's trotting into the kitchen, waiting at my feet for his "treat."

He sets his leash down to eat.

"What a good boy," I coo, watching him swallow.

He immediately picks his leash up again.

"We have to wait for Andy, silly boy."

Which gives me just enough time for a cup of coffee and about five hundred words. I've been trying to write every morning, just a bit, a toe in the water. Mostly it's journaling at this point. Though I've got a few ideas. Sitting on the last pages of my journal, scrawled down before I can forget them, but then ignored until I'm ready to think about them.

Today I write about how Andy is trying to break me from my caffeine addiction and I'm trying to break him from his sugar addiction. Both of those huge risks.

As soon as the doorbell rings, Alfie scoops up his leash again, running so fast toward it that he skids and slides, the leash whipping out behind him.

"Excuse you, sir," I say.

He pays me no mind, whining as I walk at normal speed toward the door.

Andy opens it before I get there though—he and Alfie snuggling and cooing at each other in a puddle of man love.

"Got you a surprise," Andy says, standing up and dusting some of Alfie's hair off his jeans.

"Flowers?" I ask, looking around.

"Better," Andy says, holding up a large-ish box.

"What is it?" I ask.

"Duh, you have to open it," he says. "That's why I put a bow on it."

He did indeed, though otherwise, it's just in its Amazon box.

When I peel back the lid, I'm greeted by two abominably pink roller skates. "Whoa," I say, shading my eyes. "The 80s called. They want their skates back."

"I knew you'd like them," he says.

"How do you know I even know how to skate?" I say, pulling them out of the box. They have pastel rainbows on the sides.

"I figured if you didn't then that would just be more of an excuse for me to hold your hand."

"As you jog beside me?" I ask.

"Of course not," he says. "I bought myself a pair as well."

"Pink?" I ask.

"No," he says. "But they do flash, like light-up shoes."

"Of course they do," I say.

"Put them on," he says. "I figured we could go for a skate, instead of a walk."

"But what about Alfie?" I ask. "I'm trying to be all fun and stuff, but I'm really not sure it's a good idea to roller skate with a dog on a leash."

Andy glances down. "He's the most obedient

animal on earth. You could probably even let him off leash."

It's not untrue. I purse my lips together, thinking.

Alfie doesn't understand the change though. He's still got his leash in his mouth. "Well, we're going to have to at least start with it," I say. "Or Alfie won't know what's happening."

"We can go to Ansley Park," Andy says. It has a nice path that goes around the pond. Alfie can run beside us.

"Okay," I say. "But first, we have to stop off at the Panning church. They've just finished the last window, and Pastor Dan wanted us to see it."

"We'd have to be on the sidewalk to skate to the church," Andy says. "You sure you're up for that? It's more narrow and bumpy."

"Oh, I think I'm up for it," I say.

Which is true, because much to Andy's chagrin, I *do* in fact know how to skate and am, in fact, better at it than Andy, whose hand I frequently grab when *he* stumbles, which happens every few feet. Alfie trots along beside us, unaware that I've unclipped him from his leash.

"So you were planning to save me when I fell?" I ask Andy, the fourth-ish time I catch him.

"To be honest, I hadn't thought it through in an exactly thorough way."

"What a surprise," I say as we get to the church

and I clip Alfie back into his leash. We slip our skates off so as not to scuff up the new floor and walk in the door in socked feet.

The final window—the one I used some of Mamie's inheritance money to donate—is a picture of the holy family, Mary, Joseph, and Jesus tucked into a tight circle. Pastor Dan and I worked with a local artist to get the design just right. And although the three of them are the focal point, I realize that the holy family is only holy because of the fourth—a divine father. The three working with a fourth. The number for completion only possible because of death. My brain almost explodes. If Joshua were here, he'd write a paper about it. As it is, Andy and I watch the sun rise through the window, the golden-red light hitting our faces and arms.

And Andy, sitting right here, right now, reaches over, takes my hand, and then kisses it. Alfie, realizing kissing is happening, jumps into the action, licking my other hand and Andy's bare knee.

"Dude," Andy says to Alfie. "I'm trying to have a moment."

Which is when I pull Andy's face to mine. We hover there for a moment, enjoying the warmth, and then I close my eyes as his lips brush mine.

A risk. Every time. But a beautiful one.

. . .

AUTHOR'S NOTE:

If you haven't read the other books in this series, you can find them below!

From Ashes

From Gunpowder

From Asphalt

From the Sky

Sign up for my newsletter to get the FREE story "Ready."

ACKNOWLEDGMENTS

I appreciate all the friends who support my writing. A special shout out to my ARC team for their help and support. Thank you to my editor, Carrie. And cover designers, Les and Lara.

A huge thank you to my husband, Kip Pace, for his usual support as well as helping me with the details pertaining to being a flight medic. If there are still mistakes in regards to this profession, they are due to my lack of understanding.

ABOUT THE AUTHOR

J. E. Pace is the author of the books *From Ashes, From Gunpowder, From Asphalt, From Snow,* and the short story "Ready," which you can get for free by signing up for her newsletter.

If you enjoy fantasy or memoir, you can find more of her work, written under the name Jean Knight Pace.